Isabel Shannerhorf

Louisa —

Ky.

Sept 17th 1923,

POLLY AND THE PRINCESS

"WHAT IS IT?" HE ASKED AS HE CAME UP

POLLY
AND THE PRINCESS

BY
EMMA C. DOWD

AUTHOR OF
POLLY OF THE HOSPITAL STAFF,
POLLY OF LADY GAY COTTAGE,
DOODLES, ETC.

ILLUSTRATED

NEW YORK
GROSSET & DUNLAP
PUBLISHERS

Published November 1917

TO
MY MOTHER

CONTENTS

CONTENTS

POLLY AND THE PRINCESS

CHAPTER I

WAFFLES AND DEWLAPS

THE June Holiday Home was one of those sumptuous stations where indigent gentlewomen assemble to await the coming of the last train.

Breakfast was always served precisely at seven o'clock, and certain dishes appeared as regularly as the days. This was waffle morning on the Home calendar; outside it was known as Thursday.

The eyes of the "new lady" wandered beyond the dining-room and followed a young girl, all in pink.

"Who is that coming up the walk?"

Fourteen faces turned toward the wide front window.

Miss Castlevaine was quickest. Her answer did not halt the syrup on its way to her plate.

"That's Polly Dudley."

"Oh! Dr. Dudley's daughter?"

1

"Yes. She's come over to see Miss Sterling. They're very intimate."

"Miss Sterling?" mused Miss Mullaly, with a sweeping glance round the table. "I don't believe I've seen her."

"Yes, you have. She was down to tea last night. She had on a light blue waist, and sat over at the end."

"Oh, I remember now! She's little and sweet-looking. Somebody told me she had nervous prostration. Too bad! She is so young and pretty!"

A tiny sneer fluttered from face to face, skipping one here and there in its course. It ended in Miss Castlevaine's "Huh!"

"I think Miss Sterling is real pretty!" Miss Crilly, from the opposite side, beamed on the "new lady."

"She has faded dreadfully," asserted Mrs. Crump. "They used to call her handsome years ago, though she never was my style o' beauty. But now —" She shook her head with hard emphasis.

"She has been through a good deal," observed Mrs. Grace mildly.

"No more'n I have!" was the retort. "If

2

she'd stop thinking about herself and eat like other folks, she'd be better."

"Nervous prostration patients have to be careful about their diet, don't they?" ventured Miss Mullaly.

"She hasn't got it!" snapped Mrs. Crump.

"She thinks she has." Miss Castlevaine's thick lips curved in a smile of scorn.

"If she can't digest things, it won't do her much good to eat them," interposed Miss Major positively. "Nobody could digest these waffles — they're slack this morning."

Miss Castlevaine gave her plate a little push. "I wish I needn't ever see another waffle," she fretted.

"Oh!" exclaimed the "new lady," "I don't understand how anybody can get tired of waffles!"

"Nor I!" laughed Miss Mullaly's right-hand neighbor. "I shall have to tell you about the time I went to Cousin Dorothy's wedding luncheon.

"I never had eaten waffles but once; that was at my aunt's. She had gone to housekeeping directly after the wedding ceremony, and was spoken of in the family as 'the bride.' I had been her first guest, and, as she had treated me to waffles, I thought waffles and brides always went together. So when I was included in the invitation to Dorothy's wedding luncheon, my first thought was of waffles. I said something about it to my brother, and Ralph was just tease enough to lead me on. He told me that the table would be piled with waffles, great stacks of them at every plate! Like a little dunce I believed it all and went to that party antici-pating a blissful supply of waffles. In vain I looked up and down the elegant table! I ate and ate, but never a waffle appeared! Finally, when I could stand it no longer, I piped out, 'Cousin Dorothy, please can I have my waffles now?' Of course, my mother was dreadfully mortified, for some of the guests were strangers, and very great people; but Dorothy took it as a mighty good joke, and even after I was married she used to laugh about my 'w'awful' disappoint-ment. I've not gotten over my appetite for waffles either! I believe I could eat and relish them three times a day."

"You couldn't! Just wait till you've had 'em fifty-two times a year, five years running — as I have!" Mrs. Crump's lips made a straight line.

"Mrs. Crump has kept tabs on her waffles," giggled Miss Crilly. "How many does this morning make — five hundred and —?"

"Sh!" nudged Mrs. Bonnyman at Miss Crilly's elbow.

Two youngish women entered the room. They were the superintendent and the matron.

Upstairs, meanwhile, Miss Juanita Sterling, in bed, and Polly Dudley, seated on the outside, were having a familiar talk.

"I should n't think you 'd want to die till God gave you something to die of," Polly was saying wistfully. "I think He must want you to live, or He would give you something to die of. Perhaps He has some beautiful work for you to do and is waiting for you to get well and do it."

"Polly, I cannot work! And there is no lack of things for me to die of!" Impatience crept into the sweet voice. "Being in prison is bad enough even with good health; but to be sick, wretched — the worst kind of sickness, because nobody understands! — and to grow old, too, grow old fast — oh, I wish God would let me die!" The little woman gave a sudden whirl and hid her face in the pillow.

5

"Don't, Miss Nita!" Polly's voice was distressed. She stroked the smooth, soft hair. "Don't cry! You're not old! You're not old a bit! And you're going to be well — father says so!"

"That won't take away the dewlap — oh!" cried Miss Sterling fiercely, "I don't want a dewlap!"

"Dewlap?" scowled Polly. "What's a dewlap?"

"Polly! You know!" came from down among the feathers.

"I don't!" Polly protested. "Is it some kind of — cancer?"

"Cancer! Polly!" Miss Sterling laughed out.

"Well, I don't know what it is." Polly laughed in sympathy.

"Look here!" The little lady raised herself on her elbow and lifted her chin. "See that!"

Polly peered at the fair, pink skin.

"What? I don't see anything."

"Why, that! It's getting wabbly." Her slim forefinger pushed the flesh back and forth.

"Oh!" Polly's face brightened. "I remember! That's what Grandaunt Susie called it! She said she used to have an awful one — it hung 'way down. And she cured it! You'd never dream she had one ever!"

"Oh, yes, you can do away with such things if you have money — if you can go to a beauty-doctor!" The tone was bitter.

"No, she did n't!" hastened the eager voice. "She did it herself!"

"Of course, if you have expensive creams and all the paraphernalia —"

"But she did n't — she said so! She just used olive oil!"

"How old was she?" Miss Sterling inquired with a now-I-'ve-got-you air.

"She was seventy when she had the dewlap; now she's seventy-three or four."

"Polly Dudley! I don't believe it!"

"Why, Miss Nita, I'm telling you the solemn truth!"

"Yes, yes, child! I did n't mean you! But this Aunt Susie —"

"Oh, she's just as honest! Why, she's mother's grandaunt, and she's lovely! She was sick and could n't do anything, and her hair was thin and her cheeks hung down and she was all wrinkles and she had the dewlap — she said she looked dreadful. Now you ought to see her!

She's perfectly well, and her hair is as thick, and it's smooth and solid all under her chin, and her face is 'most as round as mine!"

"How did she work the miracle?" Miss Sterling's eyes twinkled.

"Why, I guess by massage and exercises. She did n't take anything. She did lots of stunts; she had piles of them for her legs and arms and neck and face and feet and all over. She made up mighty funny faces. You lie over this way, and I'll show you one.

"First you must smile — just as hard as you can." Polly laughed to see the prompt grin. "Now I'll put my hands so, and you must do exactly as I tell you." Polly's little palms were pressed against the other's cheeks, and she began a rotary motion.

"Open your mouth — wide, and then shut it again — oh, keep on smiling! And keep your mouth going all the time, while I do the massaging."

"Goodness!" Miss Sterling broke into a laugh. "I should think that was a stunt! It ought to do something." She turned on the pillow in another paroxysm of mirth.

"But you made me stop too soon," objected

Polly. "You ought to open and shut your mouth twenty-five times. 'Most everything Aunt Susie did twenty-five or fifty or a hundred times."

"I don't wonder she got well! She'd have to if she did n't die. I should laugh before I got through twenty-five times, I'm sure. What's it for, anyhow?"

"To make the cheeks plump up and not sag — oh, yours look so pink!" Polly danced over to the dresser and back.

The handglass showed a face of surprise. The thin, white cheeks had taken on a soft rose tint and — yes, an extra fullness!

"Queer!" Miss Sterling ejaculated. "I would n't have believed it!"

"Oh, let's try it again! Then you get up and go to walk with me — won't you?"

"I can't, Polly! Wish I could! But I don't feel as if I could even stand up. I suppose I shall have to go down to dinner. I don't dare not."

"Have n't you had any breakfast?"

"No. Folks that can't get up don't need to eat." She laughed sadly. "It's well I'm not hungry."

9

"But you ought —"

"Tap! tap!"

The matron opened the door while Polly was on the way.

"Mr. Randolph is at the other end of the building and will be here presently to see about the new wing."

Mrs. Nobbs was gone.

"Nelson Randolph!" cried Miss Sterling. "Hand me my blue kimono, Polly, quick! It's right there in the closet, by the door!"

She swung her feet to the floor and caught up her stockings.

"You going to get up?"

"Of course! Hurry! I believe he's coming — no, he isn't! Oh, I can get this on all right! You fix the bed! Never mind the wrinkles — plump up the pillows! Yes, hang my clothes anywhere you can find room. There! Does my hair look all right?"

"Lovely! That kimono is very becoming."

"Little flatterer!"

By the time Nelson Randolph, president of the June Holiday Home, appeared in the doorway, what he saw was a well-appointed bedroom, a little blue-clad lady demurely reading a

10

small volume, and Polly hovering near. With a perfunctory good-morning to Miss Sterling, and a genial handshake for Dr. Dudley's daughter, he passed with Mrs. Nobbs to the southwest corner of the apartment. He took a glance around the ceiling, a look from the window, and some measurements with a foot-rule; then he walked briskly across the room, nodded politely, and departed.

"What a lovable man he is!" commented Polly, as the retreating footsteps told of their safe distance.

"Is he?"

"Don't you know him?" Polly queried.

"Not very well. Probably he does n't remember me at all. He used to come to the house occasionally to see father. That was before he was married. I was only seventeen or eighteen."

"I like to look at him, he is so handsome." Polly's head wagged admiringly. "I guess he'd remember you all right, only he does n't know you're here. He has n't been president very long, just since Mr. Macy died. What are they going to build now?"

"I don't know. First I've heard of it. They have more money than they know what to do with, so they've decided to put up an L and spoil my view," laughed Miss Sterling.

"I could tell them lots of things better than an L — some new dresses for Mrs. Crump and Mrs. Albright and Miss Crilly. They've been here longest and look the worst. That brown one of Mrs. Crump's is just full of darns."

"Same as mine will be when I've been here as long," added Miss Sterling.

"Strange, when they have so much money, they don't give the ladies nice things to wear," mused Polly. "Perhaps that is what makes Mrs. Crump so cross-grained. Mrs. Albright is n't. She's sweet, I think."

"She is a dear," Miss Sterling agreed. "But she's had enough trouble to crush most women. I wonder sometimes if anything could make her blue."

"Miss Crilly's cheerful," observed Polly. "I like her pretty well."

"She is kind-hearted. If only she were n't all gush and giggle! She raves over everything, cathedral or apron trimming — it's all the same to her."

Polly laughed. "She's rather pretty, I think."

12

"Too fat."

"No, you can't call her fat; only her bones don't show. I wish Miss Castlevaine could thin up and show her bones just a little, and I do feel sorry for her because she can't curl her hair. She'd look a thousand per cent better with some little fluffs."

"Why don't you be sorry for me?"

"Oh, you don't need curly hair as the rest do!" answered Polly comfortably.

"Need it! I'm a scarecrow with my hair straight!"

Polly took the smooth head between her two palms. "You'll never be a scarecrow if you live to be a hundred and fifty!" she declared. "But the dear homely ones—it is hard on them. What do you suppose is the reason Miss Sniffen won't let them curl their hair just a mite?"

"Walls are said to have ears," replied Miss Sterling, with a little scornful twist to her pretty mouth. "It would n't be safe for me to express my opinion."

Polly smiled. "It's a shame! And it is n't fair when she has curly hair that does n't need any putting up. I just wish hers would straighten out — straight as Miss Castlevaine's!"

13

"You seem to have taken a sudden liking to Miss Castlevaine."

"Oh, no! Only I feel sorry for her, she is so fat and fretty, and her hair won't fluff a mite. It must be dreadful to think as much scorn as she does."

"And talk it out," added Miss Sterling. "I wish she would n't, for she is really better than she sounds."

"Oh, if she 'd try some of Aunt Susie's exercises, perhaps they 'd make her face thin!"

"I thought they were to make it plump."

"So they are — and thin, too, in the right places. They 'd cure her double chin."

"Anyway, she has n't any dewlap yet. When it comes it will be an awful one. I can't imagine her in that exercise you tried on me."

"Are you going to do it every day?"

"I would if I had any faith in it." Miss Sterling sighed — with a wrinkled forehead.

"Oh, you must n't pucker in wrinkles if I 'm going to rub them out!" Polly smoothed the offending lines. "Now I 'll run over home and get you that book Aunt Susie gave to mother. It tells all about everything, and it will make you have faith. It did mother."

"She does n't need it."

"No; but Aunt Susie said she'd better begin pretty soon, for it was easier to cure wrinkles before they came."

"Yes, I guess it is," Miss Sterling laughed, "and dewlaps too!"

CHAPTER II

WHEN Russell Holiday and his wife named their only child June, they planned to make her life one long summer holiday. For eighteen years success went hand in hand with their desire; then an unfortunate marriage plunged the joyous girl into bleak November. She grew to hate her happy name. But with the passing of the man she called husband much of the bitterness vanished, and she began to plan for others.

"I want this Home to be as beautiful as money can make it and as full of joy as a June holiday," she told her approving lawyer. "There must be no age limit. It shall welcome as freely the woman of forty as her mother or her grandmother. I will gather in the needy of any sect or race, — the oppressed, the disabled, the sorrowful, and the lonely, — and as much as can be give to them the freedom and happiness of a delightful home."

In just one week from the day the ground was broken for the big building, a drunken chauffeur

16

drove the donor and her lawyer to their death, and the institution was continued in a totally different way from that intended by the two who could make no protest.

To be sure, it stood at last, in gray granite magnificence, on the crest of Edgewood Hill, a palace without and within; but to those for whom it was built had never come, through the years of its being, a single June holiday.

It was this that some of the residents were discussing, as they crocheted, knitted, or embroidered in Miss Major's room on a dull May morning.

"Too bad June Holiday could n't have lived just a little longer!" Mrs. Bonnyman sighed.

"What would she say if she knew how her wishes were ignored!" Miss Castlevaine shook her head.

"Regular prison house!" snapped Mrs. Crump.

"Well, I'm glad to be here if I do have to obey rules," confessed a meek little woman with grayish, sandy hair. "It's a lovely place, and there has to be rules where there's so many."

"There don't have to be hair-crimping rules, Mrs. Prindle — huh!"

As the curly-headed maker of the hated law walked across the lawn, Miss Castlevaine sent her an annihilating glance.

"Is that Miss Sniffen?" queried Miss Mullaly, adjusting her eyeglasses.

Miss Castlevaine nodded.

The others watched the tall, straight figure, on its way to the vegetable garden.

"She has the expression of a basilisk I saw the picture of the other day," spoke up Mrs. Dick.

"What kind of an expression was that?" inquired Mrs. Winslow Teed. "I saw a stuffed basilisk in a London museum when I was abroad, but I can't seem to recollect its expression."

"Look at *her!*" laughed Mrs. Dick. "She has it to perfection."

Miss Crilly's giggle preceded her words.

"She's like a beanpole with its good clothes on, ain't she? But, then, I think Miss Sniffen is real nice sometimes," she amended.

"So are basilisks and beanpoles — in their proper places," retorted Miss Major; "but they don't belong in the June Holiday Home."

"Are her rules so awful?" inquired Miss Mullaly anxiously.

"I don't like them very," answered the little Swedish widow.

"Mis' Adlerfeld puts it politely," laughed Miss Crilly. "I'll tell you what they are, they are like the little girl in the rhyme — with a difference, —

'When they're bad, they're very, very bad,
And when they're good, they're horrid!'"

"I heard you could n't have any company except one afternoon a week," resumed Miss Mullaly, after the laughing had ceased, — "not anybody at all."

"Sure!" returned Miss Crilly. "Wednesday afternoon, from three to five, is the only time you can entertain your best feller."

"Why, Polly Dudley was here Thursday morning!"

"Now you've got me!" admitted Miss Crilly. "She's a privileged character. She runs over any blessed minute she wants to."

"And she brings her friends with her," added Miss Castlevaine, — "David Collins and his greataunt's daughter, — Leonora Jocelyn, — Patricia Illingworth, and Chris Morrow, and that girl they call Lilith, besides the Stickney boys up in Foxford — huh!"

19

"She must be pretty bold, when it's against the rule," observed Miss Mullaly.

"No," dissented Mrs. Albright, "it isn't boldness. Polly runs in as naturally as a kitten. The rest don't come so very often. I shouldn't say they'd let 'em; but they do."

"There's never any favoritism in the June Holiday Home — never!" Mrs. Crump's brown poplin bristled with sarcasm.

"Maybe it's on Miss Sterling's account," interposed Mrs. Albright. "She thinks so much of Polly, perhaps they hope it'll help to bring her out of this sooner."

"Don't you believe it!" Miss Castlevaine's head nodded out the words with emphasis. "Dr. Dudley's a good one to curry favor with."

"Is Miss Sterling a relative of his?" asked Miss Mullaly.

"No. Haven't you heard how they got acquainted? Quite a pretty little story." Mrs. Albright settled herself comfortably in the rocker and adjusted the cushion at her back.

The others, who were familiar with the facts, moved closer together and nearer the window, both to facilitate their needles and their tongues.

"It was the day after Miss Sterling came, along in September," the story-teller began, "and she was up in her room feeling pretty lonesome — you know how it is."

Miss Mullaly nodded — with a sudden droop of her lips.

"She stood there looking out of the window toward the back of the new hospital, — it was building then, — and she saw a little girl climbing an apple tree. She watched her go higher and higher, after a big, bright red apple that was away up on a top branch. Miss Sterling says she went so fast that she fairly held her breath, expecting to see her slip; but she did n't, she's so sure-footed, and it would have been all right if she had n't ventured on a rotten branch. When she stepped out on that and reached up one hand to pick the apple, the branch broke, and down she went and lay in a little heap under the tree.

"Well, Miss Sterling said she felt as if she must fly right out of that window and go pick her up. But it did n't take her many minutes to run down the stairs and out the front door — she did n't stop to ask permission — and over across lots to Polly. She was in a dead faint, but in a minute she came to, and Miss Sterling ran up to the house and got Dr. Dudley and his wife, and they carried her in, and Miss Sterling went too. The Doctor could n't find that Polly was hurt at all, only bruised a little — you see, the branches had broken her fall, and she was all around again in a few days. Miss Sterling was pretty well upset by it, so that the Doctor came home with her, and she had to go to bed, same as Polly did! It made quite a stir here.

"Ever since then Polly has run in and out, any time of day, just as I hear she does at the hospital. She's that kind of a girl, never makes any trouble, and so nothing is said."

"I guess I shall break lots of the rules before I know what they are."

"You'll learn 'em soon enough, don't you worry! There's a long list; but you'll get used to 'em after a while — we have to. There's nothing like getting used to things. It's a great help."

CHAPTER III

IT is a shame, Miss Nita!" Polly was saying. "To think of it — that you can't curl your hair even to go to a wedding! I wonder if father or mother could do anything."

"Oh, no!" cried Miss Sterling, in sudden terror. "Don't, I beg of you, let them say a word to Miss Sniffen! She'd turn me right out!"

"I should wish she would, if I were you."

"Where could I go? I'd have to sit on the sidewalk!"

Polly laughed.

"No, Miss Nita," catching one of the slim white hands and pressing it against her cheek, "you come right over to our house when Miss Sniffen turns you outdoors, and we'll take care of you!"

"It isn't anything to laugh at," sobbed the little woman.

"I know, I'm wicked to laugh; but I had a picture of you sitting on the curb in your nightgown, and I could n't help it!"

23

Then Miss Sterling laughed too.

Shortly she fell to crying again. "I did want to look nice at Cousin Jennie's wedding, as nice as I could, and I do think it is downright mean!" She hammered out the last words with desperate force.

Polly stood by her side, distressed into silence.

"You don't know that she'll let you go anyway, do you?" she asked presently.

"Yes, she said I could, and then I asked her if I might curl my hair. She snapped out a disagreeable 'no,' and I turned and came upstairs."

Polly was doing some hard thinking.

"Queer, Jennie should marry at her age," Miss Sterling resumed after a brief pause, wiping her eyes dry. "She is forty-one, only two years younger than I."

"Are you forty-three? Nobody'd ever guess it." Polly gazed at her critically. "I wonder if I could n't curl your hair at the last minute, and smuggle you downstairs, all wrapped up, so Miss Sniffen would n't know. You could wet it out the next morning."

Miss Sterling shook her head with a wee smile. "I would if I dared, but I don't. If Miss Sniffen were n't there to see, Mrs. Nobbs would be, and

24

nothing escapes her eyes. No, 't would be too much risk."

"Maybe it would," Polly admitted, and then paused to listen. "It's three o'clock and I must go. I halfway promised David and Leonora I'd come down there this afternoon. I guess they're a little bit jealous of you. It's handy to run over here, and they're so far away. I should think you'd get tired of me, I come so much."

"Tired of you!" echoed Miss Sterling. "You are the only bit of cheerfulness I have to look forward to. Last night I could n't sleep; I was just upset after seeing Miss Sniffen, and my head felt wretched. But I kept saying to myself, 'Polly will be here in the morning!' and that helped me through the night. You don't know — you never will know! — what a comfort you are!" She pulled Polly down and gave her a little squeeze.

"And then I did n't come this morning after all!" cried Polly in sudden contrition. "That was mean! But I had some things to do for mother, and Chris wanted me to help him with his stamps, and so I did n't get to it. I'm sorry."

"Dear child! I don't expect you to spend all your time with an old gray-haired woman who has n't the mite of a claim on you."

"Gray-haired!" chuckled Polly. "You can't find one gray hair. I dare you to try!" She shook a threatening finger.

"Don't have to try. I know just where there are two — right in there." She bent her head.

"Oh, they're only a little pale!" laughed Polly. "They are n't really gray. But I must go, Miss Nita. Good-bye."

"If you come across the Board anywhere downstairs, you may give it my compliments."

"Does the Board meet this afternoon?" whispered Polly. "It would n't be compliments I'd give them!" She waved her hand, and the door shut.

Yes, the Board was in session, the Board of Managers of the June Holiday Home. A little hum of voices came to Polly's ears from a room at the left. "I wish —" She stopped midway between the staircase and the front entrance, her forehead wrinkled in thought.

A maid came from the rear of the house, duster in hand.

"Oh, Mabel!" Polly began in a low tone,

"would you mind taking a message to the Board for me?"

The girl, with a shade of surprise on her face, said, "Certainly, Miss Polly, I'll take it in. Who shall I give it to?"

"Mrs. Beers — she's president. Tell her, please, that I have something very important to say to the Board, and ask her if I can come in now, or pretty soon — whenever it won't interfere with their business."

The maid knocked and disappeared. In a moment she returned.

"She says you can come now."

There was very evident curiosity mingled with the smiles of greeting.

"I happened to think," Polly began at once, "that maybe you could do something to help out matters. I've been up to see Miss Sterling, and she is feeling pretty bad because she can't curl her hair to go to her cousin's wedding, and I did n't know but you would fix things so she can."

"'Fix things'?" scowled the lady at the head of the table. "You mean, put on an electric attachment?"

"Oh, no!" Polly came near disgracing her-

27

self by a laugh. "But it's against the rule, you know, to curl your hair, and Miss Sterling asked if she could n't, just for the evening, and Miss Sniffen said no."

The ladies gazed at one another, plain surprise on their faces. Then they looked questioningly at their presiding officer.

"The Board never interferes with the superintendent's rules — " began Mrs. Beers.

"Unless it is something we especially don't like," put in the member with a conscience.

The president sent a severe glance down the table.

"I thought, maybe, just for this once, you'd fix it so she could — she would wet it all out before breakfast." Polly was very much in earnest.

"There's altogether too much complaint among the inmates," spoke up a fat woman on Mrs. Beers's left. "They should be made to realize how fortunate they are to have such a beautiful Home to live in, instead of finding fault with every little thing and sending people to try to wheedle us into giving them something different from what they have."

"Oh, Mrs. Puddicombe!" burst out Polly,

"Miss Sterling did n't send me at all! She does n't know a thing about it! I never thought of coming in until I passed the door — then it occurred to me that maybe you would like to help her out. It's pretty hard to have to go to a wedding with your hair all flat, just as they do it at a hospital — I don't believe you'd like it yourself, Mrs. Puddicombe."

Several smiles were visible. A titter escaped the youngest member.

Mrs. Puddicombe's broad face reddened under her amazing labyrinth of screwlike curls.

"These charity people," she resumed irrelevantly, "never know when they're well off. Why, this Home is the very gate of heaven! Just look at that new rug in the library — it cost three hundred dollars! But who appreciates it?"

"Well, I should rather walk over a thirty-cent rug than every time I turned round have to have a rule to turn by!" Polly tossed out the words impetuously.

"You're a saucy girl!" returned Mrs. Puddicombe. "You'd better go home and tell your father to teach you good manners."

The president rapped for order.

"I beg your pardon, if I was saucy," Polly hastened to say. "I did n't mean to be. I was only thinking —"

"That will do," interrupted Mrs. Beers. "There has been too much time given to a very trivial matter."

Polly walked away from the June Holiday Home in the company of uneasy thoughts. She feared she had made matters worse for her dear Miss Nita.

CHAPTER IV

A JUNE HOLIDAY

THE wedding night brought no recall of the negative answer which Miss Sniffen had given to Juanita Sterling, although the little woman hoped until the last moment for some sign of relenting.

But Polly was on hand to braid the thick, soft hair into a becoming coronet, and to assert that she knew the bride wouldn't look half so pretty.

Several days after, Polly danced in, her face full of the morning.

"You feel pretty well, don't you?" she began in her most coaxing way.

"A little better than usual," Miss Sterling laughed. "What do you want me to do?"

"You know David and Leonora and I went down to Fern Brook last week," Polly began deliberately, seating herself in the rocker which Miss Sterling did not like, "and ever since then I've been wishing it would come a lovely day for you and me to have a little picnic all by ourselves. Or we might ask one or two others, if you like. Will you, Miss Nita? You'll break my heart if you say no — I see it coming! Just say, 'I should be de-e-lighted to go!'"

"Oh, I'd love to, but —"

"No, there is n't a 'but' or an 'if' or anything! We're going! Who else do you want?"

"You crazy child! I'm afraid it will use me up. I don't dare risk it. We'll have to take the trolley — and the walk across lots — oh, I can't, Polly!"

"Yes, you're going! I've made up my mind! The trolley ride won't hurt you; you'll have nothing to do but to sit still, and the walk is n't long."

"Remember, I have n't been off the grounds, except for the wedding, in months."

"I don't forget, and it's awful. You felt better the day after the wedding."

"Ye-s, but —"

"We're going! It's decided!" Polly jumped up. "Say quick who we'll invite, and then I'll run down and beg permission to go on a picnic — unless you'd rather."

"Mercy — no! I guess that's one reason why I have n't been away; I have n't had life enough to want to unwind red tape."

"I shall love it," laughed Polly. "Shall we ask Mrs. Albright? She's nice."

"Yes, and how would you like Mrs. Adlerfeld? I think she's pretty lonely."

"First-rate! She is sweet, and she talks the dearest way. Hurry up now, and get ready! I'll be back in no time with the passports."

"Why, I don't know," Miss Sniffen hesitated. "How far is it, do you say?"

"We take the trolley out to Grafton Street," Polly explained slowly, "and then we go 'cross lots just a little way to the dearest grove and a lovely little brook that tumbles over the stones — oh, it's beautiful! Can't you go with us, Miss Sniffen?" cried Polly in a burst of generosity, shivering the next minute for fear her invitation would be accepted!

"No, thank you," actually smiled the superintendent; "my business does n't include picnics, and I doubt whether it would be wise for Miss Sterling to go so far away from the Home. It might cause trouble — and unnecessary expense; the others may go if they wish."

"Oh, Miss Sniffen, please let Miss Sterling go! That's one reason why I want it, because I think it will do her good," wheedled Polly, adding tactfully, "Father says it often makes the nerves better to get the muscles tired."

"Yes, I think that myself. Of course, it would do her no real harm, if you could manage to keep her from getting wrought up and having one of her tantrums."

"Oh, I promise you I'll bring her home as good as new!" declared Polly recklessly. And with profuse thanks she darted softly away.

The four walked sedately down the long stairs in repressed glee, the three ladies waiting on the piazza while Polly registered their names, destination, time of starting, and expected return, in the daybook on the secretary's desk.

"Red tape all wound up!" she finally announced in a whisper, and the quartette proceeded to the corner below, to be in readiness for the car.

Juanita Sterling appeared to have lost her weak nerves somewhere on the way, as the four left the road behind them and made a path through the clover into the distance.

"I want to sit right down and enjoy it!" she exclaimed, dropping among the blossoms. "Hear that bird! It's a bobolink — it is! Oh, me! Oh, my! I have n't heard a bobolink for — I'm not going to bother to think how long. It is glorious!"

"This is n't anything compared to the woods and the brook," asserted Polly.

She put down her lunch-basket and snipped off some clover heads.

"Those are full of honey, Miss Nita, — taste! They are n't buggy a mite."

Like bees they sipped and sipped, and laughed and said foolish things like children at a merry-making.

Suddenly Miss Sterling sprang to her feet.

"The day is going," she cried, "and we must get there quick! Come!"

The "just a little way" of Polly's lengthened on and on until the three who were not accustomed to country fields looked in dismay toward the long line of trees which seemed so very far off.

"Are you fearfully tired?" Polly would reiterate, and "Not a bit!" Miss Sterling would lie with complacency, while Mrs. Albright grew wondrously jolly in her effort to keep everybody from realizing the truth.

When, finally, they stepped into the dim, cool wood, melodious with the gurgle and splash of hurrying water and the lilting of unseen birds, nobody remembered the hot, weary way she had come.

Miss Sterling, stretched upon a bed of vines and moss, announced that she was in "heaven."

Little Mrs. Adlerfeld looked across in answering sympathy.

"It makes me so glad and happy, it hurts," she said, her hand upon her breast.

"I knew you'd love it!" exulted Polly, dropping lightly between the two and laying a hand upon each. "Let's come out here every week!"

Nobody objected. Mrs. Albright wagged an approving smile, Mrs. Adlerfeld continued her dreamy gaze into the brook, the invalid was too drowsy to speak.

"Go to sleep, all of you!" Polly commanded gayly. "I'll have a red-and-green luncheon for you when you wake up!"

She bounded off along the slippery pine-needled path and disappeared behind a curtain of foliage.

Miss Sterling awoke with a start — where was she? Then the events of the morning flashed into view, and she smiled contentedly.

Mrs. Adlerfeld, leaning back against a stone,

was peacefully nodding, and a gentle snore from the other of the trio told that Polly's order had been obeyed.

Where was Polly? Miss Sterling looked around, but she was not in sight. Even with the springing of a sudden fear she caught the sound of distant talking — a man's voice! She rose to her feet and stood irresolute, listening. Then she smiled. That was Polly's laugh! In a moment two figures rounded a clump of young pines. Juanita Sterling caught her breath — the man walking beside Polly was Mr. Randolph!

The president of the June Holiday Home found a welcoming hand as he strode up the piney path.

"Were n't you surprised, Miss Nita?" cried Polly. "He's going to have us arrested for trespassing on his land!" — with a roguish glance toward the owner.

"Then we shall have to invite him to luncheon, shan't we?" Miss Sterling's blue eyes held pleasant twinkles. "It is too pleasant to-day to go to jail!"

The gentleman chuckled.

"Oh! will you stay?" begged Polly.

"You'd better!" urged Miss Sterling. "There

are Banbury turnovers and chicken sandwiches!"

"It is hard to refuse —" he began.

"Oh, I knew you could n't say no when Miss Nita asked you!" sang Polly delightedly. "Nobody can! Except Miss Sniffen!" she added conscientiously.

"Miss Sniffen" appeared to pass unnoticed. Polly suddenly remembered her handful of wintergreen sprigs and berries, and the sleepers awoke to join the merriment and the little pungent feast.

"I came up," Mr. Randolph explained, "to look over some trees that a man wants, and I rather think I ought to go directly back; but," he went on with a whimsical laugh, "I guess business won't know it if I steal this June holiday. It is a good while since I had one." His face grew instantly grave.

"You have to catch June holidays quick," smiled Mrs. Adlerfeld wistfully. "They don't stay!"

"No, they don't stay," Mr. Randolph agreed gravely. "But," he brightened, "you of June Holiday Home have them all the year round." He looked from one face to another.

38

Mrs. Albright smiled a wordless response, the swift color flushed Miss Sterling's face, while fun played about Polly's mouth.

"You have a pretty good time there, don't you?" he persisted.

His eyes were bent on Miss Sterling; yet Mrs. Albright kindly interposed with the safe assertion, "It is a beautiful place."

"Yes, it is beautiful," he replied, scanning the cheery, wrinkled face. "Any town should consider it a great privilege to have such an institution within its borders. Mrs. Milworth — or June Holiday, as she preferred to be called — was a wonderful woman. I am glad to be in a position to help in the carrying-out of her plans."

Miss Sterling smiled a little queerly. Polly opened her lips, then shut them tight, and finally announced quite irrelevantly that she was hungry.

One of Mrs. Dudley's prettiest tablecloths was spread on a little piney level close to the brook, and Polly set out the paper plates and cups and the boxes of food.

"Which do you like best, Mr. Randolph, coffee or chocolate?" Polly queried anxiously.

"I will answer as a little boy of my acquaintance did, — 'Whichever you have the most of.'"

"Well, you see, we have only one, and I do hope you don't like coffee best."

"I don't!" he declared. "I always drink chocolate when I can get it."

"I'm glad I brought it, then!" cried Polly. "You cut the cake, please, Miss Nita. I'm afraid I could n't do it straight."

The little feast was ready at last, appetites were found to be of the keenest sort, and everything went merrily.

"I have never had the pleasure of a meal at the Home," — Mr. Randolph was eating a Banbury turnover with plain enjoyment. "I suppose you ladies are treated to this sort of thing every day."

"We have a pretty good cook," answered Miss Sterling discreetly; "but these pies are of Mrs. Dudley's make. Polly brought the lunch."

"Oh!" The man's eyebrows raised themselves a little. "Then I should say, Mrs. Dudley is an excellent Banbury pie-ist."

"I shall have to tell her that," laughed Polly. "It will please her very much."

"Nothing delights a woman more than to have her cooking praised," laughed Mrs. Albright.

"I learned that years ago." Mr. Randolph smiled reminiscently. "When I was first married, I think I must have been a rather notional man to cook for. My wife seldom did much in the kitchen, but one day she made a salad. As it did not exactly appeal to my appetite, after one taste I remarked that I was not very hungry. To my dismay she burst into tears. It was her favorite salad, and she had made it with unusual care, never dreaming that I would not like it as well as she did. Ever afterwards I ate the whole bill of fare straight through."

"It sometimes takes courage to do that," smiled Mrs. Albright. "I hope you had a good cook. How much people think of eating! I don't blame 'em either. Nobody enjoys anything better than — for instance, a lunch like this."

"Robert Louis Stevenson did," spoke up Mrs. Adlerfeld. "I read in my day-to-day book this morning — I can't quite remember — yes, this is it: 'After a good woman, and a good book, and tobacco, there is nothing so agreeable on earth as a river.' I did not think then I should be eating my dinner right on the bank of a little river!" She gazed down lovingly on the water swirling and foaming among the stones.

"Stevenson ought to know," said Mr. Randolph with a pleased smile. "So he is one of your favorites as well as mine!"

"Yes, I like him very." Her little sunny face beamed with pleasure. "His book is more educating as many things said by a teacher."

"He is a good teacher."

"I wish he had not put in tobacco," scowled Mrs. Adlerfeld. "There are a many things better as tobacco."

"You have not tried it," he returned. "Stevenson knew because he had tried it."

The little woman shook her head decidedly. "I have been suffered a many times by tobacco." Then a smile broke mischievously. "You may smoke after dinner, Mr. Randolph."

The man laughed. "I was not pleading for myself," he protested. "This is sufficiently soothing —" His hand made a comprehensive sweep. "Tobacco would be superfluous."

Miss Sterling had risen and gone over to the

lunch-box, where she was trying to open a second thermos bottle.

"Let me do that for you!" He sprang to help her.

She stepped back heedlessly, her foot slipped, and with a sharp cry she fell on the smooth slope.

Polly and Mr. Randolph reached her together.

"Are you hurt?" Polly's voice was distressed.

"Any damage done?" The man's tone was cheery, yet concerned.

She laughed bravely.

"Oh, no!" taking the proffered hands and trying to rise. Then she sank back, catching her breath hard.

"It's just my ankle — but it is n't hurt!" she declared fiercely. "Let me try it again."

She stood on her feet. "I guess I'm all here," she laughed; yet even with the words her face grew white.

Mr. Randolph caught her, and she drooped limply against him.

He laid her down gently, and at once she opened her eyes.

Mrs. Albright was rubbing her hands. "You will be all right in a minute," she said cheerily.

"I am all right now," Miss Sterling maintained. "How stupid of me to faint! I won't have a sprained ankle — so there!"

The rest laughed, though a little uncertainly.

Polly, like a true doctor's daughter, was examining the injury.

"It does n't swell, so it can't be sprained," she decided positively.

Miss Sterling sat up and supplemented Polly's inspection. "Merely a strain. I'll be able to walk in a little while."

"You'd better not tax it," Mr. Randolph advised. "I am glad my car is so near. I drove in as far as the road was good."

"Oh!" Miss Sterling's voice was grateful. "I was wondering how I could ever walk over to the trolley."

"You would not have had to do that in any case, but my car is ready whenever you care to return."

"The ride will be a lovely ending to the day," Miss Sterling assured him, "and, if it won't hinder you, suppose we don't go any sooner on my account."

Four o'clock found the picnickers leaving the wood, the injured one assisted on either side by Polly and Nelson Randolph.

The way was not long, but time after time it took all the pluck of which Juanita Sterling was mistress not to stop in the path and cry out that she could not go a step farther.

Her escorts were solicitous.

"Lean on me more, Miss Nita," Polly would urge. "I'm awfully strong. Favor your foot all you can."

"Had n't I better carry you the rest of the way?" asked Mr. Randolph when she could no longer hide her pain.

Her thanks were gracefully given, but she refused to proceed except upon her own feet.

"It is nothing," she insisted. "I shall be all right in a moment."

Never did hospitable inn look more inviting to a weary traveler than did the waiting car to Juanita Sterling.

"You sit in front," advised Polly, "it will be much easier for you."

"Certainly!" the man exclaimed, throwing open the other door.

But before Polly could stay her she had

stepped to the running-board — and was on the back seat!

"You are naughty!" Polly pouted.

Miss Sterling laughed softly.

The man said nothing, only helped Mrs. Adlerfeld to a place beside him.

The cooling, sunlit air was delightful. It was long since Miss Sterling had been in an automobile, and the car rode as easy as a rocking-chair. She drew deep breaths, and half forgot that her ankle was still throbbing from its recent effort.

"Feel equal to a little longer ride?" suddenly inquired the driver, throwing the query toward Miss Sterling.

"Equal to anything!" was the happy reply.

"Oh, that will be nice!" cried Polly, squeezing her friend's arm, and beaming on her right-hand neighbor.

"Am I going too fast for you?" was the next question.

"Not a bit!" — "It is lovely!" — "The faster the better!" came in merry succession from the back seat.

They spun along the smooth road with greater speed, and the freshness of the country was brought to them in one steady sweep.

46

"This is glorious!" breathed Miss Sterling.

"I never rode in one of these cars before," confessed Mrs. Adlerfeld blithely.

"Indeed!" a pleasant light flashed in the driver's eyes. "And how do you like it?"

"Oh, I like it very!" The wrinkled face was radiant. "It makes me so glad and happy!"

"We will have another ride some day," was the unexpected response, which made the little Swedish woman fairly gasp in delight.

The gayety of the party came to a sudden end when Mr. Randolph drove into the Home grounds.

"Please, not a word to anybody about my fall," said Miss Sterling in a low voice, as she was helped from the car.

"Is that wise?" It was asked in a surprised tone.

"Extremely wise," was the smiling response. "I might wish to go picnicking again, you know." Her twinkling eyes met his puzzled face.

"As you will," he promised gravely.

There was time for no more. The others were waiting.

Polly kept beside Miss Sterling who walked

without a limp and gave no sign of the torture she was undergoing.

"Go right upstairs!" whispered Polly. "I'll report for all of you when I come down."

"You need n't go up, the rail will be sufficient."

But Polly would not relinquish her charge until she saw her safe in her room.

"How came you to be riding with the president of the Home?" Miss Sniffen looked down sternly on Polly.

"Oh! did you see us come? Was n't it lucky — nice that Mr. Randolph had his car? And was n't he good to bring us?"

"Was the meeting by arrangement?" questioned Miss Sniffen severely.

"Oh, no! I was so surprised! We all were! He happened to go over there to see about some trees, and so stayed to luncheon. We had a lovely time! Was n't it queer it happened to be his land?"

Miss Sniffen's thin lips drew themselves into a sarcastic line.

"'Happened!' There seems to have been a number of *happenings*."

"I know it," Polly agreed demurely, looking

at her watch to make sure of the time. "We came in about five minutes ago, Miss Sniffen. It was twenty minutes of six just before we got here."

"What time did you leave the picnic grounds?"

"I think it was four o'clock."

"Did you come directly back?" Miss Sniffen's hard eyes fastened on Polly's face.

"Oh, no! We had a beautiful ride! We went 'way out on the Flaxton road, along by the river. Don't you think Mr. Randolph is a very lovable man?"

"I think it was entirely out of place for you to spend the day in the woods with an unmarried man. I shall look into it."

Polly's brown eyes grew big and wondering. "Why, Miss Sniffen, I don't see what harm there was! We had the loveliest time!"

The superintendent did not reply. She turned deliberately and walked down the great hall.

Polly watched her a moment, the wondering look still in her eyes. Then she sped swiftly toward home. She hoped Miss Sniffen would not find out about Miss Nita's ankle.

CHAPTER V

MISS LILY AND DOODLES

THE long line of choir boys issued decorously from the side door of St. Bartholomew's. The running, pushing, scuffling, and laughter were reserved for the next street. Sly nudges and subdued chuckles were all that the most reckless indulged in under the shadows of the church.

At the foot of the steps stood a slender, white-haired woman with stooping shoulders. She scanned each face as it emerged from the dim passageway, and her own grew a bit anxious as the boys passed. Then it suddenly brightened with recognition. Doodles had appeared.

The woman stepped forward to meet him. "Excuse me," she hesitated, "but are you the one who sang that solo, 'Take heart, ye weary'?"

The boy smiled his modest answer.

"Oh, I want to thank you for it! I've been waiting till you came, and I was so afraid I'd missed you after all, for I probably shan't have

50

another chance. I wanted you to know how much good it has done me."

"Has it?" Doodles looked his pleasure.

"Oh, it was beautiful!" she said tremulously. "I never heard anything like it! I always enjoy your singing, and am so disappointed when you don't sing alone; but seems to me this piece was sweetest of all!"

"I guess you'll like the one for next Sunday," Doodles told her, — "'And God shall wipe away all tears.'"

"Oh!" It was mingled longing and regret. "That must be beautiful! I wish I could hear it — seems as if I must!" Her voice broke a little. "But I'm afraid I can't. I shan't be here next Sunday."

"That's too bad! I'm sorry!"

"It can't be helped. I am glad I could come to-day and hear you — it does me more good than sermons!" Tears made the blue eyes shine.

"Perhaps I shall sing it some other time when you are here," Doodles suggested hopefully.

The woman shook her head. Her reply was soft and broken. "I shan't ever be here again."

"Oh!" Doodles was instantly sympathetic.

Then a gleam lighted his sorrowing face. "I'll tell you what," he began hurriedly, "I'll come to your house and sing for you this afternoon — that is, if you'd like me to," he added.

Such joy flooded the tearful eyes! "Oh, you dear boy! if you would! I don't know how to thank you!"

"That's all right! I'd love to do it. Shall I come early, right after dinner, or —"

"Oh, come early! It is so good of you!" The tears threatened to overflow their bounds.

Doodles glanced down the street. "What is your address, please? I have to take the next car."

"Why, yes! I forgot! I live at 304 North Charles Street."

"Thank you." He lifted his cap with a bright smile. "I'll be there!" he promised and was off.

The woman watched him as he hailed the passing car. He saw her from a window and waved his hand. She returned the salute, and then walked slowly away.

"I hope he won't forget the number," she said to herself, "he did n't take it down. And I never thought to give him my name!"

Doodles easily found the place the woman

had designated. The house was small and dingy, and two grimy babies were playing on the doorstep.

"Miss Lily's upstairs, in back," answered the girl to whom the inquiry had been referred. "I guess it's her you want. Ther' ain't nobody else, 'cept Miss Goby, an' she's a big un."

The top of the dim flight was nearly reached when a door opened and threw a stream of light on the stairway. The boy saw his new friend waiting for him.

"Walk right in!" she said cordially. "It's awfully good of you to come!"

The room was in noticeable contrast with the rest of the house. Here everything was neat and homelike, although there was little attempt at ornament. Doodles was soon seated in a cushioned rocker and listening to the little old lady's grateful talk.

"When you spoke of that new song, 'God shall wipe away all tears,' it did seem as if I just could n't miss hearing you sing it! But I never dreamed that you could do such a thing as to come and sing it to me here. I wish I had a better place for you to sing in, but I've had to take up with 'most anything these days."

53

The lad hastened to assure her that he was accustomed to sing in a small room, and that it made no difference to him where he was.

"Then you don't mind not having an organ or piano or anything?" The tone was anxious.

"Not a bit," he smiled. "I never used to have accompaniment — I can sing anywhere."

After the first note Miss Lily sat motionless, bending forward a little, her hands clasped in her lap, her eyes on the singer. Whether she saw him was doubtful, for her tears fell fast as Doodles sang the comforting words.

"And God shall wipe away all tears from their eyes; . . . and there shall be no more death, neither sorrow, nor crying, . . . neither shall there be any more pain: . . . for the former things are passed away."

With silence the listener suddenly dropped her face in her hands and began to sob.

In a moment Doodles was singing again, and soon she grew calmer. When he stopped she was ready to talk.

"I don't see what makes me cry so!" she broke out, with a great effort fighting back the tears. "I'm all upset anyway. It is so lovely having you sing — right here! You don't know! I'm afraid I shan't ever want you to stop." She laughed quiveringly.

"More now?" he asked.

"If you are n't tired," she hesitated.

"Never!"

He sang again.

In the doorways upstairs and down people were listening. The little house on North Charles Street had never heard such music within its walls. As the song ceased, applause came, — uncertainly at first, then louder and steady.

The two in the back room looked at each other and smiled.

"I guess they like it as well as I do," Miss Lily said.

In response Doodles sang "Only an armor-bearer," still one of his favorites, and at its close the approval of those outside was prompt and long.

Many other songs followed; apparently the audience grew.

"They'll tire you out," the little lady fretted.

The boy shook his head decidedly, beginning for the second time, "And God shall wipe away all tears."

"Oh, it is like heaven itself!" Miss Lily breathed. Then she sighed softly. "What if I had missed it!"

"I think I shall have to go now," at last Doodles said; "but I will come and sing for you again any time, if you like, — any time when you are here." He rose and picked up his cap.

"Oh, my dear boy, I'm not ever coming back! I'm" — she began to sob, and Doodles could scarcely make out the words — "I'm going — to the — poorhouse!" She broke down, and her slight shoulders shook pitifully.

The boy stood as if stunned. Then he stepped near. "Don't cry!" he said softly, "don't cry!"

"Oh — I can't help it!" she mourned. "I've kept up — I thought maybe I should n't have to go; but my eyes have given out, and I can't earn anything only by sewing — and I can't sew now! To think of me in the poorhouse!"

"I'll come and sing for you there!" cried the boy impulsively.

"Oh! you would n't — would you?" She clutched at the only straw of hope.

"Of course, I will! I'd be glad to!"

"You're awfully good!" She wiped her eyes.

"I did n't mean to entertain you with tears," she smiled. "Seems as if I might stop, but I can't." Her eyes were wet again.

A sudden light illumined the lad's face. He opened his lips, then shut them.

"How soon do you expect to go?" he asked.

"Some time the last of the week, the man thought." She swallowed hard. "He said he'd give me time to pick up my things — he was real good."

"I'll see you again before the last of the week," promised Doodles, putting out his hand.

She clasped it in both of hers.

"You are just a dear — that's what you are!" she said tremulously. "And you don't know how I thank you! I can't tell you what it has been to me!"

As the singer passed down the stairs curious eyes peered out at him; but he did not know it. His heart was full of Miss Lily's grief, although overspreading it was the beautiful thought that had come to him so suddenly a moment ago.

CHAPTER VI

"BETTER THAN THE POORHOUSE"

POLLY was on the veranda when Doodles came.

"Why, Doodles Stickney! I was just thinking of you! How did you know I wanted to see you this morning?"

"I did n't," he laughed; "but I wanted to see you!"

"I'm so glad — oh, I forgot! I'm due at the dentist's at ten o'clock! Maybe I can get off."

"No, no! I could n't stay till that time anyway. I came down on business —"

"Dear me!" laughed Polly, "how grand we are this morning!"

"I don't know whether it is 'grand' or not — it depends a good deal on the president of June Holiday Home. I'll tell you all about it," dropping into a chair beside Polly.

He related the incidents of the day before, of Miss Lily's meeting him at the church door, of his singing to her in the afternoon, and finally of her distress at going to the poorhouse.

58

"And I happened to think if she could only come to the June Holiday Home —"

"Lovely!" cried Polly. "I don't see why she can't!"

"Nor I, but somebody may. I thought I'd see you first and maybe you'd give me a little note of introduction — you know Mr. Randolph so well, and I never spoke to him."

"Certainly I will! I'll go right and do it now! Chris will want to see you — I'll send him out."

The note that Doodles carried away with him was in Polly's best style.

Dear Mr. Randolph: —

This is to introduce my friend Doodles Stickney, or to be perfectly proper, Julius Stickney. He will tell you about Miss Lily, and I do hope you will make a place for her at the Home. I have never seen her, but I know she is nice, or Doodles would n't like her or take so much trouble to get her in. I feel awfully sorry for her. It must be dreadful to have your eyes give out so you have to go to the poorhouse.

Miss Sniffen made a terrible fuss because you stayed at the picnic with us — or because we stayed with you. Anyway, she scolded Miss Nita like everything. I'm afraid we can't ever have a picnic again. She began on me when I went to report our arrival — she happened to be at the desk. You know you have to report as soon as you get in, and I said I'd do it for the crowd. Miss Nita could n't because her ankle ached so. It turned black and blue — just awful! She would n't say a word to anybody, and father sent some liniment by me. The first smelt so strong Miss Nita did n't dare use it for fear they 'd suspect, so father sent her another kind. He said it was n't quite so good as the smelly sort, but her ankle is a whole lot better. Don't you think she is brave? I don't know what Miss Sniffen would say if she knew about that. We've all kept whist.

This is a pretty long letter, but I knew you'd want to hear about Miss Nita's ankle. You will let Miss Lily in, won't you?

Yours with hope,
POLLY MAY DUDLEY.

Thank you ever so much for that beautiful ride! I shall never forget it.

Doodles walked into the great office of the Fair Harbor Paper Company and asked to see Mr. Randolph.

"We hired a boy last week. We don't want any more." The clerk was turning away.

"Oh, I'm not applying for a place!" cried Doodles, his voice full of laughter. "I wish to see the president on business."

The young man scowled, irritated by his blunder, and surveyed the boy with a disagreeable sneer.

"Well, he's too busy to attend to kids. What do you want anyhow?"

Doodles hesitated. He did not wish to tell his errand to this pompous young person.

"Please say to Mr. Randolph that I would like to see him on important business about the June Holiday Home."

"Who sent you?"

"No one; but I have a letter of introduction."

"Oh, you have! Hand it out!"

Doodles made no move toward his pocket.

"I wish to give it to Mr. Randolph himself," he said gently.

"Well, you can't see him. He's busy now."

"I will wait," replied the boy, and took a chair.

The clerk went behind the railing and sat down at a desk.

Doodles looked out on the street and watched the passers. Occasionally his eyes would wander back to the office and over the array of men and women bent to their work, then they would return to the wide doorway. He felt that he had small chance to speak with Mr. Randolph until he should go to luncheon, and that, he argued to himself, would not be a very good time to present his business. He wished that the unpleasant young clerk would go first — he would like to try some other.

Men and women came and went, some of them disappearing in the rear, where, undoubtedly, was the man he sought. If only he dared follow! Finally the offensive youth came out through the gate and over to where he sat.

"Here, you kid," he began in an insolent tone, "you've hung round here long enough! Now beat it!"

Into the soft brown eyes of Doodles shot an angry light.

The other saw it and smiled sneeringly. He did not count on the lad's strength.

In a moment the indignation had passed. There was none of it in the quiet voice. "Good-day, sir!"

Doodles was gone.

A plan had instantly formed in his mind. He would get himself a lunch, and then wait outside the office until Mr. Randolph appeared. That was the only way. It never occurred to him to give the matter up.

One restaurant was passed; it did not look

inviting. The next was better, but flies were crawling over the bottles and jars in the window. He went on.

"It will cost more, I suppose," he muttered regretfully to himself, as he entered a neat café where the door was opened to him by a boy in livery.

"Bread and milk," he ordered of the trim maid, and he smiled to himself contentedly at the daintiness with which it was served.

The milk was cool and sweet, and Doodles was hungry. The whistles and clocks announced that it was noon, and soon afterward people began to stream in. Women with shopping-bags and bundles, men with newspapers, hat-less working-girls; but everywhere were courtesy and low voices. Doodles was glad of his choice.

He sat eating slowly, wishing he knew at what time he would be most likely to meet Mr. Randolph, when he stared at a man coming toward him — it was the president of the Paper Company! The boy drew in a delighted breath — what great good luck!

Mr. Randolph sat down at a little table not far away. He looked tired, the lad thought, and he decided to wait until the close of the meal, if he could manage to make his own small supply of milk last long enough.

"Nothing more, thank you," Doodles told the maid who came to ask. "This milk is very nice," he added, which brought out an answering smile.

At last the president had reached his fruit. The boy's last crumb had vanished long ago, and he thought he might venture across to the other table.

"May I speak with you a moment, sir?" he asked softly, taking the letter from his pocket.

"Certainly." The man bowed with his accustomed courtesy.

"Polly Dudley gave me this for you."

At mention of the name a pleasant light overspread the grave face.

The lad watched him as he read. The light deepened, then the brows drew together in a scowl. Doodles wondered what Polly had written.

"This lady is a friend of yours, I take it." The keen gray eyes looked straight at the boy.

"Yes, sir," Doodles smiled, "though a very new one. I never saw her till yesterday."

The eyes bent upon him widened a little.

The lad told his story as simply as possible, touching lightly upon his own part in it. "And so," he ended artlessly, his appealing brown eyes looking straight into the steady gray ones, "I thought, even if there were rules and patches and things she did n't like, it would be better than the poorhouse."

A little amused smile replaced the hint of surprise on the man's face.

"Where do you sing?" he asked abruptly.

"At St. Bartholomew's Church, Foxford."

"Did you come down expressly to see me about this?"

"Yes, sir," answered Doodles.

"How did you know I was here?"

"I did n't." A smile overspread the small face. "I waited at your office until" — he hesitated an instant — "I thought I would find you after I had had a lunch."

"Get hungry?"

"Oh, no, sir!"

Mr. Randolph eyed him questioningly.

"The young man thought I'd waited long enough," was the gentle explanation.

"So he told you to go!"

65

"I guess he got tired of seeing me there," smiled Doodles.

"Did you wait long?"

" 'Most two hours."

"Tall, light-haired fellow, was it?"

The boy assented.

The president mused a moment and then resumed: —

"In any case your friend will have to make an application. I think I will let her take a blank. Have her fill it out, and you can send it down to me. I will attend to the rest."

Doodles rose from his chair, feeling that it was time to go, yet he could not forbear one question.

"Do you think she can come to the Home?" His tone betrayed his solicitude.

"I will do the best I can for her, Master Stickney." Mr. Randolph had also risen, and he smiled down into the upturned face. "It will have to be referred to the Committee on Applications, but I will see that it is put through as quickly as possible."

Doodles decided to see Miss Lily before going home, so it was still early afternoon when he entered the little house on North Charles Street.

"Why, you dear boy!" The little lady had him in her arms. "How good of you to come! I was thinking this morning, what if I should n't ever hear you sing again — and now here you are!"

"I told you I 'd come," laughed Doodles.

"Yes," smiled Miss Lily; "but people forget. I guess you are n't the forgetting kind."

"I did n't come to-day to sing," the boy began slowly. Now that the moment was at hand he felt suddenly shy at disclosing his errand. "I happened to think yesterday of the June Holiday Home down in Fair Harbor, and I wondered if you would n't rather go there and live than to go — anywhere else."

For an instant Miss Lily stared. "That beautiful place up on Edgewood Hill? — me? — go there?" Her mobile face showed a strange mingling of astonishment, fear, and joy.

"Certainly! Should n't you like to?"

"'Like to'! All the rest of my life? — Oh, I can't believe it!"

"I don't know that you can get in," Doodles hastened to explain; "but I went to Fair Harbor this morning to see Mr. Randolph — he 's the president of the Home. He does n't know yet for certain, but he has sent you a blank to make out, and then it's got to go to a committee. He said he'd do the best he could for you, — he is a very nice man!"

"And you have taken all this trouble for me?" Miss Lily's hands went up to her face. The tears trickled down and fell on her dress.

"It was n't any trouble," asserted Doodles. "I thought maybe there was no chance, and so I would n't tell you till I found out." The lad took the paper from his pocket.

Miss Lily wiped her eyes. "I can't see to write," she said tremulously; "that is, not well, and the doctor said I must n't try." She looked mournfully at the boy.

"I'll do it for you," he proposed cheerily. "Then if there's anything to sign you can do it with your eyes shut. I love to write with my eyes shut and see how near I come to it!"

"I never tried," she admitted, "but perhaps I could."

"It says first, 'Your name in full.'" Doodles looked up inquiringly.

"Faith Lily," repeated its owner mechanically. Then she started across the room. "I'll get you a pen and ink," she said.

Doodles wrote with careful hand. "That's a pretty name," he commented.

"I always liked it," she smiled. "But I'm afraid my faith has been going back on me lately. I did have a good deal. I thought the Lord would n't let me go to the poorhouse, then it seemed as if He was going to. Only a little while ago I thought He must have forgotten me — and now this!" Her dim eyes grew big with wonder and thankfulness. "Even if I can't go, I shall be glad you tried to get me in; it will tell me I have one friend."

"The next is, 'Time and place of birth.'"

"I was born August 3, 1847, in Cloverfield, Massachusetts."

"'Name of father,'" read Doodles.

"Jonathan Seymour Lily."

There were many questions, and the boy was a slow writer. It took no little time to place all the answers. But the end of the list was finally reached without blot or smudge. Doodles surveyed his work with gratification.

"I guess I have n't made any mistake," he said, reading it over. "Now if you can just put your name there, it will be done."

Her hand trembled and the letters were wavering, but when Doodles declared it was "splendidly written," she smiled her relief.

Tuesday, Wednesday, Thursday went by, and Doodles heard nothing from Mr. Randolph. He began to be afraid that the committee had decided against his friend, and although his mother told him that such procedures always take considerable time, he grew more nervous with every mail-coming. When Saturday morning brought him no word, he decided to go over to Miss Lily's.

"I don't know that she could read the letter if she had one," he said in dismay. "Why didn't I think of that before!"

His first glimpse of the little woman corroborated his worst fears. Her eyes were swollen with weeping, and her face was haggard and despairing.

"Can't you go?" he ejaculated.

"I haven't heard a word!" she answered mournfully. "I didn't know but you had."

"No, I haven't. That's why I came over."

She shut the door and made him sit down.

"I guess I'll have to go to the poorhouse after all," she began in a hushed voice, as if fearful of being overheard.

"Oh, I would n't give up! Mr. Randolph said it would take time."

"But I can't wait! The woman thought I was going, and she's rented my room, and she won't let me stay another night! I have n't quite enough money to pay up, and she says she shall keep my trunk and furniture — oh, to think I have come to this!"

The little woman's distress was agonizing to Doodles.

"Now, don't you worry!" he pleaded. "You are coming straight home with me to stay at our house over Sunday, and next week we shall probably hear."

"No, no! — your mother — your mother won't want me!" she sobbed. "I can't go to make her all that trouble!"

" 'T won't be a bit of trouble!" he insisted. "She will like to have you come! We all will! We'd better go right away, too. Is your trunk packed?"

"Pretty much; there are a few little things to put in." She found herself yielding to the stronger will of the boy. Going to the closet, she brought out some articles of clothing which she began to fold.

71

"Is all the furniture yours?" Doodles asked, looking around on the meager array.

She shook her head. "Only the rocking-chair and the couch and that little chair you're in and the oil heater and the pictures —" She ran her troubled eyes over the things enumerated, as if fearing to forget some of her few remaining possessions. "Oh, yes! there's my bookshelf! I must n't leave that."

"Suppose I make a list of them," suggested Doodles. "I think maybe we'd better have them taken over to our house — Blue can come this afternoon and see about it. Blue's my brother, you know."

"But Mrs. Gugerty won't let me have them!"

"She will if you pay up."

"Yes, but I can't! I gave her the last cent I had!" Her voice quivered.

Doodles took out his purse and counted over his change.

"No, you're not going to pay it!" she cried. "I shan't let you!"

"I'm afraid I have n't enough," smiled the lad ruefully — "only sixty-seven cents."

"I owe a dollar and a quarter," she admitted.

"Blue can pay it when he comes for the things," returned the boy, dismissing with a careless "That's nothing!" the little woman's protest.

Miss Lily looked around for the last time with a cheerful smile.

"Somehow I can't feel as bad to go home with you as I know I ought to," she said, "only I hate to have you and your folks do so much for me — and I such a stranger, too!"

"No, you're a friend," Doodles corrected.

"Yes, I am — forever and ever!" She laughed tremulously. "I don't see why you're so good to me."

"You'll like my mother!" Doodles responded with some irrelevance. "She's the best mother in the whole world!"

"I know I shall love her if she's any like her boy!" She gave him a caressing pat.

True to the word of Doodles, Miss Lily was welcomed to the little bungalow with such heartfelt hospitality that her sad, starving soul was filled with joy, and when Blue returned with her small stock of goods and put Mrs. Gugerty's receipt into her hand, her eyes overflowed with happy tears. With cheery Mrs.

Stickney and merry Doodles and Blue for companions, she had little time to worry over the possible outcome of her application to the June Holiday Home, and Sunday was passed in an utterly different way from that she had imagined a week before.

It was not until the next Wednesday that any news came from Mr. Randolph. Then the letter-carrier brought a long, thin envelope addressed to "Miss Faith Lily," and the recipient turned so white when Doodles handed it to her that he feared she was going to faint.

"Shall I open it?" he asked.

She bowed her head. Words were far away.

He drew out the paper and gave it one hurried glance. Then he swung it over his head with a glad whoop.

"You're going! You're going! You're going!" he shouted.

"Doodles!" remonstrated his mother, for Miss Lily was weeping.

In a moment, however, tears had given way to joy, and Doodles must read to her every word of Mr. Randolph's friendly note as well as the wonderful document that was to admit her to the palatial June Holiday Home.

CHAPTER VII

ROSES — AND THORNS

POLLY was in Miss Sterling's room when the box was brought up.

"Flowers!" she squealed as soon as the door had shut upon the matron's stout figure.

"Bosh!" retorted Miss Sterling. "More likely Cousin Sibyl has sent me some of her children's stockings to darn. She does that occasionally. I suppose she thinks —"

"O-o-h!" breathed Polly, for the speaker had disclosed a mass of pink — exquisite roses with long stems and big, cool green leaves.

"Now what do you think?" Polly exulted.

Miss Sterling stood regarding the roses, her face all pink and white, the color fluttering here and there like a shy bird.

"It's a mistake!" she said at last. "They can't be for me."

"Of course they're for you!" Polly pointed to the address on the cover. "Is n't there any card?" searching gently among the flowers. "I

guess Mr. Randolph forgot to put in his card!"
Polly's eyes twinkled mischievously.

"Polly Dudley, don't be silly!" The tone
was almost impatient.

"It would be lovely for him to send them
anyway!" defended Polly. "And I almost
know he did!" she insisted.

"You don't know any such thing!" Miss
Sterling was taking the roses out. She brought
them to her face and drew in their fragrance.
Then she held them at arm's length, gazing
at them admiringly.

"Aren't they beautiful!" she said softly. "I
wish I knew whom to thank."

"It looks like a man's handwriting," observed Polly.

"It might be Mrs. Lake," mused Miss Sterling, quite ignoring Polly's remark. "Mrs. Lake
has always been nice to me. Only she would
never omit her card. No, it must be somebody
else."

Polly tried the roses on the small table, on
the desk, on the dresser — where their reflection added to their magnificence. Finally they
were left on the broad window-sill, while the
two discussed possible givers. It was Miss

Sterling, however, who suggested names. Polly clung to her first thought.

"I told him you had had an awful time with your ankle, and how Miss Sniffen scolded you," — Polly lowered her voice, — "and I suppose he felt sorry —"

"How Miss Sniffen scolded me? Not about his being there?" The tone was dismayed.

"Why, yes! What harm was there?"

"Polly! Polly! You didn't say — what did you say?"

"I can't remember exactly," was the plaintive answer. "I don't see why you care, anyway. I think I said it was because he stayed with us and took us to ride."

"Well, it can't be helped," laughed Miss Sterling, "but — how could you, Polly?"

"I should think you'd be glad to have him know how Miss Sniffen acts."

"Sh! Somebody's coming!"

"I must go," Polly whispered.

She let in Mrs. Albright and Miss Crilly.

"Oh, what dandy roses!" Miss Crilly dashed over to the window. "Your best feller must sure 'a' sent 'em! Ain't they sweet? But why don't you have 'em over on that little table?

They'd show off fine there! May I?" She carried them across the room.

"Polly tried them in various places," responded Miss Sterling.

"Well, 't don't make a whole lot o' difference where you put such roses! My, but they're immense!" She stood off, the better to admire them. "Would n't I rave if they belonged to yours truly! How can you folks take them so coolly?"

Juanita Sterling laughed. "I had my time when they first came!"

"You say it all, so we don't need to," laughed Mrs. Albright. "They are beauties, that's a fact!"

Miss Crilly sat down, her eyes still on the flowers. "I don't see a card anywhere," she nodded. "Ain't that proof positive?" winking toward Mrs. Albright.

"There was none," smiled Miss Sterling.

"You don't mean you don't know who sent 'em?" Miss Crilly queried.

"Just that. Either the sender forgot to put in her card or she did n't wish me to know."

"I bet 't is n't a 'her'!" giggled Miss Crilly. "Don't you, Mis' Albright?"

That lady twinkled her answer. "I should n't wonder."

A soft knock sent Miss Sterling to the door, and Miss Castlevaine came in.

Miss Crilly showed off the roses with all the pride of a possessor.

"I guess I saw them down in the lower hall," smiled Miss Castlevaine knowingly. "There was a long box on the desk."

"You did? And ain't it funny?" Miss Crilly ran on, — "she don't know who sent 'em!"

"Perhaps Miss Sniffen could tell you."

Miss Sterling looked up quickly.

"What do you mean?" asked Miss Crilly.

Miss Castlevaine moved her chair nearer, listened intently, and then began in a low voice: "I was coming up with a pitcher of hot water, and you know there's a little place where you can see down on the desk. Well, Miss S. was there fussing over a box, and I said to myself, 'I guess somebody's got some flowers.' Then I saw her lift the cover and slip out something white. I did n't see it distinctly, for just as she took hold of it she looked up, and I dodged out of sight. When I peeked down again she was dropping something into a little drawer, and I

79

came on as still as I could. I thought then that whoever had those flowers would n't find out who sent 'em!"

"It is n't right!" Mrs. Albright's comfortable face took on stern, troubled lines.

"I'd go to the florist and find out," declared Miss Crilly.

"There's no name on the box." Miss Sterling drew a deep breath, and indignation flushed her pale cheeks.

"I did suppose we could have what belonged to us, even here! Things grow worse every day. Boiled tripe for dinner — ugh!" Miss Castlevaine's face wrinkled with repugnance.

"And only potatoes to go with it," sighed Mrs. Albright. "It's too bad we can't have green vegetables and fruit — now, in the season."

"I heard something yesterday," resumed Miss Castlevaine, "that I guess you won't like — I don't know what we're coming to! Miss Major got it in a roundabout way through one of the managers, and it may not be true; but they say they're going to cut out our Wednesday pudding and our Sunday pie!" Her little blue eyes glared at her listeners.

Juanita Sterling dropped back in her chair. "What next!" she ejaculated.

"They'll be keeping us on mackerel and corned beef yet!" snapped Miss Castlevaine. "As if we did n't pay enough when we came here to insure us first-class board for the rest of our lives! I gave them three thousand dollars — I was a fool to do it! — and I have been here only two years! If they keep that woman much longer —!" The flashing eyes and set lips finished the sentence.

"Well, ain't that great!" cried Miss Crilly. "I did n't bring any such pile as you did, Miss Castlevaine, but that is n't to the point! They 've got more money 'n they know what to do with! What they saving their old barrelful for, anyway? Not a scrap o' dessert from one week's end to another — goodness gracious me!"

CHAPTER VIII

WAITING TO BE THANKED

JUANITA STERLING sat alone with her roses, trying to think it all out. The other ladies were down in the parlor, where Mrs. Nobbs was reading aloud; but to-night Egyptian archæology had no charm for the possessor of the pink roses. How could she wander through prehistoric scenes while somebody was waiting to be thanked! Somebody — but who? The roses knew! Yet they would not tell! Little quivers of light fluttered in and out of their alluring hearts, almost as if they said, "We are telling! We are telling! Only you will not understand!" The woman gazed wistfully at them — and sighed. The secret of the roses held her through the long, still hours of the evening. What possible reason could the superintendent have had for withholding the name, unless —! She shook her head and sternly chided her cheeks for rivaling the roses. If only Polly had n't — but was it Polly? Had not that name appeared before Polly spoke? She clinched her teeth in scorn for herself. "'There's no fool like an old fool,'" she muttered contemptuously. No doubt it was Georgiana Lake. To-morrow she would write Mrs. Lake a note of thanks. There would be no risk in that. Yes, she would do it! She would be a fool no longer! And if the roses chuckled over her decision she never knew it.

The note went by the morning's mail. Its answer came in two days.

My dear Nita
You are a witch fit for the hanging! How did you know — how could you guess! — I was going to send you some of our Pink Ramblers? Only they are not quite blossomed out enough yet. When they are you shall have more than you can hold in your two small hands! But to thank me for them ahead of time! It is just like you! You always were a witch! Why don't you come to see me? I should have been up last visiting day only that the house was full of workmen, and Isabel had engagements, and somebody must stay — I was the somebody! — A visitor! Too bad! Love —
                                        GEORGIANA.

Before the pink roses had lost a petal another box was brought to Miss Sterling's door. Her fingers quivered with hope as she untied the ribbon. The address was in the same firm, open hand. A shimmer of gold met her first glance, but the scrap of white she had longed for was missing. Without doubt the pilferer had thwarted her again. She put the yellow beauties into water with half-hearted pleasure. Why could n't Miss Sniffen let her have her own! She pounded the air with her little impotent fists. She did not go down to tea. Unhappiness and worry are not appetizers.

The next morning it was whispered from room to room that the second card had been filched from Miss Sterling's box of roses. Miss Castlevaine loved so well the transmitting of newsy tidbits, that they were not apt to remain long in one quarter.

"I'd do something about it!" she declared to Miss Major. "It has come to a pretty pass if our belongings have to be tampered with before we even are allowed to see them! I think somebody ought to tell the president."

The incident, however, passed with talk, nobody being willing to risk her residence in behalf of Juanita Sterling.

When Polly Dudley heard of it she waxed wrathful.

"I never liked Miss Sniffen," she declared, "and now I just hate her!"

"Polly!" remonstrated Miss Sterling.

"I don't care, I do! I wish mother was on the Board, then I'd try to make her say something! What business has Miss Sniffen to open your boxes, anyhow? I almost know they came from Mr. Randolph, and that's why she's mad about it!"

"Polly, I hope you won't say that to anybody else. You've no more reason to think he sent them than you have to think King George sent them."

Polly chuckled.

"You haven't — intimated such a thing, have you? — to anybody else, I mean?" The question held an anxious tone.

"Why, no, I guess not," was the slow answer, "except mother. I think I said to mother that probably he was the one."

Miss Sterling shook her head with a tiny scowl. "Your mother must think me an intensely silly woman," she sighed.

"Oh, I didn't say you thought so!" Polly hastened to explain. "I only said I did."

"Please don't even suggest it again," she laughed. "I wish the mystery could be cleared up."

The sender's name was discovered earlier than they had thought possible.

Two days afterwards, Polly rushed in, her face alight, her eyes shining. "Oh, Miss Nita!" she began, and then stopped, suddenly realizing that Mrs. Winslow Teed and Miss Crilly were in the room.

"I did n't know — I thought maybe — you'd go with me to call on Miss Lily — Doodles said — Doodles is in a hurry for me to go," she ended lamely.

Juanita Sterling, amused at the sudden transition, had caught a flash of triumph in Polly's eye and wondered with a fluttering heart what she had come to announce.

"Why can't we go, too?" cried Miss Crilly.

"Miss Lily looks like a refined, cultured person," remarked Mrs. Winslow Teed.

"Oh, Doodles says she is lovely!" Polly had recovered her equilibrium.

The latest comer at the June Holiday Home received her visitors with shy courtesy. Miss Crilly and Polly soon relieved her of any embarrassment she may have felt, and talk went on blithely.

Several smiling glances thrown across the

room by Polly put Miss Sterling's mind in confusion. They might signify much or nothing, yet she found herself missing what was being said around her in wild conjecture as to their meaning. She wanted to carry Polly upstairs with her. Finally she rose to go, and Polly said good-bye, too, in accordance with Miss Sterling's hope.

They went along the corridor together, Polly squeezing her companion's arm with little chuckles of delight.

"You can't guess what I've got to tell you!" she broke out, as soon as they were at a safe distance from Miss Lily's room.

"Sh!" cautioned the other. Talk above a whisper was forbidden in the halls.

"Oh, I'm always forgetting!" breathed Polly.

Once inside the third-floor room the little woman was seized by a pair of eager arms and whirled round and round.

"He did send them! He did! He did! Now what do you think!"

Miss Sterling went suddenly limp and dropped into a chair.

"You don't know — for certain?" she cried.

87

"I do! Mr. Randolph sent you those roses — both boxes!"

The woman felt the flame in her face and turned quickly on pretense of searching for something in her sewing-basket. She was so long about it that Polly began to complain.

"You don't care very much, seems to me! I thought you'd be just as glad as I am!"

"Why, I am glad to find out who sent them, dear, as glad as can be! But I may as well be sewing on these buttons while you are talking. Now, tell me how you found out — I'm dying to know!" she laughed.

"Well, it's so funny!" Polly resumed. "You see, our Sunday-School is going to send a boy in India to college, and last Sunday we had to tell how we'd earned what we brought. A boy in Chris's class, Herbert Ogden, said Mr. Randolph paid him fifteen cents apiece for carrying two boxes of roses to the June Holiday Home. So after Sunday-School Chris went along with him and asked him if he remembered who the boxes were for. He said, 'Oh, yes, because it was such a queer name! They were both directed to Miss Ju-an-i-ta Sterling!' Chris said it was all he could do to keep his face straight.

88

And the boy went on to say he remembered the last name because it made him think of sterling silver! Was n't that the greatest?"

The exclamations and laughter satisfied even Polly.

"You'll thank him right away, shan't you?" she queried.

"I suppose I ought," sighed the possessor of the roses.

"Don't you want to?" Polly's tone showed her surprise.

"Such notes are hard to write," was the discreet answer. She bent closer over her work than there was any need. Her cheeks were pinking up again.

"I do believe you're growing near-sighted!" declared Polly irrelevantly.

"No, I guess not," she replied calmly. "This button bothered me — it's all right now," as Polly scrutinized the waist.

"I should n't think you'd hate to write to Mr. Randolph. I think he's lovely!"

"I presume he is," Miss Sterling said quietly. "I'm not well acquainted with him, you know."

"I'll write it for you," proposed Polly, "if you'd like me to."

The little woman bending over the blouse caught her breath — to think of missing the writing of that thank-you to Nelson Randolph!

"Oh, no, dear! I won't shirk my duty. It would n't look quite the thing for you to do it."

"Perhaps it would n't," Polly agreed, "though I'd just as lief."

CHAPTER IX

BLANCHE PUDDICOMBE

You're a great deal better, are n't you, Miss Nita?" Polly was saying.

Miss Sterling gave a smiling nod across the bed. She and Polly were putting on the covers.

"I think you've been growing stronger since the picnic. Maybe it was the outdoors. Father says there's nothing like it for nerves. I wish we could have another, now your ankle is all well; but it is too late for to-day. Why can't we go to walk, you and Mrs. Adlerfeld and Mrs. Albright and I? I know a lovely road out Brookside Avenue way."

"Well," agreed Miss Sterling, "if it is n't too far. I feel equal to a good deal this morning."

"Oh, that's jolly! We need n't go any farther than we choose, you know. I'll bring a lunch, so it will seem like a little picnic — things taste so much better out of doors. Is n't it lovely that you are stronger! Did you tell Mr. Randolph that you're better?"

91

"Why, no, dear, of course not! It was just a note of thanks."

"What if it was! You could have said that! He'll want to know!"

"I think he'll be able to survive the omission." Miss Sterling patted the pillow into shape and smiled over it.

"Oh, I saw him yesterday!" Polly broke out. "I forgot to tell you!"

The other waited, an expectant smile fluttering about her pretty lips.

"Blanche Puddicombe was riding with him. He had his roadster. I don't see what he takes her around so much for. She isn't a bit pretty."

"Probably she is agreeable." Miss Sterling laid down the blanket she had folded and crossed the room.

"I don't see how she can be with such a mother," Polly went on. "She fusses herself up a good deal the same way. She hasn't a mite of taste. I saw her downtown shopping the other day with a sport skirt, very wide scarlet stripes, and a dress hat trimmed with a single pink rose — the most delicate pink — and a light blue feather! Oh, yes, and a crêpe-de-chine waist of pale green!"

92

An amused chuckle sounded from the window, where Miss Sterling was straightening the curtains.

"You ought to have seen her! Her hair is black as — my shoe, and she wears it waved right down over her ears — you would n't know she had any ears! Queer, Mr. Randolph should want her riding round with him so much! You'd think he would have more sense, would n't you?"

"She has money — and youth!" was the emphasized reply, in a cold, hard tone. "Money and youth make everything harmonize — even sport skirts and dress hats!"

"She does n't begin to look as young as you do. She looks more than thirty, and you don't!"

"Polly Dudley!"

"Father says so, anyway!"

"I thank your father for the flattering compliment; but I think he must be needing glasses."

"No, he does n't need glasses!" retorted Polly. "His eyes are first-rate. Dear me! Is it eleven o'clock? I must go home! Let's start early — by two, can you?"

"Oh, I don't believe I'll go this afternoon!" The voice sounded weary.

"Why, Miss Nita! you said you would!"

"I know, but I wasn't tired then. I guess I'll have to put it off a day or two."

"You haven't done anything to tire you! You'll never get well if you don't go more!" cried Polly plaintively. "And we won't go a step farther than you like. We needn't ask anybody else, if you'd rather not — we can go all by ourselves." Polly waited anxiously.

Miss Sterling shook her head with a little sigh. "You go with the others to-day. I don't feel as if I could."

Polly finally went off, her face downcast. Coaxings had availed nothing.

CHAPTER X

"GOOD-BYE, PUDDING"

Juanita Sterling scowled a perfunctory thank-you to Mrs. Nobbs, who handed her a long box. She had come to hate those long boxes.

"I wish he'd keep his old flowers in his greenhouse!" she muttered disdainfully after the door was well shut. She gazed on the box with a sigh. Nevertheless, she untied it with hurrying fingers.

Great ruby roses sent their pent-up fragrance straight to her nostrils, and she drew it in with a breath of delight. Then she flung the box on the bed and finished putting her dresser in order, a task with which she had been occupied.

Little jerky bits of scorn were now and then directed toward the flowers, as if they were responsible for their intrusion. When their innocence suddenly suggested itself, she smiled.

"Poor things, they can't help it! How should

I feel if I were carried where I was not wanted and then should be blamed for being there!"

Contritely she took the roses from their box and put them in her prettiest vase, quite as if she would make amends. She sat down by them and looked the matter in the face.

"I can't have these where they will remind me all day long of being a silly old woman!" She considered the blossoms with a dismal face. "What shall I do with them? I'd put them in a bundle under the bed, only I'd feel so sorry for them — no, I can't do that! I suppose I could give them away — oh, there's Mrs. Crump! The very thing! Maybe they'll help her to forget her pain. I'll take them in now!" She caught up the vase and bore it triumphantly along the hall.

Mrs. Crump was on the couch.

"All for me? Why, Miss Sterling! How good you are! You can't have kept many for yourself."

"I don't want any," laughed the donor. "I'll be glad enough if you can enjoy them."

Miss Crilly and Miss Major came in.

"Mis' Crump! if you're not tryin' to beat Miss Sterling! Seems like a hospital 'stead of a

Home, so many roses round! — You don't say she's given you all hers? My, ain't you the limit o' generosity, Miss Sterling! You look lots better, Mis' Crump! Maybe it's the reflection o' the roses! Lovely color, ain't it! He must be a goner, sure! How many times a week d' they come? 'Nother card swooped, I s'pose? It beats me!"

Miss Major opened the door for Miss Castle-vaine.

"I could n't help hearing what you said about another card — who's lost one now?"

She shook her head while Miss Crilly explained. "We shall have to lock up our jewelry pretty soon — huh! How do you feel this morning, Mrs. Crump? Had the doctor?"

The invalid winced and caught her breath, as a sudden twinge shot through her arm. "I don't know as I'm any worse," she said. "I have n't slept a wink since two o'clock! No, the doctor did n't stop here! I thought maybe he would, he was in Mrs. Post's room, right next door; but Mrs. Nobbs said yesterday it was n't necessary — it's 'only pain,' you know!"

"Only pain!" laughed Miss Crilly. "Is n't that enough? Then, when I'm sick it 'll be with something besides pain — I'll remember that! And I'll have the doctor when I need him — don't you forget it!"

"What's the matter with Mrs. Post?" queried Miss Castlevaine.

"Something about her knee — she told me the doctor was going to bandage it up. It was Mrs. Post, you know!" Mrs. Crump emphasized the sentence with lowered voice and lifted eyebrows.

Miss Castlevaine nodded. "No favorites in the June Holiday Home! How did you like the dinner yesterday noon?" She smiled knowingly.

"It's good-bye, pudding, forevermore!" laughed Miss Crilly. "Did n't it seem queer not to have a bit of dessert?"

"Same as other days," returned Miss Major. "I suppose the Sunday pie will go next."

"So I heard!" Miss Castlevaine's lips thinned themselves together. "But that is n't the worst thing! Do you know about Mrs. Dick?"

"No — what?" Miss Crilly stopped smelling of the roses.

"Why, Tuesday she met an old schoolmate on the street who inquired if she had been ill.

98

Mrs. Dick said no. 'Why did n't you come to the wedding, then?' the lady asked. 'Wedding?' exclaimed Mrs. Dick; 'what wedding?' 'Why, Anita's!' (Anita is her daughter.) 'I did n't know she was going to be married, and it is n't likely I should have gone without an invitation,' she laughed. 'I invited you,' the lady said. 'It was a very informal affair, no cards, and not many guests; but I telephoned to the Home, for you to come over and spend the day. I wanted you to see Anita's pretty clothes and her beautiful presents. They said they 'd give you the message right off.' 'First I 've heard of it!' said Mrs. Dick, and I tell you she was mad! Is n't that awful? If anything happens to us, I don't know as our friends will hear of it till after the funeral — huh!"

"Is she going to make a fuss about it?" asked Miss Major.

"Of course not! She 'd probably be turned out if she did."

"What are we coming to!" For a minute Miss Crilly actually looked doleful. "I 'm going to tell all my folks that if they want me to know anything in a hurry they 'd better telegraph or send me a special delivery letter —

that'll fix 'em. My! To think of bein' invited to a weddin' and not knowin' it!"

"When I first came here," resumed Miss Castlevaine, "my cousin was dreadfully upset because they would n't call me to the telephone to talk with her. Finally she said so much they gave in, and I went down. I supposed it was the regular thing until she told me about it afterwards. She had to ask me two or three questions about something, and get my answers to know what to do."

"There should be a telephone in every room, as there is in a hotel," asserted Miss Major.

"Oh, my!" ejaculated Miss Crilly. "When you get it, send me word! Probably I shan't be here by that time, but I guess I shall be hoverin' somewhere round, and I'll know when your 'phone's in!"

"To have one in each room would be a great deal of expense," said Mrs. Crump.

"What of it!" retorted Miss Major. "Haven't they money enough? They're always building additions — now the one that's going to spoil Miss Sterling's room and Miss Twining's down below. They'd a good deal better spend it on telephones."

"They've got a new rug down in the hall," announced Miss Castlevaine. " 'Most anybody could have new rugs if they stole the money to buy them with!"

"What do you mean?" was Miss Crilly's quick query.

"You'd better not say anything about it; but I heard that Miss Twining wrote a poem for a Sunday-School paper and got eight dollars for it —"

"My!" put in Miss Crilly.

"And," went on Miss Castlevaine, "she bought a new shirt waist. When she wore it Mrs. Nobbs asked her where she got it. Like a simpleton, she told the whole story, so pleased to have earned the money, and never dreaming but that it was her own! What did they do but make her give up the seven dollars she had left! They did let her keep the waist — she needed it badly enough." Miss Castlevaine shook her head, while comments flew fast.

"I'm sorry for Miss Twining," sympathized Miss Crilly. "She's the kind that won't sputter it all out, as I should; she'll cry herself sick over it!"

"If we cried for all the hard things we have

here," said Mrs. Crump, "we should n't have any eyes left!"

"I wonder if the directors know how things are going," observed Miss Major.

"I bet they ain't on to it!" Miss Crilly wagged her head decisively.

"But who'd dare tell 'em?" queried Mrs. Crump.

"Excuse me!" giggled Miss Crilly.

CHAPTER XI

"SO MYSTERIOUS"

ARE you busy?" asked Miss Leatherland at the threshold of Miss Sterling's room.

"No, indeed! I was wondering whether I'd go out on the veranda or sit here and mull. I'm glad you've come. Take this chair — it's the easiest."

"Then I'll leave it for you." She started toward another.

"No, I don't like it!" Her hostess laughingly pushed her back. "I'm too short for that one. I'm always wishing I were as tall as you."

Miss Leatherland blushed at the little compliment and smiled over it.

"I don't know but I'm meddling in what is none of my business," she began shyly. "At first I thought I would n't say anything; then I decided I would do as I'd wish to be done by. I certainly should want to know anything of this kind — though perhaps you know already."

"What is it? Nothing dreadful, I hope."

"Oh, no! Only it shows — unless she has told you — how things are going downstairs."

She hesitated, as if not knowing just how to say what she had come to tell.

"You were home about four o'clock yesterday, were n't you?"

"Yes."

"I met all of you down in the hall, you remember, and I thought it was along there. Have you heard anything about a telephone message that came for you while you were away?"

"No — was there one?"

Miss Leatherland bowed her head and drew her chair nearer.

"This afternoon I went up to call on Mrs. Macgregor, and yesterday, it seems, she had business with Mr. Potter, of the Fair Harbor Paper Company, and was in his office waiting for him to come in. It was about three o'clock, she said. Mr. Potter's office is next to the president's, and the door was just ajar. Mrs. Macgregor has very sharp ears, and she happened to be sitting close to the door, so could n't help hearing. She says Mr. Randolph called up the Home — she knew the number, she uses it so

104

much — and asked for Miss Sterling. I suppose they told him you were out, for he said he was sorry and inquired if they knew when you were coming home. Evidently whoever was at the 'phone did n't tell, for he said if you should come in by half-past four to ask you to call him up. Probably she offered to deliver his message, for he said no, he'd like to talk with you, and then he rang off. Mrs. Macgregor asked if Mr. Randolph was a relative of yours, and I said I thought not."

Miss Sterling shook her head.

"I don't see why Miss Sniffen or Mrs. Nobbs, or whoever 't was did n't do as Mr. Randolph asked them to — I don't see why! It's getting so we can't tell anything!" Miss Leatherland looked distressed.

"Things are growing queer," was the quiet response. "I don't know what Mr. Randolph could have wanted, but I surely have a right to be informed about it."

"If you should ask Miss Sniffen, please don't say anything about me, she might think I'd interfered. I only thought you ought to know it."

"I'm mighty glad you told me," Miss Sterling smiled across into the perturbed face, "and I shall certainly not speak of the matter to Miss Sniffen or any of them."

"I guess you are wise not to," agreed Miss Leatherland. "Anybody that would do things she has done, you don't know what she'd do!"

Polly heard of the little episode with mingled dismay and delight.

"Oh, I wonder if he wanted you to go to ride!" she burst out. "Only you won't ever know! Dear me, I wish we had waited till the next day for our walk! Isn't it too bad you weren't home?"

"We had a nice time!" laughed Miss Sterling.

"Didn't we! But it's a shame for you to miss a ride with that lovable man!"

"Polly, why will you? He didn't say anything about a ride! Probably it was simply some little business matter."

"But what?"

"I haven't the least idea."

" 'T was a ride! I know it just as I knew he sent the roses! I was right about the roses!"

"Rides and roses aren't the same!"

"No, rides are better — more good-timey.

106

Dear, dear! I'd been wishing he would ask you—and now!" Polly sighed. "Anyway, he wanted to talk with you about *something!*" she chuckled. "But it's so mysterious!"

She said good-bye and then came back.

"I happened to think," she whispered, "why can't you come over to our house and telephone to him? He'll never know where you are."

Miss Sterling shook her head. "It would n't do! They'd ask me what I was going for — and I could n't tell!"

"Do they always ask that?" scowled Polly.

"Always!"

"Then let me telephone!"

"No, no! We'd better leave it to work itself out. I am not supposed to know anything about it." She laughed uncertainly.

"It's a shame! Oh, everything about him always gets mixed up with trouble! I wish it did n't!"

Juanita Sterling made the same wish as she sat alone in the hour before bedtime. What could Nelson Randolph have wanted of her? And why did Miss Sniffen and her subordinates strive so strenuously to keep her from communicating with him or knowing of any attention that he paid her? She wrestled with the hard question until the bell for "lights out." Then she noiselessly undressed in the dark.

Sleep was long in coming, yet her nerves did not assert themselves unpleasantly, as usual. In fact, she had forgotten her nerves, in the strange, vague gladness that was half pain which flooded her being. She would berate herself for being "an old fool," though conscious at the same time of little, warming heart-thrills that exulted over her reason. As Polly had said, the president of the June Holiday Home had wished to talk with her about *something* — that of itself was as surprising as it was mysterious.

CHAPTER XII

JUANITA STERLING was making her bed when the soft tap came.

"What shall I do?" Miss Crilly whispered tragically, slipping inside and shutting the door without a sound. Her eyes were big and frightened. "I've kept out of Mis' Nobbs's reach thus far, but I s'pose I can't very long! They are lookin' everywhere for Mis' Dick—you know she was n't down to breakfast, and I'd no idea she'd come — all the while the rest o' you were lookin' for her. At half-past five this mornin' *I see her go away with the milkman!* I happened to be at my window. I could n't sleep, 't was so hot, and I sat down there to get a breath o' air. He come along and sent in the boy with the milk, same as he gen'ally does — I see him lots of times. But was n't I astonished when Mis' Dick come marchin' out, all dressed up in her Sunday togs, and got in and rode off with him! She had her big suitcase — it must ha' been all cut an' dried beforehand! What do you s'pose it means? I'm scart to

109

death! I do' want to squeal on Mis' Dick — I always liked Mis' Dick! An' if they ask me, I can't lie it out! Oh, what would you do?" Miss Crilly came near being distressed.

"Why," answered Miss Sterling, "I think I should keep still unless I were asked. In that case I should tell all I knew."

"Oh, dear, I hate to squeal!"

"Maybe you won't have to. I hope not!"

"What do you s'pose she went off with Mr. Tenney for?"

Miss Sterling shook her head.

"He's a widower! You don't s'pose —?" Miss Crilly giggled.

The other shrugged her shoulders.

"Well, anyway, there'll be a row till she's found! Gracious! I was so upset I could n't eat much breakfast! I told Mis' Albright finally — I could n't keep it a minute longer. Then I came up here. You don't s'pose she's gone luny, do you? She was so upset about goin' to that weddin'!"

"No, it is n't that!" decided Miss Sterling. "Mrs. Dick is not the kind to go crazy."

"Somebody's comin'!" Miss Crilly darted to the closet and shut herself in.

Mrs. Albright and Mrs. Adlerfield appeared.

"I thought Miss Crilly was here." Mrs. Albright looked about in surprise.

Miss Sterling nodded significantly toward the closet.

Mrs. Albright opened the door, and laughed.

"Come into daylight, you silly! Nobody's going to eat you up! They've found out!"

"They have? How?"

"One of the maids saw Mrs. Dick go by the window, and she ran to see where she was going; but she did n't dare tell at first. Finally, she did, and they're going to send out to Mr. Tenney's."

"My! I'm glad I ain't in Mis' Dick's shoes!" Miss Crilly emerged from the folds of Miss Sterling's petticoats. She brushed back her disordered hair and drew a long, laughing sigh. "Is n't it lovely they've found out! I b'lieve I'd have been luny myself in a little while if they had n't!"

"Nonsense!" pooh-poohed Mrs. Albright. "You could n't stay luny more'n half a twinkle! You'd have to come out of it to laugh!"

"Sure, I would!" Miss Crilly agreed. "My! How do folks live that don't laugh!"

"You are in no danger of dying from that disease," returned Mrs. Albright.

"No, I guess I ain't. My mother used to say that she believed if I had to live with the Devil himself, I'd keep on laughing."

The quartette settled down to calm, now that the danger was over, but the talk still ran on Mrs. Dick.

"She's been married twice before, has n't she?" asked Miss Crilly.

"Before what?" chuckled Mrs. Albright.

"O-h! Did I? That's one on me, sure! Well, maybe it is 'before' — who knows! What else could she be goin' off at half-past five with the milkman for? Might not be a bad thing either — guess he's all right. 'Most anything 'd be better 'n bein' under Miss Sniffen and her crowd!"

"Where did Mrs. Dick live before she came here? Did you know her?" Mrs. Albright inquired.

"I knew of her," Miss Crilly answered. "She kep' boarders over Kelly Avenue way. She used to teach school years ago. Her first husband died and all her children, then she took boarders and married one of 'em — this Mr.

Dick. He did n't live long — only long enough to run through what she'd saved up. He drank. She's worked hard all her life, I guess. I like Mis' Dick! She's good company."

"I like her very," agreed Mrs. Adlerfeld. "She has been nice to me a many times. If she goes to marry, I think it will no harm anybody, and I wish her the best things in the world."

The little Swedish woman voiced the larger number of Mrs. Dick's associates in the Home. Slighting remarks were heard from Miss Castlevaine and a few others, but in almost any case they were to be expected.

On the second day of Mrs. Dick's absence Miss Crilly appeared in Mrs. Bonnyman's room, where some half-dozen of the ladies were chatting.

"She is married!" she announced in a stage whisper, — "married to the milkman — oh! oh! oh!" Miss Crilly sat down in the midst of eager questioning.

"They say she wrote a note to Miss Sniffen yesterday, but I did n't get my news from her — no, sir-ee! It came pretty straight, though, — I guess it 's so all right."

"What'd you say, Mis' Albright? Yes, she

was married day before yesterday — went to the minister's! She told somebody she just could n't stand it here another minute."

"I wonder if she's ever seen him much," said Miss Major.

"My, yes! She's known him for years — used to be her milkman when she kept house! He is n't any stranger! Oh, don't I wish I could see her!"

"Maybe she will come over and call on us," observed Mrs. Prindle.

"If she dares," spoke up Mrs. Bonnyman.

"Well, I'm glad for her!" declared Miss Crilly. "Would n't it feel good to be cut loose from rules! Dear me! We're so tied up it seems sometimes's if I must scream!"

"I don't think people outside know how things go here," put in Miss Mullaly. "Why, everybody congratulated me on getting in! I thought I was going to have the time of my life!" She laughed deprecatingly.

"It is the time of our lives — the worst time!" snapped Miss Major.

"Well folks can get along some way," said Miss Sterling; "but Heaven save the sick ones!"

CHAPTER XIII

ALONG A BROOKSIDE ROAD

Oh, here you are!" cried Polly from the doorway, just beyond Mrs. Bonnyman.

"Been looking for me?" Miss Sterling smiled.

"Everywhere!" Polly dropped beside her friend. "No, Mrs. Bonnyman, don't get a chair for me! I like this! Besides, I'm not going to stay. It's too lovely outside to be cooped up in the house. Why can't we all go to walk?"

"Oh, that's the ticket!" Miss Crilly jumped up. "I'll have to change my togs first — will you wait for me?"

Polly nodded and smiled, as Miss Crilly skipped off.

"Will you all go?"

Miss Sterling rose.

"You will, Miss Nita?" Polly clung to her hand.

"Yes, but not with this dress on."

"I bid many thanks to you," said Mrs. Adlerfeld quaintly; "I shall like to go very."

115

Having made sure of the others, Polly ran off to make her invitation general, stopping at various doors on her way downstairs.

"Shall we go two by two, like a boarding-school?" giggled Miss Crilly, as the little party left the Home grounds.

"Let's go any old way!" Then, glancing beyond Miss Crilly, Polly gave a glad cry, — "David and Leonora!" and flew to meet the two who were just at the hospital entrance.

"Will you come to walk with us?" she invited. "Or I'll stay if you'd rather."

They declared that they would much prefer the walk, and Polly was soon making the introductions where they were needed. Many of the ladies were well acquainted with Polly's friends.

David at once appropriated his old-time chum, and Leonora skipped over to Miss Sterling.

"Ther' 's so many of us we ought to march abreast, clear across the street, as they do in processions!" Miss Crilly was in high spirits.

The road Polly had chosen led through an avenue of old elms and thence out into the wide country. Past the city milepost, not far distant from the Home, a little brook purled along, overswept by willows.

"Is n't this beautiful!" cried Miss Major. "And here are raspberries — oh!"

The party broke ranks and scattered among the bushes, eager for the fruit that was just in its prime.

"Do you suppose they belong to anybody?" queried Mrs. Prindle, a bit anxiously.

"If they do they don't love 'em a whole lot," Miss Crilly returned. "See those! They are so ripe they almost fall to pieces lookin' at 'em! But they're sweet as sugar!" She plumped them into her mouth.

Soon they strolled forward by two's and three's, but long before the young folks and a few others had begun to be tired, several were lagging behind, Miss Twining among them.

"Are you coming back this way, Polly?" she called.

"Why, I thought we would n't. What's the matter?"

"Used up," she smiled.

"Oh, I'm so sorry! I've gone too far, have n't I? You sit down somewhere and rest, and I'll stay with you. The others can go on, if they like."

"Guess I'll wait, too." Miss Sterling dropped wearily to the grass.

Mrs. Adlerfeld, Miss Lily, Mrs. Albright, and Miss Castlevaine lined themselves beside her.

"I don't know what possessed me to come on such a long walk!" fretted Miss Castlevaine.

"Why, I never thought that anybody could be tired!" said Polly contritely. "Why did n't you speak sooner?"

"Oh, we'll be all right by the time you get back!" laughed Mrs. Albright. "Now run along, every one of you! Shoo! Shoo!" She waved her skirts toward them.

It took a good deal of urging, however, to induce Polly to leave Miss Sterling. Finally she ran off with David, calling back that she would n't be gone long.

The afternoon slipped away, and the air grew cooler. The exhausted ones gathered strength and now and then rambled about a little, wondering why the others did not return. They watched longingly the point of road where the party had disappeared, even Miss Lily peered vainly into the empty distance.

Miss Castlevaine looked at her watch for the twentieth time. "It is a quarter past five!" she frowned. "Where can they be!"

"We may as well sit down while we wait," laughed Mrs. Albright. "Wandering round in a circle won't bring them any quicker." She lowered herself plumply beside Miss Sterling.

"Now don't you go to worrying!" she said. "They have n't been eaten up by bears or carried off by hawks. Probably they are having so good a time they have forgotten to come back."

The sun dropped lower and lower. The wayside shadows thickened. A robin on the topmost branch of a locust sang a solo.

"There they are!" cried Miss Castlevaine.

The others looked eagerly down the road.

The thud of hoofs came out of the hush.

"Oh, it's only a team!" was the disappointed contradiction. "I saw the dust and thought they were coming."

The buggy whirled up, the driver lifted his hat with a smiling bow — and was gone.

"Mr. Randolph and Miss Puddicombe!" commented Miss Castlevaine. "Who was he bowing to? Not me!"

"I have met him," responded Mrs. Albright.

"Oh! Maybe it was you, then. But he was looking at Miss Sterling!"

"She knows him, too, and so does Mrs. Adlerfeld."

"Oh!" repeated Miss Castlevaine. "I see him riding with that Miss Puddicombe a good deal lately. Guess she's trying to catch him."

"They are coming now for certain!" exclaimed Mrs. Albright.

Away in the distance the returning party could be discerned. Soon there was a waving of eager hands. The forward ones started on a race.

"It's Miss Crilly and the children!" Mrs. Albright laughed. "Isn't she game!"

Polly and David were ahead.

"Are you tired out waiting?" called Polly.

"Have you been to Buckline?" twinkled Mrs. Albright.

"Almost!" answered David.

"We've had such a time!" laughed Polly.

"Time!" burst in Miss Crilly. "We'd been goners, sure, if we hadn't jumped like fleas! My! You oughter seen Miss Mullaly — if she didn't go hand-springin' over that wall!"

120

"But what was it?" cried Mrs. Albright.

"A cow!" — "An ugly old cow!" — "She went bellowin' like Sancho Panza set loose!"

"Did she chase you? What did you do?"

"She was coming for us, and we jumped over the wall! We were on our way home," explained Polly.

"And David wanted to go and drive her off, so we could get by," put in Leonora; "but I held on to him!"

"I could have done it as well as that man," insisted David, looking somewhat disgusted at the lack of faith in his ability.

"He 'most got away from us!" laughed Miss Crilly. "We all had to grab him!"

"Did the cow's owner come?" Miss Castlevaine queried.

"We don't know who it was," answered Polly. "We were hiding behind some bushes the other side of the wall."

"Such a combobbery as that cow cut up! My! I thought she'd knock the man into slivers!" said Miss Crilly.

"But she did n't!" observed David.

"No," said Polly, "he drove her off finally."

"And we beat it!" giggled Miss Crilly.

"We thought you would wonder what had become of us," smiled Leonora.

"We did," agreed Mrs. Albright, "and somebody else will be wondering that same thing, if we don't march home about as fast as we can!"

Polly's cool and charming sweetness was all that saved the party from Miss Sniffen's very apparent displeasure, the tardy ones agreed. Supper had been served at least five minutes before they filed into the dining-room; but their astonishing appetites, which gave a relish even to soggy corncake and watery tea, almost counterbalanced any fears for their future walks with Polly.

Juanita Sterling sat down wearily in her own room. "I wish I had stayed at home!" she sighed.

CHAPTER XIV

POLLY PLANS

FATHER," Polly began thoughtfully, "I've been thinking — you remember I told you about our walk the other day and how tired Miss Nita and some of the other ladies were before I even thought of such a thing —" Polly stopped questioningly.

"I remember," smiled Dr. Dudley.

"So don't you think it would be nice — until they grow stronger, you know — for them to ride instead of walk?"

"Very nice, indeed. Do you want me to take them?"

"I wish you could," laughed Polly, "but I know you don't have time. I happened to think, though, why could n't we have the car some morning, while you are busy in the hospital? Evan could drive for us."

"A very good plan," the Doctor nodded musingly. "You wish to go with them, I take it."

"Yes, I think I'd better. I know, one more

123

could go if I did n't; but I guess they'd be more lively with me along than if they went with just Evan."

"If I were going I should certainly want you, too," twinkled the doctor.

"Oh, dear! We don't have as many good rides together as we used to, do we?" Polly bent down from the arm of Dr. Dudley's chair where she was sitting and cuddled her cheek against his.

"No," he replied, "we'll have to borrow an hour some day and run away."

"Would n't that be fun! Oh, let's!"

"I think we'll do it, then I can get re-acquainted with you."

Polly chuckled. "As if you did n't know me clear through, from head-top to toe-tip!"

"I feel quite like a stranger lately. I come in here and ask, 'Where's Polly?' and your mother says, 'She is over at the Home,' or, 'She's gone to walk with Miss Sterling.' When I see Miss Sterling I shall tell her what I think of it."

"You might tell me," suggested Polly demurely, "and then I can repeat it to Miss Nita."

"I prefer to say my say to her," the Doctor replied with no hint of a smile. "You might not say it strong enough."

A wee chuckle escaped Polly. "What are you going to tell her?" she coaxed.

"That she can't have my girl so much without paying for her."

"Oh," laughed Polly. "Miss Nita does n't have any money."

"It would be of no use in this case. Do you suppose you can be paid for in money?"

"Oh, you dearest, funniest man! I wish you could see Miss Nita more — you would n't wonder I like to go there. She is so lovable."

"I do not doubt it. How is she now — better?"

"Ever so much better! She does n't say anything lately about wanting to die. I wish she had nice things to eat — I don't see how she stands sour bread and so much corned beef and mackerel and sausages."

Doctor Dudley shook his head musingly. "It is too bad — a magnificent building, and wretched household management."

"I wonder why they keep Miss Sniffen," Polly said.

"Probably she is agreeable to the trustees, and nobody calls their attention to anything wrong."

"Yes, I've seen her—when some of the officers came. She is as smiley as a goose! I hate her smile; it looks as if she did n't mean it."

"She is evidently not the woman for the place. I am sorry." The Doctor glanced at his watch and rose abruptly.

"Got to go?"

"I ought to have gone earlier."

"Oh, dear! I wish other folks did n't need you all the time!" mourned Polly.

He stepped back and kissed her. "That is the penalty of more money," he smiled.

"More fame, you mean!" she retorted and heard a little chuckle as he passed out the door.

Polly did not plan long without acting, and within an hour she was on her long walk to Colonel Gresham's, to talk over her scheme with Leonora and David.

She found Mrs. Gresham just starting to meet a train.

"I'm so sorry I can't stay," she told Polly, "and Leonora and David are not at home! But the Colonel is out in the stable. He will be de-

lighted to see you. I'll call him." She turned
to a bell button.

"Oh, no, please!" interrupted Polly. "I'd
rather go there. I haven't seen Lone Star for
an age!"

"You'll find them chatting together, as
usual," laughed the little lady, and Polly
skipped off as soon as Mrs. Gresham had
driven away.

"Good afternoon, Miss Dudley." The Colonel extended his hand.

"Seems to me you're pretty formal," smiled
Polly.

Colonel Gresham laughed, a gentle, mellow
laugh, quite in harmony with the happy-lined
face and the graying hair.

"I wish I had a chair to offer you," he said,
looking about him, as if expecting one to pop
into sight. "I suppose I'm indebted to David
and Leonora for this visit."

"No, Colonel Gresham, I came to see you
especially this time. I was going to ask them
what they thought of a little plan I have; but
they are not necessary — and you are!"

"Ah! a plan? I wait on your pleasure!" The
Colonel bowed with mock gravity.

"Thank you!" chuckled Polly. "Perhaps you won't when you know about it. But I want to see Lone Star first — oh, he's just as beautiful as he ever was!" She patted the neck of the handsome creature and stroked his nose.

The horse whinnied at the attention and eyed her with seeming delight.

"I believe he remembers me, and I have n't spoken to him for — oh, how long is it?"

"My memory cannot extend so far." Colonel Gresham was evidently in a whimsical humor this afternoon.

Lone Star was made happy with more caresses and a full measure of oats, and then the Colonel and Polly walked slowly up to the house.

When Polly unfolded her plan in regard to the Home ladies Colonel Gresham's face lighted with interest.

"You can have two of my cars," he said, "on one condition — no, two — that I may drive the big one and that you will sit on the front seat beside me."

"Oh, it won't be a bit hard for me to say yes to that!" Polly smiled. "I should like it! Let me see, five and four are nine, and four makes

thirteen — why, they can all go — or all that
are well enough! Won't that be lovely!"

" 'Lovelicious,' I think!" The Colonel
looked demurely down at Polly.

"How much I used to say that!" Polly
laughed. "Well, I truly think this will be —
three cars! Won't they be surprised! But we
must squeeze in Leonora and David somewhere! Probably the ladies would n't all care
to go, anyway. You are so good to let them
have the cars — I never thought of two — or
that you could go with us! I can't thank you
half enough!"

Before Polly went home a ride was arranged
for the next morning, and her heart skipped
joyfully all the long way, thinking how happy
Miss Nita and the rest would be.

Directly after luncheon she ran over to the
Home.

"You look glad about something," Miss
Sterling told her.

"You will be when you know," chuckled
Polly. "What do you think! — you're going
to ride with Colonel Gresham to-morrow morning!"

"With Colonel Gresham! He has n't invited me!" Miss Sterling's knitting dropped into her lap.

"I have — or I'm going to! Oh, it will be lovely!" Polly's brown eyes shone. "Colonel Gresham is going to let us have his two biggest cars, and he will drive the seven-passenger one. Then father says we may have ours with Evan to drive, and we're going to take as many of the ladies as we can and have a beautiful ride! What do you think of that?"

"It's overwhelming! Catch me if I drop!" The gray-blue eyes were dancing.

Polly squeezed her ecstatically. "I want you in the car with me, and now let's see how many can go and which ones to ask."

It was a pleasant task, though really a little puzzling, for there were sixteen ladies of the Home, and only ten or eleven were to be counted among the weaklings. Nobody must be offended and nobody must feel hurt. So with David and Leonora, it was a hard matter, after all, to decide on the invitation list. Miss Sterling, however, was a wonderful assistant. Polly was sure she could never have disposed things so happily if it had not been for her wise Miss Nita.

CHAPTER XV

"LOTS O' JOY"

THE morning was as clear and balmy as a festival day should be, and the cars were at the door of the June Holiday Home at three minutes before nine o'clock.

"Let's go early," Juanita Sterling had said, "while the day is fresh from the hand of God." And in accordance with her wish Polly had appointed the hour.

Most of the ladies were in Sunday attire, their wardrobes holding few changes between "everyday" and "best."

Juanita Sterling handled her small stock of apparel so that, plain as it was, it had an air of distinction. Little deft touches here and there added character and daintiness to any garment that she wore. Some of the less fortunate realized this as they rode out of the Home gate that July morning, and one or two were actually envious of the little woman who sat in Colonel Gresham's beautiful car and responded so merrily to the Colonel's sallies.

"I guess Miss Sterling has ways of getting her nest feathered that some other folks don't know anything about," whispered Miss Castlevaine to Miss Major.

"No such thing!" was the prompt retort. "She knows how to put her feathers on, that's all."

"Knowing how don't change colors as I've ever heard — huh! Look at that white dress! They don't give me white dresses!"

"Probably she had it when she came. She hasn't been here a year yet, you know," replied Miss Major.

"They won't make over mine," complained the other.

"Oh!" broke in Mrs. Albright, "look over there! Isn't that magnificent?"

Fields and slopes of varying green, wooded hills, and mountains in the blue distance — these made the picture that had called forth the exclamation.

"Magnificent!" echoed Miss Major.

Miss Castlevaine looked, but said nothing. The darkness of envy and discontent still dimmed her eyes.

Juanita Sterling, in the car ahead, was yielding herself to the bountiful joy of the moment and had forgotten disagreeable things. Polly and Colonel Gresham kept up a steady run of pleasantries, much of which came easily to her quick ears, and she found herself smiling with them even while her eyes were feasting on the ever-changing landscape.

"Does n't Mrs. Dick live somewhere out this way?" inquired Miss Mullaly.

Miss Sterling did not know and in turn asked the Colonel.

"Tenney, the milk dealer? His farm is over there to the left a mile or two. Would you like to call on the bride?"

"Yes, I should! Would n't you, Polly?"

"First-rate! Let's!" was the eager answer.

So at the next cross-road the car was turned that way.

"I'm awfully glad you thought of it!" Polly turned to say.

"I did n't think of going there," Miss Mullaly admitted, "but I'd love to. Won't she be surprised!"

Surprised, indeed, was the former Mrs. Dick. She was on her way from garden to kitchen when the procession of cars came into view, and, her overflowing basket in hand, she halted on the side lawn until the party should pass by. A bunch of automobiles did not appear every day on the Tenney Farm road. Instead of going past, however, the big car ahead steered straight for her, and she recognized her friends! Down went her basket, and she skipped over the grass with the agility of a girl of fifteen.

"How do you do — Miss Sterling and Polly — and all of you! Well, I am astonished!— And if there are n't Miss Twining and Mrs. Bonnyman — why, are you all here?"

"Pretty nearly," answered Polly, who had jumped from the car and was clasping the speaker's hand.

Mrs. Tenney was soon surrounded by her Home associates and was so overwhelmed by the suddenness of the call that she almost forgot to invite them into the house.

"Oh, we can't stay!" declared Mrs. Albright. "We are just out for a ride, and those of us in the rear cars were about as surprised as you were. We'd no idea that Colonel Gresham was headed for your place — we did n't know you lived here till we saw you!"

134

"Dear people!" broke in Miss Sterling, "where are our manners? I'll confess, I forgot! Mrs. Tenney," with twinkling eyes she extended her hand, "I wish you every possible joy for all the days and years to come!"

Amid much laughter more good wishes followed, until somebody remembered that the morning was slipping away, and they were far from home.

"Well, say, why can't you all come out here sometime and spend the day? 'T won't make a mite of difference when. We always have enough to eat, and I am generally right here. I'd love dearly to have you. Pile 'em all in, if you can! Sit in each other's laps — any way to get 'em here! They're going to keep up the rides, are n't they?"

An instant's silence was broken by Polly. "Yes, we are!" she promised. "Colonel Gresham and father are going to let us have the cars until we're able to walk ten miles on a stretch!"

This sally was greeted by a shout, and the party climbed into the cars and were off, goodbyes mingling with the noise of the motors.

"Anybody getting tired?" asked Colonel

Gresham, as they swept into the village of Clare.

None would admit fatigue, and on whirled the cars, leaving the handful of houses behind. Presently they entered the broad street of an old town, where houses with gambrel roofs and quaint porches neighbored in quiet dignity with towered mansions and verandaed bungalows. Colonel Gresham drew up his car at a little shop, and he and David disappeared through the doorway. They soon came back with their hands full of ice-cream cones, which they distributed and returned for more.

"Is n't this cream lovely!" beamed Leonora to the back seat of the third car.

"Delicious!" responded Mrs. Albright.

"As good as I ever tasted!" declared Miss Major.

Miss Castlevaine nibbled hers for a moment longer before she spoke.

"My cousin goes automobiling a great deal," she said, "and she makes her own cream — solid cream it is, too! — and she has something that she puts it in so that she can slice it off as she wants it. It keeps ice cold for an indefinite time."

"I have heard of such contrivances," said Mrs. Albright politely.

"No cream could be better than this," asserted Miss Major confidently.

Miss Castlevaine drew her lips into a smirk.

"Trust the Colonel for buying the best of everything!" went on Miss Major. "What a man he is! I wish he were one of the directors of the June Holiday Home."

Miss Castlevaine's face stiffened into an expression of superiority, as if she could divulge things detrimental to the Colonel if she wished. But nobody appeared to regard her, and the cars jogged on.

Mrs. Adlerfeld, meanwhile, wore a look of saintly rapture.

Polly turned to say, "Isn't the air nice this morning?"

"Here it is beautiful!" smiled the little Swedish woman. "I have lots o' joy!"

Colonel Gresham threw her an admiring glance. "Glad you like it," he said.

"Oh, I like it very!" she responded. "I hope it did n't tired you to drive him."

"Not a bit!" he laughed.

"It looks more play as work," she smiled.

He nodded brightly back to her, and then turned to Polly. His tone was too low to carry to the seat behind.

"Why did n't you tell me what a charming little woman we had with us?"

"Is n't she sweet!" beamed Polly. "Did n't you ever meet her before?"

"Never! I'm going to invite her to ride with me — all alone, just to hear her talk!"

Polly chuckled. "I wish you would," she told him.

"She'd go, would n't she?"

"Of course! Why not?"

"I'll warrant that sour-looking elephant in the back car would n't!" laughed the Colonel. "She's that kind!"

"Oh! I guess you mean Miss Castlevaine. She's the biggest one there is. But she is very nice — sometimes."

"The times are few and far between, are n't they?" he twinkled.

Polly laughed, but said apologetically, "She's been pleasant to me."

"She ought to be; but over at the Tenneys' she looked as if she'd like to be somewhere else. She seemed to keep on the edge of things."

"She doesn't always come in with the rest — feels a little above some of them. She is very proud of her Russian ancestry. Her mother or grandmother was a duchess."

"I thought she was proud of something," observed the Colonel, "and it couldn't be her good looks."

"I think you are pretty hard on her," protested Polly.

"Am I?" he smiled. "Is she a particular friend of yours? You'll have to excuse me."

"Oh, she isn't an especial friend, but I feel sorry for her because she has to wear such old clothes — and she loves pretty things."

"Why doesn't she get pretty things, then, while she is about it?"

"She can't!" cried Polly. "She has to take what Miss Sniffen gives her."

"Oh, I see! Well, I reckon I'd look sour if I were dependent on that Miss Sniffen for clothes."

Polly chuckled. "I can't imagine it!"

"It would come pretty hard!" Colonel Gresham shook his head musingly. "It is a shame that those women are not better treated! I'll take them to ride as often as I can — you tell them so, Polly!"

139

"I will!" Polly beamed her delight. "It's lovely of you! It will do them no end of good. They stay cooped up in the house too much. You see, there's so much red tape about going out even for a little walk, that sometimes they'd rather stay at home."

"I'm going to talk to Randolph about it when I get a chance. He is too sensible a man to let this sort of thing go on."

"Oh, but you must n't make him think there has been the leastest mite of complaint! If anybody finds a word of fault, she'll get turned out! They're afraid of their lives!"

"This little woman back here does n't look afraid."

"No, she's different." Polly cast a look at her.

Mrs. Adlerfeld caught it and smiled back, a bright, happy smile, as if, indeed, she had "lots o' joy."

CHAPTER XVI

THE HIKING CLUB

"OH, Miss Nita! What do you think?" Polly burst into the room full of excitement. "Chris has gone!"

"Gone? Where?"

"To Australia!"

"Not alone?"

"Oh, no! His father is with him. We never knew he was coming — till there he was! For a minute Chris hardly knew him! Isn't that queer? But he didn't look like himself. His hair is cut close to his head! What do you suppose he did it for? It isn't becoming! But, oh, you ought to have seen Chris! He jumped right into his father's arms and cried and cried and cried! Mr. Morrow cried, too, almost as hard as Chris! We had a pretty exciting time!"

"When was it?" put in Miss Sterling.

"This noon. Mother did finally persuade him to stay to dinner — he wasn't going to! I don't see why he was in such a hurry to get away! Oh, I shall miss that boy awfully! He is

141

always just so — never cross or pouty, or anything. Sometimes he has been pretty blue — I suppose thinking of his father and wondering why he did n't come. It has been almost two years! It won't seem a bit natural without Chris. I shall have to come over here and bother you more than ever." Polly sighed a bit sorrowfully and dropped on a hassock at Miss Sterling's feet.

"You know you could n't come too often, my dear."

"I feel sometimes as if I were a nuisance," laughed Polly. "I guess Miss Sniffen thinks so. She looks at me so queer when she meets me in the hall."

"It is only her way. She can't have anything against you."

Polly shook her head doubtfully; then she smiled. "I did kind of pacify her the other night when we were late from our walk, did n't I? I was afraid I could n't, but I was n't going to let her know it!"

"It was funny the way she came round," Miss Sterling agreed.

"That makes me think," Polly broke out, "when are we going to have another walk?"

"I — don't — know," sighed the other. "Walking is such an effort! I get so tired I can't sleep."

"That's too bad!" mourned Polly. "But don't you think it's because you stay in the house so much? If you went oftener maybe you'd get used to it and it would n't tire you."

"Perhaps. I don't know."

"We were planning, only yesterday, Chris and I, to start a walking club — and now he's gone! But I suppose the rest of us can have it," Polly went on. "We thought we'd ask David and Leonora and Patricia, — she and her mother are just home from the shore, — and Doodles and Blue and all of you folks here."

"All the ladies?"

Polly nodded.

"They're not all equal to it. You forget how old some of them are."

"Anyway, they are n't too old to be asked!" laughed Polly.

"No, and it is a good idea. Sometimes a club will have a stronger pull on anybody than just an incidental invitation."

"That's what we thought — dear, dear, it's too bad Chris had to go!"

"I'm sorry, but I imagine he is happy enough to be with his father."

"Yes! He looked like another boy after his father came. Well, we'll have to do without him."

"How can Doodles and Blue be in? They live eighteen or twenty miles away."

"Oh, they can come down by trolley, or we can go up there," replied Polly easily.

Miss Sterling laughed. "You forget that we have n't any money for trolley fares."

"I never thought! They'll have to come here, then. Anyway, they've got to belong! Doodles is the sweetest boy! I used to wonder if he would change any when he was able to run and play — I did n't know but he'd get to be — coarser, you know; but he is just the same. Blue is nice, only he is more like other boys — Doodles is n't!"

"Miss Lily has been telling me of how he went to sing to her. She just idolizes him."

"I know she does. The other day when I was up to see her she could n't talk of anybody else. There is n't much doubt but that she will join the club if she can see Doodles oftener."

"She seems to be fairly strong; her trouble is only with her eyes."

144

"I guess it will do her eyes good to go out-doors more. I wanted to call it the 'Hiking Club'; but Chris was afraid the name would frighten some of them — they'd think a 'hike' meant more than just a walk."

"Mrs. Post is quite lame yet, and Mrs. Grace is having rheumatism. They could n't go at present. Miss Twining's heart bothers her. She said she should n't dare attempt so long a walk again."

"As the one the other day? That was n't long for a well person."

"But most of us are not well — if we were we should n't be here."

"I'll ask them all, anyway!" Polly insisted. "Can't we have our first meeting here in your room, Miss Nita?"

"Certainly. When is it to be?"

"I think to-day would be a good time — about two o'clock. It is n't very pleasant out, raw and chilly. I'll go round and invite them now. Will you come, too?"

"No, I'll sit here and read. You run along and get your hikers, and then come back and tell me about it."

CHAPTER XVII

GRANDAUNT SUSIE AND MISS SNIFFEN

POLLY aroused more enthusiasm among the ladies than Miss Sterling had thought possible. Almost everybody, even Mrs. Grace, with her rheumatic knee, was eager to join the new club.

It was agreed that those who were able should take a tramp together twice a week and should walk on the veranda, ten times its length, at least once a day.

Polly was unanimously elected president, Miss Major for corresponding secretary, and David Collins for treasurer.

"The club will be bankrupt from the start," laughed Miss Crilly. "What do we need a treasurer for?"

"Oh, they always have one!" insisted Polly. "Maybe the money'll come."

"Sure! Somebody might donate a million dollars to us — and what should we do without anybody to take care of it!" Miss Crilly chuckled happily.

146

The work of organization being disposed of, Mrs. Bonnyman asked what was to be done next.

Polly did n't know.

"Oh, we must adjourn!" declared Miss Major. "That is the principal event of most business meetings."

Accordingly, with much giggling from a few of the members, the new club voted to adjourn until the next Monday.

"Oh, dear! it's raining hard!" cried Polly. "I thought maybe we could go for a little walk, just to mark the day."

"Can't we do something here — have some game or other?" suggested Miss Crilly.

"I say!" burst out David, "I forgot! Mother told me to be at home by half-past three, and it's almost that now. Will you come, Leonora, or wait for the shower to be over?"

Leonora preferred a walk in the rain to one alone, so they hurried into their raincoats and were off.

"Our company's dwindling," observed Miss Crilly, as the door shut upon Mrs. Post and Mrs. Crump, "but I don't want to go home yet — need I, Miss Sterling?"

"Certainly not! I want you all to stay. Polly, you are queen of ceremonies — what shall we do next?"

"We might try some of Grandaunt Susie's exercises," twinkled Polly.

"Just the thing!"

"Who's Grandaunt Susie, pray?" Miss Crilly was frankly curious.

"Mother's grandaunt," explained Polly. "She was miserable, and these exercises made her strong enough to do almost anything. She is seventy-three, — or was when she was here, a year ago, — and father himself says she does n't look a minute over thirty-five!"

"Oh, my! Let's try 'em! I want to look 'not a minute over thirty-five'!" Miss Crilly waved her hands excitedly.

"How do you begin — this way?" Miss Mullaly sprang to her feet, threw out her chest, and worked her arms up and down.

"Oh, no!" cried Polly. "That is not it at all! You take them lying down!"

"Mercy!" cried Miss Lily.

"I'd like that!" declared Mrs. Albright.

"Good and easy!" Miss Crilly nodded.

"Yes, they are every one to be practiced in

bed, before you get up in the morning," resumed Polly.

"What if you don't wake early enough?" asked Mrs. Prindle with a shrug.

"Then you're late for breakfast or lose your chance of going back to thirty-five!" laughed Miss Crilly.

"How can you thrash your arms round in bed?" Miss Mullaly queried.

"You don't have to. It is n't like gymnastics."

"Well, do tell us, Polly! I'm just crazy to begin!" Miss Crilly laughingly shook Polly's shoulders.

"There are so many of them," Polly drew a long, laughing breath, "I hardly know which to take first. There is one for the legs — that would help in walking. But you'll have to lie down first."

Miss Crilly and Miss Major hurried to the floor, Miss Mullaly following.

"Oh, lie on the bed!" cried Miss Sterling.

"This is all right," asserted Miss Crilly. "Go on, Polly!"

"You want to turn just a mite on your right side. Now make your right leg firm, and put

your left toes against the top of your right foot,
— yes, that's it! — and tense the muscles of
your left leg — hard! Now relax! Tense again!
Relax! You must n't do it too long at first, but
that's the way — tense and relax, ten times on
this side and ten on the other."

"Whew! takes some strength! Why don't
you try it, girls? It's fun! Miss Sterling will
let you have her bed — we'll make it over
afterwards. Try it, Mis' Albright, and you,
Miss Leatherland, it'll do you good!"

"Yes, go ahead, as Miss Crilly says," urged
Miss Sterling. "I've practiced that, and I
think it has made me stronger."

Polly's class was increased to five, but the
others could not be induced to make any attempt.

"There's another that's pretty good," went
on Polly. "It's for both sides, alternate, but
you can learn it on your right. Bend up your
left knee, and take your left ankle in your left
hand — now pull hard, leg and hand both!
That's right. Pull and then relax. Here's another; bend your knee — the upper one, and
take it in both hands and pull hard! Relax,
and then pull again."

"I wish there was an exercise to make thin folks fatter," observed Miss Mullaly.

"I know some that'll make your cheeks plump and round," said Polly.

Little squeals of doubt greeted the announcement.

"I don't believe they'd make my face round," laughed Miss Leatherland.

"Yes, they would! Would n't they, Miss Nita?"

"I can't swear to it, as Polly does; but this I do know—it plumps and pinks them for a little while. Polly says her aunt told her that after enough practice the plumpness would stay."

"Oh, what is it?" queried Miss Mullaly eagerly.

"I'll try it on Miss Leatherland if she'll let me," offered Polly. "It will be more of a test on her, because she is thinnest."

"Certainly you may, but I can't quite believe it will do what you say it will."

"Just you wait!" chuckled Polly. "First you must smile, a big, big smile! Not quite hard enough!—Yes, that's better! Now, while I press my hands against your cheeks and massage them this way, you must open and shut your mouth — no, wider than that! — a little wider — just as wide as you can! Keep on smiling all the time!

"There! now I'll let you look in the glass — see how your cheeks have plumped out! Oh, but you look pretty!"

"Doesn't she!" Miss Crilly jumped up, the better to see. "Look! everybody! My, how pretty!"

"'Pretty!'" scorned Miss Leatherland. Yet the pink rose higher.

"Polly! is this the right way?" Miss Mullaly was doing her best, but not well enough to satisfy the instructor.

"The middle of your hand must come up high on your cheek," explained Polly. "Yes, that's it! And twenty-five times you must open and shut your mouth."

"Polly," broke in Miss Sterling, "when you can, I wish you'd tell Mrs. Prindle how to make her hair grow."

"Yes," added Mrs. Prindle, "she says you know a way of massaging the scalp, and my hair is so thin!"

"You'll have to take it down, I guess — so you can get at it all over," said Polly.

"Do you know it will really help it?"

"Grandaunt Susie said her hair was so thin you could see through it, and when she was at our house it was as thick as — as thick as mine."

"Oh, I'm going to try that — my hair's all coming out!" Miss Lily drew her pins from the thin coil.

Mrs. Grace and Mrs. Adlerfeld made their heads ready for manipulation.

"You just put your hands this way, right up under your hair,"— Polly spread out her fingers, — "and clutch at the scalp hard, as if you were going to pull it off. Go all over the head, again and again for five minutes—two or three times a day. Aunt Susie says it will make the hair grow like fun."

"Oh, Miss Polly, will you be so kind as to show me just how it goes, please?" Miss Twining was shaking down her scanty locks.

"It's very easy," Polly smiled. She liked the shy, gentle Miss Twining. "This is all there is to it," working her hands under the soft blond hair. "The only trouble is, it tires the hands out pretty quick."

"Oh, yours must be tired! I should not have asked you!"

"No, no! Mine are all right. I was thinking only of yours. Now, try it yourself. Yes, that's the way! You have it!"

"Polly!" Miss Crilly was on the floor, hugging her knee.

"I'm here!" laughed Polly.

"Do you know anything that will scare away a double chin?"

"Yes, I do!"

"Oh, jolly! What is it?"

"I'd like to hear about that!" spoke up Miss Castlevaine.

Polly thought a moment.

"You'll have to lie down — flat on your back — no, you go over on the bed, Miss Castlevaine, and I'll tell you how to do it."

"Don't get up, Mis' Albright!" cried Miss Crilly. "I can learn how here just as well!" She lay back, her eyes on Polly.

"I'll put this pillow right under your shoulders — so. Now throw your head —"

A sharp rap halted the sentence. Mrs. Albright sat up. The door was flung open before Polly reached it.

"Ladies! what does this mean?" Miss Sniffen stood there, resolute and merciless.

154

Nobody answered.

Miss Twining and Miss Lily began hurriedly to gather up their disheveled hair. Miss Castlevaine arose haughtily. Polly's tongue was quickest to recover itself.

"I was only teaching the ladies some exercises to make them strong. We are not doing any harm, Miss Sniffen."

"I infer that it makes them stronger to pull their hair down." The tone was smoothly sarcastic.

"Oh, that!" returned Polly, with a tiny smile; "I've been telling them how to massage the scalp, so as to make their hair grow."

"Very necessary, indeed! And I suppose their hair grows faster if they stretch themselves out upon the bed and the floor! I'm ashamed of you!"

"Oh, Miss Sniffen!" protested Polly, "you have to lie down to take these exercises! The book says so!"

"Book!" snapped the angry voice; "I'll book you all for what you won't like if I ever catch you in such unladylike postures again! You must be in your second childhood! Now march to your rooms, every one of you!" She waved her hand peremptorily toward the doorway, and the culprits filed meekly past her — all but Miss Castlevaine. She walked with stately step and head held high, as became the great-granddaughter of a duchess.

"I think you would better go home now, you have worked mischief enough for one day!" She addressed Polly in a slightly mollified tone.

"Why, Miss Sniffen, I can't see what harm there is in trying to get well and strong. I should think you'd like the ladies to be better. Father and mother think these exercises are fine! Mother's Grandaunt Susie told us about them. They made her as good as new!"

"We won't discuss the matter," replied the superintendent in a hard voice. "You need not remain to talk it over with Miss Sterling."

"I'm going — right now!" Polly caught up her coat.

"Good-bye, Miss Nita!" She swept past Miss Sniffen with a curt bow.

The door tight shut, Juanita Sterling fisted the air in the direction of the departing superintendent. Then she drooped her head and sobbed.

CHAPTER XVIII

VICTOR VON DALIN

For several days the weather was showery, not very pleasant for walking, and Polly stayed away from the June Holiday Home.

"What will Miss Nita think!" she mourned. "Miss Sniffen has probably forgotten by this time that she sent me home. Would n't it do for me to go over for just a little while this forenoon, while the officers are all busy?"

"I think you had better wait until Saturday," her mother decided.

So Polly sighed and ran off to write a little note to her beloved friend. It was warm in her own room, and she carried paper and pencil out to her favorite seat on the veranda.

She was there when a man came up the front steps, a white-haired man. He walked with a firm, quick step, and when he saw her he came over to where she sat. He took off his hat with a courteous bow.

"May I ask," he said in a low, pleasant voice,

"if you know a lady in the June Holiday Home named Adlerfeld, Mrs. Elise Adlerfeld?"

"Oh, yes, sir! I know her very well; that is, I know Mrs. Adlerfeld. I am not sure that her name is Elise."

"Her husband's name was Hans Adlerfeld."

"I don't know anything about him," Polly replied; "but there's only one Mrs. Adlerfeld there. She is a dear! I love her!"

The man's face flushed with pleasure. "Then you may, perhaps, help me. I have sought her these two years, and only now have I found her! I went to the door, and the lady told me I could not see her till next Wednesday! I cannot stay. I must go back to New York, and I must see her before I go. I begged the door-keeper to allow me to speak with my friend for only a short moment; but she would not. She said it was not visitor's day. Then I thought perhaps a neighbor might help me. So I come to you. I ask you, is there any way I can get inside to her, or she can get out to me? I beg of you, my dear young lady, will you help me? I must see her to-day! I cannot stay even till to-morrow!"

"That is just like Miss Sniffen!" declared

158

Polly. "She is the superintendent. She will never let anybody in except on Wednesday afternoon. It is a shame! I don't know —" She hesitated. "Perhaps mother will let me go over and tell her. Please take this chair, sir. Mother will see you about it; she will know better than I what to do."

"Tell her, if you please, that it is Victor von Dalin, an old friend of Mrs. Adlerfeld's, in Sweden, who desires to see her."

"Oh! are you really from Sweden?" beamed Polly. "How delighted she will be!"

"I have not been in Sweden these two years; but I knew her well when we lived there, a long time ago."

Polly ran off, full of excitement. How pleased the dear little woman would be! To think Miss Sniffen should refuse him entrance! She explained the matter to her mother.

"I will go right down," said Mrs. Dudley. "We must find some way to bring them together without arousing suspicion."

It was finally decided that Polly should go over to the Home and up to Miss Sterling's room, as usual, leaving Miss Sterling to see Mrs. Adlerfeld and to give her Mrs. Dudley's

159

invitation to spend the rest of the day at her house.

Happily, Miss Sniffen was not in sight as Polly made her quick way to the third floor.

"You dear child! Then you're not sick! I was afraid you were."

Miss Sterling held her at arm's length, to make sure of her health.

"Sick? Not a bit!" laughed Polly. "Mother thought I'd better not come until Miss Sniffen had had a chance to forget she sent me home —that's all! I was n't coming till to-morrow, but something happened—the loveliest thing!"

"What?"

"Come, sit down, and I'll tell you!"

"I can't imagine what it is!"

"No, you can't! You could n't guess if you had a year to do it in! The nicest man has come from New York to see Mrs. Adlerfeld, and they would n't let him in here! Was n't that mean! So he came over to our house, to ask if we knew her and could help him out. He used to know Mrs. Adlerfeld in Sweden, and he's bound to see her! Oh, he's so lovable! His hair is as white! But he does n't look old. Can't you come over pretty soon and see him?

160

Though I don't know as you'd better. That might give it away — to have two come! Mother wants you to tell Mrs. Adlerfeld that she would like to have her spend the day with us. Make her come just as quick as she can. You can tell her that it is Mr. Victor von Dalin that is there—isn't that a sweet name? Oh, I do hope she will come! He'll have a fit if she doesn't! Wasn't Miss Sniffen horrible the other day? When we were having such a good time! I must go — no, I guess I'll wait till you've been up and found out. Then I can tell him."

Polly waited and waited, wondering, after five minutes, why Miss Sterling did not come back.

"Dear me!" she thought anxiously, "I hope Mrs. Adlerfeld hasn't fainted or anything!"

The time dragged slowly away. Ten o'clock went by. Polly wandered restlessly around the room. She took up a book, but could not read. Once she started to go down the hall to find out; then she concluded she had better not. She looked out of the window, but could think of nothing but the worrying fact of Miss Nita's prolonged absence.

At last she heard her light step in the corridor. She sprang to the door.

"What in the world —"

Miss Sterling motioned for silence, and they hurried to the further side of the room.

"I knew you'd be frantic," she began; "but I could n't help it. Just before I reached Mrs. Adlerfeld's room I heard Mrs. Nobbs's voice in there, so I stopped at Mrs. Albright's. I knew it would be all right to tell her, they are so intimate. She is pleased as we are. But it did seem as if Mrs. Nobbs never would go! Oh, the dear woman is so excited that I don't know whether she will get dressed straight or not! Mrs. Albright is helping her. His coming has upset her completely. But it is a happy upsetting! You can see that! I am so glad!"

"Will she come right over?"

"If they'll let her. I presume they will."

"If they don't, I'll make a fuss!" threatened Polly. "I'll go after Mr. Randolph."

Miss Sterling laughed. "You won't have to do that."

"You have n't ever found out what he wanted to talk with you about over the wire, have you?" Polly asked.

162

"No, and I never shall." Miss Sterling's lips took a sorrowful droop.

"You will, too! I'll ask him myself some day!"

"No, no, you must n't!"

"You'll see!" Polly laughed and said a soft "Good-bye!"

Miss Sterling motioned her back.

"Be sure to come over to-morrow morning and tell me all about it!" she whispered.

Polly returned earlier. She appeared at four o'clock.

"I could n't wait another minute!" she said. "The two dears are sitting out on the veranda, up in the corner where the vines hide them from the street, and their heads are close together and they are talking earnestly in that queer lingo that nobody else understands! Oh, they are having the loveliest time! They were at our house to luncheon, both of them, and they're going to stay to dinner! He will take the 7.30 train for New York. We've all enjoyed it so much! Father and he just took to each other. You ought to have heard them talk! I believe he knows every book that ever was written! We had such fun! Father and mother never saw Mrs. Adlerfeld very much, and they think she is just charming. They used to go to school together in Sweden. His wife died three years ago, and he has a son and daughter, both married. The daughter lives in Stockholm and the son in Newark. Mr. Von Dalin is librarian in one of the big libraries — oh, I wish you could see him! Dear me, I must run back, for they may want something!"

Without doubt Polly was extraordinarily excited.

CHAPTER XIX

"A MOONSHINE PARTY"

NEXT Tuesday is Miss Lily's birthday!" Polly made the announcement in lowered tones.

"How old is she?" asked Miss Sterling.

"I don't know. Doodles told me when he was down the last time. You know he wrote out her application, and I suppose he had to give the date. He said would n't it be nice if we could celebrate it."

"But how? Celebrations and June Holiday Home are not on speaking terms."

"Well, Doodles proposed that we all come up to his house, and his mother would make a birthday cake. But we should n't let them do it all. Mother would furnish the salad and some of the other things. Then, I don't doubt Patricia would help, and Leonora and David."

"I wish I could." Miss Sterling shook her head sadly.

"Now, Miss Nita, don't you feel that way! If you do, I'll give it all up!"

"But I may be sorry, may n't I, that I can't help anything along?"

"No; because you do help along. It is n't just money and cake and such things."

"I like cake!" She smiled whimsically.

"Oh, why don't I bring you some! We had a lovely raspberry layer cake when Mr. Von Dalin was here, and I never thought to bring over a mite! Mother says I am growing careless, and I'm afraid she's right!"

"Dear child! I don't want you to bring me cake! I said that only in fun."

"You shall have some, all the same! Is n't the table here any better?"

Miss Sterling wrinkled her face into an answer. "The last cook is the worst we've had yet."

"Too bad! Colonel Gresham said he was going to see Mr. Randolph about things; but I dare say he has forgotten it."

"I hope he won't think I've been complaining to you." Miss Sterling looked alarmed.

"No, I cautioned him. Probably he will never think of it again."

"I rather hope he won't. My fear of the Powers is amounting almost to terror."

"Oh, Miss Nita, don't be afraid! That will

make you go back! You must n't have a bit of fear!"

Miss Sterling laughed softly. "Well," she yielded — "let's talk about the birthday celebration."

"You have n't stopped being afraid." Polly scanned the other with keen eyes. "But never mind, we'll go ahead with the plans. I love to plan! Don't you?"

"I like it too well; but I've seen so many of my projects burst into nothing all in a minute that I've been trying lately to content myself with everyday happenings."

"I'm sorry you've had so much trouble, Miss Nita," said Polly plaintively.

The little woman smiled. "I ought not to have said that. I'm better, you know! How are we to get up to Foxford?"

"Oh, in automobiles! Did n't I tell you? Colonel Gresham will let us have two, and Mrs. Illingworth one, and father ours. I don't know how many will go from here, but there'll be David and Leonora and Patricia and me, besides the Colonel and the chauffeurs. You don't think but that Miss Sniffen will let them all go, do you?" Polly added anxiously.

"Perhaps." Miss Sterling mused over it. "I can't tell; I've lost the map of Miss Sniffen's mind."

"Did you ever have it?" laughed Polly.

"I think once I had a facsimile of it."

Polly chuckled. Then she shook her head doubtfully. "I wish Miss Sniffen — was n't Miss Sniffen," she mused vaguely. Suddenly she brightened. "Why can't we tell Mr. Randolph about it and ask him to ask Miss Sniffen?" She waited eagerly for the answer. It was not quick to come.

Miss Sterling bent her head in thought, while the color fluttered on her cheeks.

"I'm afraid it would n't be best," she said finally with a deep breath. "He might —"

"Oh, bother!" Polly broke in; "I was so sure that was a brilliant thought of mine! And now you turn it down just like any common idea!"

"My dear child, it is n't that the idea is not brilliant, but it seems to me it would be — would be — just a little out of place!"

"It would n't be — a single bit!" insisted Polly. "Is n't he the president of the Home?"

"Yes; but he is n't in this, and would n't it look as if we were ignoring Miss Sniffen?"

168

"Maybe it would," assented Polly submissively. "I had n't thought of that."

"You have said nothing to Miss Lily about it?"

"Oh, no!" Polly replied. "We've only talked it over at home and with the Greshams."

"I suppose I'll have to parley with the Powers," smiled Miss Sterling ruefully.

"*I* don't want to!" Polly frowned. She thought a moment, tapping her teeth with her thumb. "Oh, I know!" she burst out joyously. "You can't object to this! Colonel Gresham's the one to do it—because he's going, too. He'll drive his big car. I thought it would n't do to have father, for she'd think I got him to do it. But Colonel Gresham would win anybody if he tried."

Miss Sterling nodded approvingly.

"Are n't you glad I thought of it?"

"It looks the best thing."

"It is! Guess I'll go and ask the folks now! Will you come?"

"No, thank you! Run on alone — you'll do it best without any assistance."

Polly laughed happily. She was too excited to insist on even Miss Nita's company.

169

It was a good hour before she returned, having been rapturously welcomed upstairs and down and kept as long as possible.

"Everybody is delighted with the idea!" Polly dropped to the hassock at Miss Sterling's knee. "They're all going—if they can! — except Mrs. Post and Mrs. Prindle. Mrs. Post has had a pull-back and she can't walk at all, and Mrs. Prindle's cold is worse. I think the rest will just fill the cars."

She counted up, and found seats and occupants to agree.

"I'm wondering whether to have Mrs. Adlerfeld or Miss Lily sit with Colonel Gresham — which would you?" Polly was all alight with her planning.

"The Colonel would enjoy Mrs. Adlerfeld best. Miss Lily would be too shy to say anything."

"So she would! I only thought of her because she's the birthday girl. Oh! You can't imagine how surprised she was — I thought she'd better know it right away, and not try to be secret about it."

Miss Sterling smiled assent.

"She looked as if she were going to cry,"

Polly went on; "but then I said something funny, and she laughed. I could see she was wonderfully pleased that Doodles should propose it. I'm glad he did, for I guess she does n't have very much to make her happy.

"Oh, I forgot! What do you think Mrs. Adlerfeld calls it? I happened to say we thought it was so nice it came when the moon was full, and she said, 'Thank you, I shall be so glad and happy to go! I am very fond about moonshine nights!' Is n't that just lovely? I'm going to call it a 'moonshine' party! It is ever so much prettier than 'moonlight.' Won't Colonel Gresham be pleased to have Mrs. Adlerfeld sit with him!"

CHAPTER XX

THE weedy roadside was a witching tangle of shadows, and the air was drowsy with spicy, wind-blown scents, as four motor cars swept on their merry way to Foxford.

Juanita Sterling, in the last of the procession, watched the gay little imps dance across the windshield and thought glad thoughts. It was going to be a worth-while evening she felt sure, and it was good that her left-hand neighbors, Miss Major and Mrs. Winslow Teed, had each other to entertain, and she was free to anticipate and ponder and to feast her heart on the visions of the night.

The sometimes insisting opinions of Miss Major and the familiar "When I was abroad" of Mrs. Winslow Teed seldom obtruded on her dreams. Once, however, she came to her surroundings with a start.

"No," Miss Major was asserting, "Nelson Randolph is not the man for the place. He takes some things for granted and lets other

172

things drift. If we had a good, live president, our superintendent would get her walking ticket instanter."

"A little strange he does n't marry again. His wife has been gone for some years, has n't she?"

"Five last June. They say he is devoted to her memory. I don't take much stock in such devotedness — so far as men are concerned. When he finds some pink and white doll that is sufficiently captivating he will go through with another wedding ceremony."

"That makes me think of a Danish couple I met in Florence," began Mrs. Winslow Teed; "she could n't have been over nineteen or twenty, and he was eighty at least. She —"

Miss Sterling was again absorbed in her own thoughts and never heard what became of the poorly-mated travelers.

Doodles and Blue ran down from the veranda as the cars speeded up the slope to the little bungalow, and they were quickly in the midst of a joyous circle.

Polly and David, alighting from the third car, ran back to help Miss Sterling and the others.

"Oh, Miss Nita! Was n't the ride lovely?" Polly squeezed her friend's arm. "Say, did you know, at the very last minute Miss Sniffen sent over word that Mrs. Bonnyman could n't go? She had the toothache, and so mother came in her place! Oh, I did wish you were in our car! I wanted to say, 'Is n't that beautiful?' and 'Just look at this!' "

"You could talk to David," laughed Miss Sterling.

"Oh, yes, I did some! But Mrs. Crump was jabbering to him most of the time. Have n't you ever been out here before? Why, I thought you had! — How d' y' do, Doodles!"

The three went up the steps hand in hand.

"Is n't that the loveliest, biggest moon you ever saw?" exclaimed Polly.

While they lingered to look at it a car flashed up the road and turned in at the entrance.

"Somebody going to the Flemings'," remarked Doodles carelessly.

"No, it's coming here!" returned Polly. The lights blazed toward them.

They waited, and a man stepped out.

"Mr. Randolph!" breathed Polly, as he emerged from the shadows.

174

"I feel somewhat like an intruder," said the president, as he grasped the hand of Doodles. "When Colonel Gresham invited me I told him my coming was impossible. Then things cleared up a little — and here I am!"

A visible stir succeeded Nelson Randolph's entrance. Mrs. Stickney and Colonel Gresham welcomed him most cordially, and Polly, as president of the Hiking Club, greeted him with a characteristic little speech.

Presently the unexpected guest was moving easily among the others, passing from group to group with hearty handshakes and happy words, at last coming face to face with Juanita Sterling.

She had watched him nearing her corner, the while politely attending to Miss Leatherland's intermittent chit-chat and vainly trying to banish from her mind the recent assertions of Miss Major. With his first word, however, they fled, and she found herself talking to the president unabashed and unafraid.

"I am glad to have the opportunity of telling you how much I thought of those beautiful roses," she said; "I never saw handsomer ones."

"It is good to know you enjoyed them. I hoped to have the pleasure of taking you out to Adalina Park in the height of the rose season." Was there an inquiry in the eyes that bent to hers?

She felt the flush sweep up her cheeks. "I should have been delighted to go," she replied. Hurriedly she tried to think of something to add to the brief sentence, but her mind was confused, and the seconds slipped by.

"I was sorry it happened so," he went on; "but we will try it again. Adalina Park is in its full glory now, and there are pretty drives outside of the parks." He smiled whimsically.

Then came the question that put her in doubt whether she should tell him the truth or not — "When should I be most likely to find you disengaged?"

"Almost any time," she answered, having decided that she would leave him to discover why she had not responded to his invitation. "Work is never pressing at the Home."

"Isn't it?" A puzzled look flickered in his eyes — or was it only her fancy?

A little flutter about the piano told that somebody was to play or sing. David took

176

the seat and began a prelude. Then he sang
in a clear, fresh voice: —

> "Red as the wine of forgotten ages,
>   Yellow as gold of the sunbeams spun,
> Pink as the gowns of Aurora's pages,
>   White as the robe of a sinless one,
> Sweeter than Araby's winds that blow —
> Roses, roses, I love ye so!"

"Who is that boy?" Nelson Randolph asked.
"Some relation of Colonel Gresham's, isn't he?"

"His grandnephew, David Collins."

"He has a fine voice."

"Excellent. Polly Dudley has a sweet voice,
too. I hope she will sing before the evening is
over. And Doodles is wonderful! Have you
ever heard him?"

"No. He told me he was in the choir at
St. Bartholomew's."

"There he comes! Oh, Polly is to play for
him!"

A very sympathetic accompanist was Polly.
Juanita Sterling listened in surprise and wonder. How could such a child do so well!

> "Young Davie was the brawest lad
>   In a' the Lairnie Glen,
> An' Jennie was the bonniest lass
>   That e'er stole hearts o' men;

But Davie was a cotter's lad,
   A lad o' low degree,
An' Jennie, bonnie, sonsie lass,
   A highborn lass was she."

Applause burst upon the hush that hung on the last note. It was insistent — it would not be denied. Doodles must sing again.

"He is a marvel!" Nelson Randolph spoke it softly, as the young singer returned to the piano.

He gave the second verse of the song, which before he had omitted, and then sang the dainty little love song, —

Dusk, and the shadows falling
   O'er land and sea;
Somewhere a voice is calling,
   Calling for me!"

Yet even that did not satisfy his audience. So he returned once more and gave in an irresistibly rollicking way a song in Yankee dialect, the refrain to which, —

"Oh, my boy Jonathan is jest as good as gold!
An' he always fills the wood-box 'ithout bein' told!" —

tagging as it did the various topics of the old farmer's discourse upon his son, never failed to bring laughter from his hearers.

At the end the applause was long and urgent;

but Doodles had run away, and would not come back.

Polly slipped up to Miss Sterling.

"Will you play for us now? — please, Miss Nita!" seeing a refusal in the eyes that met her own.

"I am not in practice. I should hate to break down before all these people," she smiled.

"There is n't one mite of danger!" Polly asserted confidently. "Do come, Miss Nita! Mr. Randolph, I wish you 'd coax her to come! She can play magnificently!"

"Polly!"

"She can!" Polly addressed the president.

"I don't doubt it," Nelson Randolph declared, "and I should be delighted to hear her."

"You would n't be delighted at all," Miss Sterling laughed. "You would want to stop me long before I had finished one page. My fingers would be lost in no time."

He dissented with courtliness, and Polly wheedled until Doodles and Blue came to add their urging to hers; but in the end they had to let Miss Sterling have her way, which was to remain outside of the entertaining circle.

So Polly sang, "Such a li'l' fellow," and

"Daisytown Gossip." Then Mrs. Winslow Teed was beguiled into singing the old song of "The Beggar Girl," and if her voice were a bit uncertain, on the whole it was sweet and received well-earned applause.

Games interspersed the music, and it was discovered that the president of June Holiday Home, as well as the eldest of the Home residents, was quite as clever in guesses as the young folks.

Either by chance or intention, — Juanita Sterling could not decide which, — Nelson Randolph appeared to have established himself for the evening at her side. Others came and went, but the president stayed.

"I wonder when we shall hear Caruso," she said. "He is on the programme; I think they must be waiting until the moon is high."

"Caruso?" he repeated with a puzzled look. "Not —"

"No, not the great Caruso," she smiled; "the little Caruso."

"But what has the moon to do with his singing? I am in the dark."

She laughed out. "I don't wonder! I supposed you knew about Caruso. He is a won-

derful mocking-bird that belongs to Doodles.
He can — but wait! You will hear him soon,
if I'm not mistaken."

Blue was at the window, gazing skyward. He
raised the curtain high, and the moonlight
streamed in. A large cage was placed on a table
in the direct beams. Suddenly the lights were
out.

A mellow fluting broke the hush, — and
Caruso was in song!

Few of the guests had ever heard his like.
He was a score of performers in one. The notes
of a dozen birds issued in quick succession from
that one little throat, clear, sweet, delicious.
Then, without warning, came the unmistakable
squeal of a pig, the squawking of hens, the yelp
of a puppy, which in a moment merged into a
little carol, and then — Caruso was singing
"Annie Laurie"!

The concert reached a sudden end, and the
audience came to itself in such applause as
none of the other performers had won.

"Are there any more astonishments in store
for me?" asked Nelson Randolph, as the clap-
ping dwindled to a few tardy hands. "When
the Colonel invited me to come up this evening

I did not anticipate a concert of this nature. He said they were to have 'a little music,' but you know what that generally means."

"I know," nodded Miss Sterling smilingly. "I wonder, after such an admission, that you were willing to risk it."

"Oh, I did n't come for the music!" he returned. "Nevertheless, it is worth going more than twenty miles to hear. Polly and Doodles and David would make a good concert by themselves — and now the mocking-bird! I never heard anything equal to his performance! He is a wonder!"

"He can whistle 'Auld Lang Syne,' too. I think he does it quite as well as 'Annie Laurie.'"

The applause had started again, and the lights, which had been turned on, went out. The audience quieted at once.

Soft and sweet came the tones of a violin.

"Doodles," breathed Miss Sterling.

Nelson Randolph bent his head to hear, and nodded in answer.

Softly the player slipped into "Old Folks at Home," and the tune went on slowly, lingeringly, as if waiting for something that did not come. Again it was played, this time with the voice of Doodles accompanying.

Meanwhile Polly was tiptoeing noiselessly from group to group and from guest to guest, with the soft-breathed word, "No applause, please!"

Over and over sounded the sweet, haunting melody, until not a few of those unfamiliar with the methods of the patient teacher and his singular little pupil, wondered, with Miss Crilly, "what in the world was up."

Then, just as almost everybody's nerves were growing tense, Caruso took up the air and carried it on bewitchingly to its close.

"How can he do it!" — "Wasn't that perfectly beautiful!" — "Did you teach it to him, Doodles?" — "My! but he's a jimdandy, and no mistake!" These and a score of others were tossed about as the lights went up.

"I must have a nearer view of that singer," declared Nelson Randolph. "I'm sure he can't look like an ordinary mocker; he must show the marks of genius in his feathers!"

Miss Sterling laughed. "He is certainly surprising. Doodles told me he was trying to teach him a new song, but I was not prepared for anything like this."

183

"Who could be! — Come!" he invited. "Let's go over and see him!"

Juanita Sterling unavoidably brushed Miss Crilly on the way across, and smiled pleasantly, to which that middle-aged merrymaker responded with a whispered, "Ain't you swell, a-goin' with the president all the evening!"

Miss Sterling flung back a laughing shake of the head, and passed on.

Nelson Randolph scanned the slim gray bird in silence. Then he turned to his companion.

"It does n't seem possible that this little fellow could do all that!"

Doodles smiled across the cage. He was giving Caruso the tidbit which he had well earned.

"How long does it take you to teach him a song?"

"I've only taught him one, Mr. Randolph. He was several months learning that. He knew 'Annie Laurie' when he came, and Mr. Gillespie taught him 'Auld Lang Syne.'"

The bird had finished his little feast and stood nonchalantly preening his feathers.

"Caruso!"

The mocker lifted his head and gave a short

184

whistle. Then he went on with his interrupted toilet.

Nelson Randolph laughed softly.

"Caruso!" began Doodles again. "Caruso!"

The bird looked up and whistled as before.

Doodles bent closer. "Can't you sing 'Auld Lang Syne' for Mr. Randolph? He has never heard it, you know."

The mocker stretched a wing and let go a mellow strain.

Softly Doodles began to sing, —

> "Should auld acquaintance be forgot,
> And never brought to mind?
> Should auld acquaintance be forgot,
> And days of auld lang syne?"

The bird had stood listening, and now caught up the air with vigor, carrying it on with a surety that was as astonishing as it was delightful.

Nelson Randolph shook his head in admiration. "Marvelous!" he cried; "marvelous!" He put his hand in his pocket — "I wish you liked pennies!" he laughed.

"His pennies are meal worms," said Doodles with a grimace. "I'll get him one."

"Ugh! How can he?" laughed Miss Crilly, as the bird disposed of the dainty.

His reward seemed to incite him to further song, for straightway he launched into a gay little medley that set his hearers laughing and admiring at once.

"The birthday supper is ready!" announced Blue informally from the door of the dining-room.

Doodles ran quickly to Miss Lily's side and they took place at the head of the little procession.

Colonel Gresham and Mrs. Adlerfeld came next.

"Oh, I'm so glad!" thought Juanita Sterling, catching a sight of the little Swedish woman's happy face.

The company speedily divided itself into two's, and Miss Sterling, with a bit of a heart flutter, found herself walking beside the president of June Holiday Home. Just ahead were Patricia and David. Where was Polly? She and David were always together — everywhere. But now she and Leonora were side by side. Strange! — but wonderings were lost in the pleasant calls of the occasion.

In the smallish dining-room a long table gave seats to everybody, and no one was crowded.

186

THE PARTY ITSELF

Nothing elaborate had been attempted, all was simple and homelike. Except for the curious decoration above the seat of honor, and the birthday cake with its pink and white frosting, there was little to distinguish it from an every-day repast.

Talk and appetite went merrily hand in hand, and the "birthday girl," as Polly and Doodles insisted on calling her, grew actually gay.

When she had cut the cake, and everybody's plate was empty, Doodles asked her to pull a pink ribbon hanging from the umbrella-like contrivance over her head.

With a half-frightened face and fingers that trembled, she plucked at the dainty string. Nothing happened.

"Pull harder!" urged Doodles.

She made another attempt — and gave a little cry, for tumbling about her came birth-day gifts in wild array.

Into her lap plumped an embroidered pin-cushion, on one shoulder drooped a muslin and lace apron, over her head was draped a white silk waist, while all around, on floor and table, were other articles, besides packages of various sizes tied with pink and white ribbons. In the laughter and confusion, presents too bulky or too frail to be risked in a fall were placed near her, — a long box of pink roses, a tall vase of cut-glass, a big, big box of candy, a pretty bon-bon dish, a small fern, and a little begonia with lovely pink blossoms.

To be thus suddenly surprised, and at the same time to be made the attractive point of so many eyes, was more than Faith Lily's composure could bear. Her lip quivered like a little child's, her blue eyes filled with tears and over-flowed — she began softly to sob.

Doodles looked distressed. Then he did the best thing possible.

He took up the pincushion. "Mrs. Dudley made you this," he said, "and this is from Leonora," — he held the apron for her to see. "Isn't it pretty? Turn round a bit and I'll tie it on!"

The crying ceased, and the tension had passed. Miss Lily smiled down on the apron with happy eyes.

"Here is a handkerchief that Polly embroidered for you," Doodles went on, "and this box of chocolates is from Mr. Randolph. Colonel Gresham gave you the roses — just smell them!" He lifted the box to her face.

THE PARTY ITSELF

"Oh!" breathed Miss Lily in delight.

"The china dish is David's present, and these cards are from Mrs. Albright and Mrs. Bonnyman and Miss Crilly. This beautiful waist — that's from Patricia, and the box of handkerchiefs from her mother, and the booklet from Miss Castlevaine, and the photograph from Miss Major. Oh! the vase is from the 'Hiking Club,' — and I don't know about the packages."

Miss Lily beamed on her riches, upon Doodles, upon the whole tableful.

"Why," she exclaimed softly," I don't see how you came to do it! I never thought of having a single present! Oh, it's beautiful of you!" Her voice trembled. "I can't thank you half enough, but I shall love you, every one, as long as I live!"

Doodles was picking up the small parcels scattered on the floor.

"Will you have these now?" he nodded.

"Oh, yes!" she said, eagerly as a child.

Everybody seemed interested in the unwrapping. They were simple gifts, but Miss Lily fingered them lovingly, even to the plainest little card.

The telephone called Blue into the next room. He returned almost at once.

"Mr. Randolph," he said, "some one wishes to talk with you."

They were rising from the table as the president came back.

"I am sorry to say good-bye so early," he told them; "but a New York man is waiting to see me on important business and has to return home on the 11.45 train. So I must get down to him as soon as possible."

He came over to Juanita Sterling with a little rueful smile.

"I hoped to have the pleasure of taking you home, but —" He shook his head. "We'll make up for it in a day or two," he finished blithely.

Her eyes met his. Something she saw there sent a warm flush to her cheeks, and she looked away.

"You will hear from me soon." He held out his hand. "Thank you for giving me so much enjoyment this evening — good-night."

That was all. Simple courtesy, Juanita Sterling told herself two hours later; but now — her heart was filled with a quivering joy that was almost pain.

On the homeward ride she found herself seated next to Miss Major, with Miss Castlevaine just beyond.

"We seem to be shifted round," Miss Castlevaine observed. "I came up in the second car, Dr. Dudley's; but Mrs. Winslow Teed has my seat — I was in front with the chauffeur. So I took the first vacant place I saw."

"She rode up with us."

"Then it is all right. I see David Collins has got Patricia Illingworth in tow — he came with Polly. I wonder if they've had a quarrel."

"I never knew them to quarrel," said Juanita Sterling.

"Oh, don't they? Well, it looks like it now. He took Patricia out to supper, too."

"So he did," responded Miss Major. "I didn't think of it in that light. We've had a nice evening, anyway. It seems good to get out of the rut."

"Yes," answered Miss Castlevaine grudgingly; "but they'll have to keep this up, now they've begun, or there'll be more fusses than a few!"

"What do you mean?"

"Why, everybody'll have to have a birthday party, or the rest'll be jealous."

"Oh, yes, I see! But they could n't do it for all."

"Then there'll be trouble! And I don't know as I should blame them any. Why should one of the family have all the good times and loads of presents, and nobody else have anything — huh!"

"It has n't established a precedent by any means," asserted Miss Major.

"Indeed, it has! And they ought to have thought of that before they began."

"I doubt if any such thing ever occurred to Polly and Doodles," interposed Miss Sterling. "They were thinking only of giving Miss Lily a pleasant birthday. I am glad she had so many presents."

"Well, Mr. Randolph meant she should have enough candy for once, did n't he? A five-pound box certainly! If she eats it all herself, it'll make her sick! I don't suppose she ever had so much at one time before, and she won't use any judgment about it. It would have been in a good deal better taste to have given her a simple pound box."

"Oh, no!" laughed Miss Major. "I'd rather have a five-pound box any time! And so would you!"

"I suppose he's used to that size," retorted Miss Castlevaine. "He probably gives 'em to his girl by the cartload — huh!"

"Who is she?" queried Miss Major.

"Why, that Puddicombe girl! He is engaged to Blanche Puddicombe — did n't you know it?"

"No, I had n't heard."

"Well, he is! They say the wedding is n't coming off till next spring. I guess he's bound to have all he can get out of his freedom till then — he won't have much after he's tied to that silly-pate!"

"She looks it all right! Her mother is n't any too smart."

"No, and the Puddicombe side is worse. We used to think that Si Puddicombe knew less than nothing! And Le Grand Puddicombe —"

Juanita Sterling edged a little closer into the seat corner. She had no interest in Le Grand Puddicombe. She stared into the night. A raw wind struck her face. Thick clouds had suddenly shut out the moon, and a chill overspread the earth. All was dark, dark, except for the flashing lines ahead. The steady pur-r-r-r-r-ing of the car was in the air, Miss Castlevaine's monotonous voice ran on and on; but the little woman at the end of the seat realized nothing except the insistent words knelling through her brain, — "Engaged to Blanche Puddicombe! Engaged to Blanche Puddicombe!"

It was not until she was in her room, with the door safely locked, that she commanded herself sufficiently to answer the clanging voice.

"I don't believe it! I don't believe it!" she burst out. "It's a lie! — a miserable, sneaking lie!"

"Engaged to Blanche Puddicombe! Engaged to Blanche Puddicombe!" was the mocking retort.

She dropped on her knees by the bedside and covered her face with her hands.

"Oh, God," she whispered, "forgive me for being a fool!"

CHAPTER XXI

TWO OF THEM

POLLY came early the next morning to talk over things.

"You got all tired out, did n't you?" she exclaimed, meeting the wearied eyes.

"Oh, no!" denied Miss Sterling. "I did n't sleep quite as well as usual, but I'm all right."

"I'm glad it is only that. You look almost sick." Polly scanned the pale face a little doubt-fully. "I'm worried about David — he acted so queer last night."

"What's the trouble? They were talking of it coming home."

"About David? — or me?"

"Miss Castlevaine spoke of David's being with Patricia, and was wondering if you had quarreled — that's all."

"No, there has n't been a word!" cried Polly disgustedly. "But I suppose he is jealous of Doodles — such a silly! He's a lovely boy, if he were n't always getting jealous of every-

195

body. He wants me to stay right with him every minute and not speak to anybody else!"

"That is foolish."

"I know it, but that's David Collins!"

"I wonder —" she stopped.

"What?" asked Polly.

"I was only thinking about Colonel Gresham. Perhaps it was jealousy that caused the estrangement between him and Mrs. Jocelyn."

"Maybe — I never heard what it was."

"Possibly it is in the blood, and David can't help it."

"He need n't be a goose just because his grand uncle was! It is n't as if we were grown up!"

Miss Sterling gave a little laugh.

"I don't care, it is n't!" insisted Polly. "If I were eighteen and engaged to him, of course, I should n't expect to go around with other boys — 't would n't be right: but now —!" Polly's face finished it.

Juanita Sterling looked gravely at nothing.

"And such a boy as Doodles!" Polly went on. "To start with, he is younger than I am, and that ought to be enough to give David some sense! Mother says she did n't see me do anything out of the way — did you, Miss Sterling?"

"Why — why, — what was it you asked, Polly? I was thinking so hard, I lost that last!"

Polly looked keenly at her friend's flushed face.

"I believe you do think I did something! What is it? Tell me right out! I shan't mind!"

"No, no, Polly! Forgive me, it was n't anything about you and David — I happened to let another thought in just for a minute — that was all. No, I don't think you did anything that a sensible boy would mind in the least. Even if you were grown up and engaged to David, you did nothing that should have caused him any annoyance."

"Oh! that's more than mother gave me credit for! — Do you really know what you're saying anyway?" laughed Polly.

"Perfectly, Miss Dudley! And I declare to you this moment that you are a model of propriety!"

"O-o-h! Don't I look awfully puffed up? Now you'll think me silly! But I've talked long enough about David and me. I'm dying to tell you how glad, glad, glad I was last evening every time I looked your way! I almost

forgot the birthday girl for thinking of you!
Was n't Mr. Randolph lovely? And did n't
you have a dandy time? Why, he kept as
close to you as if you'd been engaged to him!
He —"

"Oh, Polly, don't talk that silly stuff! I
won't hear it!" Miss Sterling got up hurriedly
and went to her work-table, apparently hunt-
ing for something in her spool basket.

"Why, Miss Nita!" Polly's tone was
grieved.

"Well, forgive me," came from over the
array of threads and silks, "but I do hate to
hear you say such things!"

"I was only telling the truth," said Polly
plaintively. "I thought you were having a
lovely time — you looked as if you were! Doodles spoke of it."

"Yes, I dare say I looked and acted like an
old fool!"

"Miss Nita! You could n't! You looked too
sweet for anything, and I guess he thought
so —"

"Polly! what did I tell you?" She came
back with a half-mended stocking.

"Are n't you ever going to let me speak of
198

Mr. Randolph again? He acted as if he were dead in love with y—"

A hand was clapped over her mouth.

"I won't hear it! I won't! I won't!" Miss Sterling laughed a little uncertainly.

Polly drew a long breath of disappointment. "I never knew you to act like this before," she mused.

"How sweetly Doodles sang!" said Miss Sterling.

"Yes," agreed Polly dispiritedly.

"And you are a charming accompanist."

"Oh! now, who's silly?"

"Nobody." Miss Sterling drew her hand from her stocking.

"It does n't seem to me that I play well at all — I long to do so much better."

"It is a rare gift to be a good accompanist, and you surely possess it."

"Thank you — you 're not saying that to counterbalance what you said about —?"

"No, I 'm not! When I say a thing I mean it."

"Perhaps some other folks do. Oh, Miss Nita! I could n't help hearing what Mr. Randolph said when he bade you good-bye—I was so near!"

199

"What if you did! There was nothing secret about it." The voice was hard and unnatural. Miss Sterling felt the flame in her cheeks.

"Well, I was almost sure that it meant he was going to take you to ride, were n't you?"

"Of course he won't ask me!" She crossed over to the work-table for another stocking.

"I think he will," said Polly decidedly. "You 'll go if he does, shan't you?"

"No, not an inch!"

"Oh, why? I'd go in a minute if he'd ask *me!*"

"Is n't there something we can talk about besides that detestable man! How did Colonel Gresham enjoy Mrs. Adlerfeld?"

"I don't know. I have n't seen him. I guess I'd better go. Mother may want me." Polly walked slowly toward the door.

"I hope I shall be in a more agreeable mood when you come next time," smiled Miss Sterling.

"I hope so," replied Polly soberly.

The door had shut, the light footfalls were growing faint, when Juanita Sterling began to sob. Her lips twitched as she tried to suppress the tears. It was no use, they would have their way, and she finally hid her face in her hands and let them go.

"Why, Miss Nita! Dear Miss Nita!" Polly had her arms around her friend's neck, crooning love words.

"I — I — did n't hear you knock!" apologized Miss Sterling.

"Never mind, you darling! I only gave one little tap — and then I — came in. You don't care, do you? If you do, I'll go right away. But I'm sorry you feel so bad! You're not sick, are you?"

"N-no, — oh, no!"

"Well, don't tell me, unless you'd rather. Sometimes I feel better to tell mother when things trouble me."

Getting no answer, she went on.

"Should you like to have mother come over?"

"Mercy — no! Don't tell anybody, Polly, — will you? — what a fool I am!"

"Of course, I won't tell — ever! But you're not a fool! Nobody can help crying when things go wrong. Miss Sniffen has n't been saying anything, has she?"

"Oh, no! I have n't seen her lately."

Polly waited patiently.

"I came back for my handkerchief," she explained. "I thought I must have dropped it — oh, there it is!"

"Was I dreadfully cross to you? I did n't mean to be, dear child!"

"You were n't a bit!" insisted Polly. "I ought to know better than to torment you about — that man. But I like him so well, I can't understand why you don't. I wish you did!"

The sobs started again, and Miss Sterling got up quickly.

"I don't see what makes me act — like this!" she exclaimed fiercely.

Polly was not obtuse. She began to think hard. Still, Miss Nita had said — Miss Nita would not lie! It was beyond her understanding.

Miss Sterling wiped her eyes.

"You know we're to go on a hike to-morrow," said Polly tentatively.

"Ye-s," feebly. Then, "I'm not going."

"Oh! why?"

"Don't want to! Should if it was n't for that!"

"Good reason," commented Polly, and she

waited for a retort, but none came. "I'm afraid David will fuss," she said finally.

"I don't blame him one mite!" Miss Sterling broke out.

"Wh-why, you said — I had n't done a thing!" Polly was plainly astonished.

"You have n't! But I don't blame David all the same." Miss Sterling smiled a queer little equivocal smile.

"Well, you two are the hardest mortals to understand!" sighed Polly. "I give it up!" She skipped toward the door. "Be ready at two, to-morrow, Miss Nita!" she called back. "If you're good, I'll let you walk with David."

CHAPTER XXII

DANCING HIKERS

JUANITA STERLING was in the little procession that started from the June Holiday Home at two o'clock. So was David Collins. They were nearly the whole line apart, and Polly skipped up and down between them.

"I'm so glad you were able to come!" she told Miss Sterling, squeezing her arm. "I have n't had a chance to speak to David yet; but I must." She sighed. "Oh, dear, I hate fusses! He's with Leonora. Say, did you see Doodles? He had to go to the music store and have something done to his violin — he said it would n't take more than three minutes. He's going to catch up with us farther along; he can take a short cut across from Columbia Street. Think of him and Blue coming clear down from Foxford just to go to walk with us!"

"It looks as if they wanted to come."

Polly laughed.

"I suppose I must n't speak to either of them, or David will be furious! I guess I'll go on and do as I like! There's Miss Crilly beckoning —

I promised her I'd walk a little way with her. Good-bye for now!"

Miss Sterling saw Doodles come up a cross street, violin in hand, and run ahead to join Polly. She chuckled softly.

"Where are we bound for to-day?" queried Miss Mullaly in her ear.

"I don't know. Polly has n't told me the route."

A motor-car whizzed by.

"Was n't that Mr. Randolph?"

"I think so," answered Miss Sterling. Her tone was indifferent.

"I've seen that lady with him two or three times. Do you know who it is?"

"Miss Puddicombe, I believe, daughter of one of the Board."

"Oh!"

The eyes of the other involuntarily followed the car.

"She dresses in all colors of the rainbow," laughed Miss Mullaly. "It's queer, how little taste some people — But maybe she is a friend of yours!"

"No, I never spoke to her. I have heard of her astonishing combinations, though."

205

Polly came running back.

"Is n't it lovely that Doodles has his violin! He says when we get tired and come to a nice place to rest, he will play to us. Are n't you tired? I want somebody to be, so we can have the music. He has learned some new pieces."

"I think there is a pretty grove not far ahead. Don't you remember it?— There's a great rock at one side, and a little clump of young birches near by."

"Oh, yes, next to a sheep pasture! That will be just the place! I'll tell Doodles!"

But before the wood was reached, the party came upon a car by the side of the road. Juanita Sterling had recognized it and longed to run away.

"Why, it's Mr. Randolph!" discovered Miss Mullaly.

"Yes, he has tire trouble, I see."

The president of the Home was already talking with those ahead.

Polly came back.

"Mr. Randolph and Miss Puddicombe," she whispered. "He is introducing her to the ladies."

Miss Sterling nodded and shrank away.

"I don't want to meet her," she objected. "I wonder if they'd notice if we should cut across this lot."

"Oh, don't! I'm afraid they would."

The other looked longingly toward the way of escape while she walked on with Polly.

Juanita Sterling and Blanche Puddicombe stood face to face, a smiling "How do you do, Miss Puddicombe!" on one side, a gushing "I'm charmed to meet you!" on the other, with a gingerly hand-shake between.

Nelson Randolph was too busy with his tire for much talking, and, as early as decency would allow, Miss Sterling by degrees slipped into the background.

"Let's go on," she whispered, taking Miss Leatherland's arm.

The others straggled after, by twos and threes.

"Why did n't you stay longer?" questioned Polly, overtaking her friend.

"There was nothing to stay for," she laughed.

"Miss Puddicombe said she would like to get acquainted with you." Polly's tone had the inflection of disappointment.

"Very kind of her," was the quiet comment.

Polly glanced whimsically at Miss Sterling's face. "I guess that is the grove you were speaking of," was what she said.

Many of the ladies were glad to stop, and scattered stones and mossy logs made pleasant resting places.

Doodles played delightfully and finally slipped into a waltz.

"Oh, my feet just won't stay still!" cried Miss Crilly. "Come on, Polly!" And the two went dancing through the wood.

"It's better over there in the pasture," said Polly, as they came to a sudden halt against a big pine.

"Let's try it!" Miss Crilly pulled her forward, and over they ran, hand in hand.

"Doodles! Doodles!" they called.

The boy and the violin were quickly there, and Patricia and the young folks ran after.

"Oh, this is lovely! Better come and try it!" —"The very dandiest place!" cried the dancers as they stopped for breath.

Miss Major, Miss Mullaly, and others came laughing into the open.

Doodles played with zest, everybody was in merry mood, and the dance went gayly on.

Polly suddenly ran into the grove for her beloved Miss Nita.

"You must! You must!" she declared, as Miss Sterling doubtfully shook her head. "You don't know how much nicer it is to dance outdoors! Come!"

She hesitated, but the music was inspiring, and impulsively tossing all else aside she skipped on with Polly.

Along the road jogged a buggy, and the driver stared at the unusual sight. Then he stopped his horse.

"What's up?" he called out. "Is it a boardin'-school or a lunatic asylum?"

Polly and Miss Sterling came whirling toward him. "Neither, sir!" answered Polly promptly. "We are dancing hikers!"

"Wh-at?" the man gasped.

But the laughing couple waltzed on.

Blue had gallantly claimed Juanita Sterling for her second dance, and as they waltzed down to the street they saw the motorists whom they had left beside the road driving toward them. The car stopped, and Mr. Randolph and Miss Puddicombe stepped out.

"It was too tempting!" he exclaimed. "We

could n't go by. Is it a free-for-everybody dance?"

"Of course it is!" answered Blue. "We are very glad to have you stop and try it with us."

The Home President turned to his companion. "Will you come?" he said.

She looked down with a scowl. "Why, Nelson, I can't dance on such rough ground!"

"Oh, come on!" he urged. "What the others can do, we can!"

"It is n't bad — really!" smiled Miss Sterling. "The sheep have nibbled it pretty smooth."

The couples whirled off, but soon afterwards Nelson Randolph was seen standing alone over by the wood.

"Guess she's the kind that goes with waxed floors and a whole orchestra," laughed Blue.

When the fiddling came to a pause Juanita Sterling found herself not far from the man whom she was endeavoring to shun.

"Let's go down to those birches!" she proposed carelessly. But she was too late, for Nelson Randolph was already coming her way.

"Too tired for another turn?" he asked.

"Oh, no, I'm not tired!" — yet her face did not reflect his smile. She wished he would go away and leave her alone. Why must she continually be meeting him! Still she could not easily refuse when he urged his request, and she yielded a somewhat grave consent.

Miss Crilly and David Collins gayly led the quadrille that followed, and even Miss Castlevaine's habitual sneer was lost in the enjoyment of the moment. But Juanita Sterling, lover of all outdoors, devotee of music and the dance, with the best partner on the ground, went through the steps, her graceful feet and her aching heart pitifully at variance.

They walked together over to the edge of the wood.

"I have business in Riverview to-morrow morning — would you like to go? The ride over the mountain is very pretty now, and my errand won't take more than five minutes."

She could feel the warm blood creep up her face. Her answer hesitated. "I am sorry," came at last, "but I'm afraid I cannot — to-morrow."

He gave a little rueful laugh. "I always choose the wrong time," he said.

"I am very sorry," she repeated truthfully.

"Nelson!" called Miss Puddicombe, as they drew near. "It is horribly impolite; but I think I'll have to hurry you a little. I want to see Grace about those tickets for the Charity Fair, and it is getting late."

"I am at your disposal," he replied gallantly. And shortly they were gone.

Polly walked home with Miss Sterling. David was devoting himself to Patricia. Polly's gay mood had passed and left her quiet and pensive. Only commonplaces were spoken — Miss Castlevaine was just ahead, and her ears were sharp. Miss Sterling knew that as soon as the seclusion of the third-floor corner room was reached Polly's heart would overflow in confidences.

"Will you come in?" For Polly had stopped at the entrance.

"Yes." A step forward. "N-no, I guess I won't — yes, I will, too!"

Miss Castlevaine looked round with a short laugh. "What's the matter, Polly? Lost your beau?"

"No, he's lost me!" was the quick retort.

"Oh, is that it?"

"Yes, Miss Castlevaine, that is precisely it!" A warning flush was on Polly's cheeks. "Thank you, Miss Nita, I'll go up for a little while," she said.

With a shrug and a little "Huh!" the descendant of the duchess passed on.

The door clicked shut, and Polly dropped into a rocker, tossing aside her hat and coat.

"What shall I do with David?" she sighed. "He barely nodded to me to-day!"

"I presume I should cruelly let him alone."

"Then 't would be good-bye, David! He'd never, never, never take the first step! And I like David!" Polly caught her breath.

"Poor little girl! I'm sorry!" Miss Sterling knelt beside her and threw an arm about her.

Polly began to sob. "I thought — he'd be decent this afternoon! I have n't — done a single thing!"

"No, you have n't!" agreed Miss Sterling. "And for that reason when he has thought it over long enough I believe he will see how foolish he has been."

"But he won't give in!" declared Polly, wiping her eyes. "Well, I can't go to him and say, 'Please forgive me!' when I have n't done anything! I guess I'll let him gloom it out! There, that's settled! Now let's talk about you!" She stroked Miss Sterling's hair, and smiled.

"You just ought to have seen you two dancing together!" she broke out in a lively tone.

"Pity there could n't have been a long mirror set up somewhere!" replied Miss Sterling.

"Well, you did look lovely!" Polly went on, ignoring the retort.

"Do you mean each of us separately or only when we were in company?" asked the other gravely.

"Oh, now, don't you make fun of me! I know what I'm talking about! Doodles said you were the best dancers he ever saw!"

"And he has seen so many!" murmured Miss Sterling.

Polly tossed her head in disapproval, but continued, "I was so in hopes he would have time to ask you to go to ride — and then she had to hurry him up! It sounded exactly as if she were jealous!"

"He invited me," said Miss Sterling quietly.

"Oh, he did?" The voice was joyful. "When are you going?"

"Never!"

Polly stared at her friend in dismay. "Miss —Nita! You don't mean —?"

"Yes, I declined the privilege!"

The brown eyes blazed. "I think you're —"

"Polly, wait! I do not wish to ride with Mr. Randolph — he is engaged to Miss Puddicombe!"

Polly's eyes grew big. "I don't believe it! — How do you know?"

"I was told so."

"Do you really think it is true?" demanded Polly.

"There is nothing else to think."

"She calls him Nelson," mused Polly — "I thought she was pretty bold! But he is too smart to be such a fool!"

"Love sometimes makes fools of the best of us."

Polly watched the red flame up in the thoughtful face beside her, and in that moment Polly grew wise.

"He does n't love that Puddicombe ninny and he never will! You should have heard her talk when he was dancing with you. I was over there. Such airs! You'd think she held a mortgage on the world!"

A soft tap on the door was followed by the entrance of Miss Castlevaine.

"Have you heard?" she whispered tragically.

"No." Miss Sterling grew grave.

Polly bent forward in her eagerness.

"You see, I went down to get a pitcher of hot water, and I heard Miss Sniffen's voice in the dining-room and so went in that way. Mrs. Nobbs was up on the step-ladder in front of the placard, so I did n't see it at first, but when I did it muddled me so I just stood there and stared. Miss Sniffen turned round and said, 'What do you want?' sharp as could be, just as if I had no business there. She felt guilty all right! You could see that! Well, if you'll believe me, I could n't think what I had gone for! And she said it again! Then I happened to see my pitcher, and that brought me to my senses, and I told her, 'Some hot water.' 'Why don't you go get it, then?' she yelled out, as if I were deaf! And I went — huh!"

"But what was it they were doing?" urged Polly.

"Did n't I tell you? They were putting up a notice in big letters, 'No talking, please.'"

CHAPTER XXIII

"HILLTOP DAYS"

WHEN Polly chanced to find her Miss Nita out she usually dropped into some other room for a little chat. On one such afternoon Miss Twining welcomed her most gladly.

"I get lonesome sitting here by myself day after day," the little woman confessed. "Sometimes I am actually envious of Miss Sterling when I happen to see you go in there."

"Then I'll come oftener," Polly declared. "I'd love to! I'm always afraid the ladies will get sick of the sight of me, I'm round here so much."

"Mercy! I don't believe anybody ever thought of such a thing. I'd be so happy to have you come to see me every day, I'd feel like standing on my head!"

Polly laughed. "I shall surely come! I should like to learn how to stand on my head — I never could seem to get the trick of it."

"I didn't say I'd *do* it!" twinkled Miss Twining; "but I declare, I believe I would try, if that would get you in here!"

"Never you fear!" cried Polly. "You'll see me so much, now I know you want me, you won't get time for anything!"

"I'll risk it." Miss Twining nodded with emphasis.

"I've wondered sometimes," Polly went on, "what I would do if I had to stay alone as much as some folks do — the ladies here, for instance. Of course you can visit each other."

"Yes, except in the hours when it is forbidden."

"Strange, they won't let you go to see each other in the evening."

"I think it is because the ladies used to stay upstairs visiting instead of going down to hear Mrs. Nobbs read. Not all of them are educated up to science and history and such things."

"I should think they would have some good books in the library, story books. Such a dry-looking lot I never saw!"

Miss Twining smiled. "They say that one night when Mrs. Nobbs was reading 'History of the Middle Ages,' she went into the parlor to find only two listeners, and right after that the rule was made forbidding them to go to each other's rooms."

Polly shook her head laughingly. "That was pretty hard on Mrs. Nobbs, was n't it? Is she a good reader?"

Miss Twining gave a little shrug. "I don't go down usually," she answered.

"Too bad! I don't wonder you are lonely. But you can read, can't you?"

"Not much by this light. It is too high."

Polly regarded it with dissatisfaction.

"Yes, it is. I wish you had one on the table. They ought to give you good lights."

Miss Twining pinched up her pretty lips with a thumb and forefinger, but said nothing.

"I was so indignant to think they took that money from you that you earned for writing a poem, I have n't got over it yet!"

"It did seem too bad," Miss Twining sighed.

"It was the meanest thing!" frowned Polly.

"For a long time I had not been in the spirit of writing, but that day I just had to write those verses, and when the paper accepted them it seemed to give me strength and courage and pleasure all at once. I was so happy that morning, thinking I could earn enough to buy me little things I want and perhaps some new books besides."

"I've felt like crying about it ever since," said Polly sadly. "You have written a good deal, have n't you?"

"Oh, yes! When I was at home with father and mother I wrote nearly every day. I had a book published," she added a little shyly.

"You did! That must be lovely — to publish a book!" Polly beamed brightly on the little woman in the rocker.

"Yes, it was pleasant — part of it! It did n't sell so well as I hoped it would. The publishers said I could n't expect it, as I had n't much reputation, and it takes reputation to make poetry sell. They said it was good verse, and the editors had been so hospitable to me I counted on the public —" She shook her head with a sad little smile. "I even counted on my friends — that was the hardest part of the whole business!"

"Surely your friends would buy it!" cried Polly.

"I don't know whether they did or not — I did n't mean that. I mean, giving away my books — that was the heart-breaking part!"

"I don't understand, Miss Twining."

"Before it was published — years before,"

went on the little woman reminiscently, "I used to think that if I ever did have books to give to my friends, how beautiful it would be! I thought it all out from beginning to end — the end as I saw it! I wrote inscriptions by the dozen long before the book was even planned. It looked to me the most exquisite pleasure to give to my friends the work of my own brain, and I pictured their joy of receiving!" She gave a short laugh.

"But, Miss Twining, you don't mean—you can't mean — that they did n't like it!"

"Oh, a few did! But I never heard from many that had read it — that's the trouble! Almost everybody thanked me before reading the book at all. When they wrote again they probably did n't think of it. One man even forgot that I had given him a copy! The funny part was that at the time he had praised the verses. Then afterwards he told me that he had never seen my book, but should so like to read it. I was dumfounded! I believe I laughed. In a moment the truth dawned upon him, and he fairly fell over himself with apologies! I made light of his blunder, but of course it hurt."

"How could he! He must have been a queer man!"

"Oh, no! he was very nice, only he did n't care enough about me or the verses to remember. I have never seen him since. "But what grieved me most of all," Miss Twining went on, "was to send books to friends — or those I called so — and never receive even a thank-you in return."

"Oh, nobody could —!"

"Yes, more than once that happened — more than twice!"

"It does n't seem possible!" Polly's face expressed her sympathy.

"I don't think I required too much," Miss Twining went on. "I did n't want people to pour out a punch bowl of flattery. But just a word of appreciation — of my thought of them, even if they did n't care for my verses. Oh, it is heart-breaking business, this giving away books!"

"I should have thought it was about the most delightful thing," mused Polly soberly.

"It may be with some writers. Perhaps my experience is exceptional — I hope so. It took away nearly all the pleasure of having a book. Of course a few friends said just the right thing in the right way and said it so simply that I believe they meant what they said. I never felt that my work was anything wonderful. I did my best always, and I was happy when any one saw in it something to like and took the trouble to tell me so — that was all."

"I should think that was little enough for any author to expect," said Polly. "I always supposed authors had a jolly good time, with everybody praising their work. I never saw anything of yours — I guess I should like it. I love poetry!"

"You do?" Miss Twining started to get up, then sat down again. "I wonder if you would care for my verses?" she hesitated. "You could have a copy as well as not." Her soft eyes rested on Polly's face.

"Oh, I should love them — I know I should!" Polly declared.

Miss Twining went over to her closet and stooped to a trunk at the end.

"There!" she said, putting in Polly's hand a small, cloth-bound volume neatly lettered, "Hilltop Days."

The girl opened it at random. Her eye caught a title, and she read the poem through.

"That is beautiful!" she cried impulsively.

"Which one is it?" asked the childlike author.

"'A Winter Brook.'"

"Oh, yes! I like that myself."

"What lovely meter you write!" praised Polly. "The lines just sing themselves along."

"Do they? The publishers told me the meter was good. I guess my ear would n't let me have it any other way."

"Do you play or sing?" queried Polly.

"I used to — before we lost our money. Since then I have n't had any piano."

"That must have been hard to give up!" Tears sprang to Polly's eyes.

"Yes, it was hard, but giving up a piano is n't the worst thing in the world."

"No," was the absent response. Polly was turning the leaves of the book, and she stopped as a line caught her fancy. Her smile came quickly as she read.

"Miss Twining!" she exclaimed, "I am so astonished to think you can write such lovely, lovely poems! Why, the June Holiday Home ought to be proud of you!"

"Oh, Polly!" The little woman blushed happily.

224

"Well, only real poets can write like this! If people knew about them I'm sure the book would sell. The poems that Mr. Parcell ends off his sermons with are n't half as good as these!"

Miss Twining smiled. "I wonder what made you think of him. Do you know — I never told this to a soul before — I have wished and wished that he would come across one of mine some day and like it so well that he would put it into a sermon! Oh, how I have wished that! I have even prayed about it! Seems to me it would be the best of anything I could hope to have on earth, to sit there in church and hear him repeat something of mine! — There! I'm foolish to tell you that! You'll think me a vain old woman!"

"No, I shall not!" cried Polly. "I should like it 'most as well as you would! It would be a beautiful happening. And probably he would if he knew them. Did you ever give him a book?"

"Oh, no, indeed! I should n't dare!"

"Why not? He is very nice to talk with."

"Yes, I know. He calls on me every year or two. I like him."

"I do, and I want him to read your poems.

Do you mind if I take this home to show to father and mother? They love poetry. — And then I'll find a way for Mr. Parcell to see it!"

"Why, my dear, it is yours!"

"Oh, did you mean that?" Polly drew a long breath of delight. "I shall love it forever — and you, too!" Impulsively she put her arms round Miss Twining's neck and kissed her on both cheeks.

"If I thought Mr. Parcell wouldn't think it queer," — hesitated Miss Twining, — "I have several copies, and I'd like to give him one; but I don't know —"

"Of course he wouldn't think it queer!" asserted Polly. "He'd be delighted! He couldn't help it — such poetry as this is! I'll leave it at his house if you care to have me."

"Oh, would you? That is dear of you! I was wondering how I'd get it to him. I'll do it right up now."

Miss Twining came back with the book, a little troubled scowl on her forehead.

"Oughtn't I to write an inscription in it? I don't know what to say."

"It would be nice," Polly nodded. "Of course you'll say it all right."

In a moment the poet was at her table, the book open before her. She dipped her pen in the ink, then halted it, undecided.

"I wonder if this would be enough, — 'To Rev. Norman S. Parcell, from his parishioner, Alice Ely Twining'?"

"That sounds all right to me," answered Polly deliberately.

"I can't say 'loving parishioner' — to a man," laughed Miss Twining a bit nervously.

"It is n't necessary," chuckled Polly.

"If he came to see me oftener I 'd love him more," said the little woman wistfully.

"He 'll come often enough now — you just wait! He has n't anybody in his church that can write such poetry as this." She patted the little book caressingly.

"I hope he 'll like it, — but I don't know," the author doubted.

"He will," smiled Polly.

In a moment the package was ready.

"It is so good of you to do it!" Miss Twining looked very happy.

"I love to do such errands as this," laughed Polly. "I 'll be in to-morrow to tell you about it."

CHAPTER XXIV

"HOPE DEFERRED"

I DID N'T see the minister," Polly reported to Miss Twining. "He and his wife were both away. So I left the book with the maid and said that you sent it to Mr. Parcell — that was right, was n't it?"

"Certainly, and I thank you ever so much. I do hope he won't think me presumptuous," she added.

"Why, how could he — such a beautiful book as yours?"

"I don't know. He might. I lay awake last night thinking about it."

"You should n't have stayed awake a minute," laughed Polly. "I would n't wonder if you'd hear from him this afternoon. Then you'll stop worrying."

Miss Twining laughed a little, too. "I'm glad I sent it anyway," she said. "It has given me something to think of and something to hope for. The days are pretty monotonous here — oh, it is so nice to have you come running in! You don't know how much good you do me!"

"Do I? I guess it's because I'm such a chatterbox! There! I have n't told you what father and mother said about your book! Father took it and read and read and read. Finally he looked up and asked, 'Did you say a lady at the Home wrote these?' Then he brought his head down, as he does when he is pleased, and exclaimed, 'They ought to be proud of her!' — just what I said, you know!"

"I am so glad he likes them!" Miss Twining's delicate face grew pink with pleasure.

"Oh, he does! He kept reading — it seemed as if he could n't lay it down — till somebody called him. And when he got up he said, 'This is poetry — I should like to see the woman who can write like that. She must be worth knowing.'"

"Oh, Polly!" Miss Twining's eyes overflowed with happy tears. "That is the best compliment I ever had in my life — and from such a man as your father!"

"Mother fairly raves over the poems," went on Polly. "She says she is coming over here next visiting day to get acquainted with you."

"I hope she will come," smiled the little woman. "I have always wished I could know her, she looks so sweet as she sits there beside you in church."

"She is sweet!" nodded Polly. "Nobody knows how sweet till they've lived with her."

Every day now Miss Twining had a visit from Polly, and every day she had to tell her that she had not heard from Mr. Parcell.

"He is only waiting till he has read the book through," Polly assured the disappointed author. "Or maybe he is coming to tell you how much he thinks of it — you'd like that better, should n't you?"

"I don't mind which way, if only he does n't scorn it and says something," was the half-smiling reply.

But as the days and weeks passed, and brought no word from the recipient of "Hill-top Days," Polly hardly knew how to comfort the sorrowful giver. She began to wish that she had not urged Miss Twining to send the book to Mr. Parcell. She even suggested making some errand to the house and asking, quite casually, of course, how they liked Miss Twining's book, but the little woman so promptly

declared Polly should do nothing of the sort
that the plan was given up at once.

At the cordial invitation of Dr. Dudley and
his wife, Miss Sterling and Miss Twining spent
a delightful afternoon and evening at the
Doctor's home.

"I feel as if I had been in heaven!" Miss
Twining told Polly the next day. "It carried
me back to my girlhood, when I was so happy
with my mother and father and my sisters and
brother. My sisters were always stronger than
I, and Walter was a regular athlete; but they
went early, and I lived on." She sighed smilingly into Polly's sympathetic face. "It is
queer the way things go. They were so needed!
So was I," she added, "as long as mother and
father lived; but now I don't amount to anything!"

"Oh, you do!" cried Polly. "You write
beautiful poetry, and you don't know how
much good your poems are doing people."

"I can't write any more — yes, I can!" she
amended. "Miss Sniffen did n't tell me not
to write. I need n't let them pay me any
money — I might order it sent to the mission-
aries! Why," — as the thought flashed upon

231

her, — "I could have them send the money anywhere, could n't I? To anybody I knew of that needed it! Oh, I will! I'll begin this very day! Polly Dudley, you've made life worth living for me!"

"I have n't done anything!" laughed Polly. "That is your thought, and it is a lovely, unselfish one!"

"It would never have come to me but for what you said! How can I ever thank you!"

"Nothing to thank me for!" insisted Polly. "But if you will have it so, I'll say you may thank me by letting me read your poems."

"Oh, I'd love to! And then you can tell me whether they are right or not!"

"As if I'd know!" chuckled Polly. "But I'll run away now and let you go to writing — I do know enough for that!" She took Miss Twining's face between her soft palms and gave her four kisses, on cheeks and temples. "Those are for good luck, like a four-leaf clover," she said gayly. "Good-bye, dear!"

CHAPTER XXV

ALICE TWINING, MARTYR

EARLY the next morning Polly ran over to the Home. She was eager to hear how Miss Twining's new plan had worked. As she neared her friend's door, however, a murmur of voices came from within, and she kept on to the third floor, making her way straight to the corner room.

Juanita Sterling met her with a troubled little smile.

"What is it?" she asked quickly, looking beyond to Mrs. Albright and Miss Crilly. Their excited faces emphasized the other's doubtful greeting.

"Nothing," spoke up Mrs. Albright, — "only Miss Twining has had a time with Miss Sniffen."

"What about?"

"Money," answered Miss Sterling wearily. "It is lucky for the rest of us that we don't have any."

"That same money?" persisted Polly.

233

"No, dear." Mrs. Albright drew up a chair beside her — "Come sit down, and I'll tell you about it. I've been telling them, and we have got a little wrought up over it, that's all."

"I should think anybody'd get wrought up!" put in Miss Crilly. "I guess it will be the death of poor Miss Twining!"

"No, no, it won't! See how you're scaring Polly!"

The girl glanced beseechingly from one to another.

"What is it? You're keeping something back!"

Mrs. Albright patted the chair invitingly. "Come here! I'm going to tell you every word I know."

"She was so happy yesterday!" mourned Polly.

"She will be again, dear."

"Looks like it!" sniffed Miss Crilly. "I believe in saying the truth right out!"

"Katharine Crilly, you just mind your own business!" laughed Mrs. Albright.

"To begin at the beginning," — she turned toward Polly, — "I was knocking at Miss Twining's door yesterday afternoon when she came up the stairs. So I went in with her and stayed a little while. She was in fine spirits. She had been to see an old friend of hers, a member of the Board, and this lady had given her the same amount of money that Miss Sniffen had —"

"Stolen!" burst out Miss Crilly.

"I'm telling this story!" announced Mrs. Albright placidly. "But Miss Twining said," she resumed, "that she had promised not to divulge the name of the lady to any one. So I don't know who it is. On her way home she had bought a book that she had wanted for a long time. I told her she'd have to look out or she would get caught reading it; but she said they always knocked before coming in, and she should have time to put it on the under shelf of her table — where the cover partly hides it. I said, 'Well, you look out now!' and she laughed and promised she would.

"In the evening, as I was sitting alone, I heard talking, and I went to my door to listen. I thought I knew the voice, and when I opened the door a crack I was sure whose room it came from. 'Oh, I'm afraid she's caught her again!' I said to myself, and I waited till I heard somebody go softly away and down the stairs. Then I stole over to Miss Twining.

"It was just as I had feared! She was reading all so nice, when without a mite of warning in sailed Miss Sniffen! Of course she asked her where she got the book, and she said it was given to her. But she would n't tell the woman's name. Miss Sniffen could n't get it out of her! She talked and threatened; but Miss Twining would n't give in. Finally she vowed she'd have it out of her if she had to flog it out! I could see that Miss Twining was all wrought up and as nervous as could be — as who would n't have been!"

"Oh!" gasped Polly. "It's just awful! Did she whip her?"

Mrs. Albright shook her head and went on.

"Miss Twining said that Amelia Sniffen used to go round in society with her youngest brother, Walter, and that she was dead in love with him. Walter fairly hated her, and never paid her the least attention when he could get out of it; but she would put herself in his way, as some girls will, until he was married and even afterwards. And when Alice Twining came here and found that Miss Sniffen had

been appointed superintendent she was almost
a mind to back out; but she had n't any other
place to go, so she stayed, and she said Miss
Sniffen had seemed to take delight in being
mean to her ever since. Well, it's a tight box
that Amelia Sniffen has got herself into this
time!" Mrs. Albright sighed.

"Please go on!" whispered Polly.

"Yes, dear. I got Miss Twining to bed, and
she quieted down a little. Finally I left her and
crept back to my room. I don't know what
time it was, — but after eleven, — I woke
dreaming that I heard my name called. I
jumped up and ran and opened the door.
Everything was still. But I waited, and pretty
soon I heard a voice in the room opposite. I
rushed across the hall — the door was locked!
'Miss Twining! Miss Twining!' I called, two
or three times. At first nobody answered; then
Miss Sniffen came over to the door and said,
'Shut up and go to bed!' I asked her to let me
in, but she would n't. I said things that I
should n't have dared to say if I'd been cooler;
but I'm glad I did! After a while I went back
to my room, and I took out my key and hid it.
I was afraid she'd lock me in. She did mean

to, but for once she got fooled. I lay still as a mouse, hearing her fumble round my door. Finally she went downstairs. When I was sure she'd gone for good I took my key and stole across the hall. Sure enough, it unlocked the door, just as I hoped it would. Oh, that poor child was so glad to see me! Miss Sniffen had come up prepared to give her a whipping! She had brought a little riding-whip with her! But the very sight of it so upset Miss Twining, in her nervous state, that she had a bad turn with her heart, — you know her heart always bothers her, — and once she gave a little cry. Of course, Miss Sniffen did n't want any rumpus, and she just clapped her hand hard over Miss Twining's mouth. She says she does n't know whether it took her breath away suddenly, or what; but she fainted! When she came to, Miss Sniffen was rubbing her — I guess she was pretty well frightened! There was n't anything more said about whipping! After she made up her mind that Miss Twining was n't likely to die right off, she and the riding-whip left."

"Oh, dear, what will become of us!" cried Miss Crilly. "We are not safe a minute!"

"You shall be!" Polly burst out excitedly. "I'm going to tell Mr. Randolph everything about it!"

"Polly! Polly!" Miss Sterling laid a quieting hand on her shoulder.

The girl threw it off. Then she caught it to her lips and kissed it passionately. "I can't bear it! I can't bear it!" she cried. "To think of you all in such danger! You don't know what she'll do!"

"I don't think we need have any fear until she gets over her scare about this," said Mrs. Albright reassuringly. "She seems to me pretty well cowed down. Her eyes looked actually frightened when I caught her off guard. You see, she's in a fix! She knows Miss Twining needs a doctor; but, of course, he would ask first thing what brought this on, and she could n't make the patient lie it out."

"I guess lying would n't trouble *her* any," put in Miss Crilly.

"Dear Miss Twining!" murmured Polly plaintively.

"She is a sweet little woman," Miss Crilly sighed.

"How is she this morning?" asked Polly.

"I hardly know what to tell you," hesitated Mrs. Albright. "I think if Miss Sniffen would keep away she'd be better. Still, when she got up and tried to dress, she fainted again. Now Miss Sniffen has told her to stay abed, and she has put a notice on her door that she is too ill to receive visitors."

"Then can't you go in?" queried Polly anxiously.

"I do," chuckled Mrs. Albright. "They'd have to do more contriving than they've done yet to shut me out!"

"Oh, I'm so glad!" cried Polly. "But she ought to have a doctor! I suppose if she did it would be that Dr. Gunnip — He's no good! Father says he's little more than a quack and he isn't safe. I wish father could see her; but he can't unless he is called. It is too bad! I believe I'll go straight to Mr. Randolph!"

"I don't dare have you," returned Mrs. Albright. "He would, of course, favor the Home, and if Miss Sniffen should hear of it —"

"Before I say anything I shall make him promise not to tell."

"I'm awfully afraid to let you do it — oh, Polly, don't!" Miss Crilly was close to tears.

"Had you rather die?" she demanded. "You may be sick yourself and want a doctor! How are you going to get him?"

"If I'm sick I bet I'll make such a fuss they'll send for a doctor — and a good one too!" cried Miss Crilly hysterically.

Polly had risen, and Miss Sterling drew her within the circle of her arm. "When the time comes we'll decide what is best to do," said she.

"I should think the time had come now!" the girl fumed. "Poor Miss Twining! It's just an outrage!"

"Oh, I forgot!" Mrs. Albright bent toward Polly, with lowered voice. "She gave me something for you, dear."

"Me?" Polly calmed at once.

"Yes. When I was with her in the night I think she feared that her heart might give out, and she said, 'If anything should happen, I wish you would give Polly those papers in my portfolio — or you may give her the whole portfolio. She will understand.'"

"Oh, I know! Yesterday morning she was planning to write some poems, and those must be the 'papers.' But perhaps she won't want me to have them now."

241

"She spoke of it again to-day," nodded Mrs. Albright. "She said she should somehow feel easier for you to keep them."

"I hope Miss Sniffen won't rummage round and get hold of them first," returned Polly anxiously.

"I guess she won't find 'em in a hurry!" chuckled Mrs. Albright. "They're in my room!"

CHAPTER XXVI

MR. PARCELL'S LESSON

POLLY carried the portfolio home with her, and later, alone in her room, read the poems it contained. Tears blurred her eyes as she read and read again the verses dated the day before. Such a lilting, joyous song it was! And now —!

"Oh, but she will get well and write again!" Polly said softly. Then she sighed, thinking of the bright plans that had so suddenly ceased.

Her thoughts went farther back, to the days of watching and waiting for the message that had never come, to the sleepless nights of grieving —

"Oh!" she burst out impetuously, "he's got to know it! Somebody must tell him how he has made her suffer! Miss Nita would do it beautifully; but I don't suppose I could hire her to! Maybe father will."

When this suggestion was made to him, however, Dr. Dudley shook his head promptly, and his impulsive daughter began at once to form other plans. "Mother would n't," she

243

told herself. "No use asking her. Dear! dear! if there were only somebody besides me! Perhaps I can coax Miss Nita —"

A telephone call broke in upon her musings, and the disturbing thoughts were exchanged for a ride and a luncheon with Patricia Illingworth. On her way home in the afternoon, the matter came up again.

"I may as well go now and have it over with," she decided suddenly, and she turned into a street which led to the home of the Reverend Norman Parcell.

Yes, he was in and alone, the maid said, and Polly was shown directly to the study.

"How do you do, Miss Polly!" The minister grasped her hand cordially. "This is a pleasant surprise." He drew forward an easy chair and saw her comfortably seated.

"Have you heard that Miss Twining is ill?" Polly began.

"Miss Twining?" he repeated interrogatively. "M—m — no, I had not heard. Is she an especial friend of yours, some one I ought to know?" He smiled apologetically. "I find it difficult always to place people on the instant."

244

His apology might not have been attended by a smile if Polly's indignant thought had been vocal. When she spoke, her voice was tense.

"Yes, Mr. Parcell, she is a very dear friend." Her lip quivered, and she shook herself mentally; she was not going to break down at this juncture. She went quickly on, ahead of the phrase of sympathy on its way to the minister's lips. "She lives at the June Holiday Home."

"Oh, yes! I remember! Her illness is not serious, I hope."

"I am afraid so," returned Polly, passing quickly toward what she had come to talk about. "I don't suppose you know what a beautiful woman she is." She looked straight into his eyes, and waited.

"No," he answered slowly, a suggestion of doubt in his tone, "I presume not. I have seen her only occasionally."

"She told me that you called upon her every year or two." Polly hesitated. "You can judge something by her poems. You received the book of poems she sent you?"

"Oh, yes!" he brightened. "I have the book."

"How do you like it, Mr. Parcell? Don't you think the poems wonderful?" Polly was sitting very straight in the cushioned chair, her brown eyes fixed keenly on the minister's face.

"Why," — he moved a little uneasily — "I really — don't know —" He threw back his head with a little smile. "To be frank, Miss Polly, I have n't read them."

Something flashed into the young face opposite that startled the man.

"Do you mean, Mr. Parcell," Polly said slowly, "that you have not read the book at all?" Her emphasis made her thought clear, and his cheeks reddened.

"I shall have to own up to my neglect," he replied. "You know I am a very busy man, Miss Polly."

"You need n't bother with the 'Miss,'" she answered; "nobody does. Then, that is why you have n't said 'thank you' — you don't feel 'thank you'!"

"Oh, my dear Polly! I am very grateful to Miss Twining, I assure you, and I realize that I should have sent her a note of thanks; but — in fact, I don't recollect just how it was —

246

I presume I was waiting until I had read the book, and — I may as well confess it! — I was somewhat afraid to read it."

"Afraid?" Polly looked puzzled.

"Such things are apt to be dreary reading," he smiled. "I am rather a crank as regards poetry."

The flash came again into Polly's face. "Oh!" she cried, fine scorn in her voice, "you thought the poems were n't good!"

He found himself nodding mechanically.

"Where is the book?" she demanded, glancing about the room.

"I — really don't know where I did leave it —" He scanned his cases with a troubled frown.

Tears sprang to the girl's eyes. She seemed to see Alice Twining's gentle, appealing face, as it had looked when she said, "I hope he does n't think I am presumptuous in sending it." She dashed away the drops, and went on glancing along the rows of books. The minister had risen, but Polly darted ahead of him and pounced upon a small volume.

"Here it is!" She touched it caressingly, as if to make up for recent neglect.

"Your eyes are quicker than mine," said Mr. Parcell, taking it from her hand.

"Read it!" she said, and went back to her chair.

The minister obeyed meekly. Polly's eyes did not leave him.

He had opened the book at random, and with deepened color and a disturbed countenance had done as he was bidden. Surprise, pleasure, astonishment, delight, — all these the watcher saw in the face above the pages.

Five minutes went by, ten, twenty; still the Reverend Norman Parcell read on! Polly, mouse-quiet, divided her softening gaze between the clergyman and the clock. The pointers had crept almost to four when the telephone called. The reader answered. Then he walked slowly back from the instrument and picked up the book.

"Miss Twining must be a remarkable woman," he began, "to write such poetry as this — for it is poetry!"

"She is remarkable," replied Polly quietly. "She is finer even than her poems."

The minister nodded acquiescently. "This 'Peter the Great,'" he went on, running over the leaves, "is a marvelous thing!"

"Is n't it! If you could have told her that" — Polly's tone was gentle — "it would have spared her a lot of suffering."

"Has she so poor an opinion of her work?"

"Oh, not that exactly; but" — she smiled sadly — "you have never said 'thank you,' you know!"

The lines on his face deepened. "I have been unpardonably rude, and have done Miss Twining an injustice besides — I am sorry, very sorry!"

"She had had pretty hard experiences in giving away her books, but I persuaded her to send one to you, for I knew you liked poetry and I thought you would appreciate it. I was sorry afterwards that I did. It only brought her more disappointment. She cried and cried because she did not hear from you. I 'm afraid I ought not to tell you this — she would n't let me if she knew. But I thought if you could just write her a little note — she is n't allowed to see anybody — it might do her good and help her to get well."

"I certainly will, my dear! I shall be glad to do so!"

"You see," Polly went on, "she fears that

249

perhaps you scorn her book and consider her presuming to send it to you — and that is what hurts. She has lain awake nights and grieved so over it, I could have cried for her!" Polly was near crying now.

"The worst of such mistakes," the man said sorrowfully, "is that we cannot go back and blot out the tears and the suffering and make things as they might have been. If we only could!"

"A note from you will make her very happy," Polly smiled.

"She shall have it at once," the minister promised; adding, "I am glad she is in so beautiful a Home."

Polly shook her head promptly. "No, Mr. Parcell, it is not a beautiful Home, it is a prison — a horrible prison!"

"Why, my dear! I do not understand —"

"I don't want you to understand!" Polly cried hurriedly. "I ought not to have said that! Only it came out! You will know, Mr. Parcell, before long — people shall know! I won't have — oh, I must n't say any more! Don't tell a word of this, Mr. Parcell. Promise me you won't!"

"My dear child," — the man gazed at her as if he doubted her sanity, — "tell me what the trouble is! Perhaps I shall be able to help matters."

"Oh, no, you can't! It must work out! I am going to see Mr. Randolph as soon as — I can. But please promise me not to say a word about it to anybody!"

"I shall certainly repeat nothing that you have told me. Indeed, there is little I could say; I do not understand it at all. I supposed the June Holiday Home was a model in every respect."

Polly shook her head sadly.

"I am there every day, Mr. Parcell, and I know! The ladies are lovely — most of them. They can't say a word, or they'd be turned out, and I've kept still too long! But I mustn't tell you any more." Polly drew a long breath. "I must go now, Mr. Parcell. I am so glad you like Miss Twining's poems! And you'll forgive me, won't you, for all I have said?"

"There is nothing to forgive, my dear."

"I don't know, maybe I've said too much; but I knew you must have lots of presents, and I kept thinking of those people that perhaps you would n't thank, and I felt somebody must tell you, and there was n't anybody else to do it. Then, as I said, I hoped you would like Miss Twining's poems well enough to tell her so. And I just had to come!"

"Polly, I am glad you came!" An unmistakable break in the minister's voice turned Polly's eyes away. "I have been inexcusably thoughtless, not only this time but many a time before. I am grateful that I still have the opportunity to give my thanks to Miss Twining."

"And you can say 'thank you' to the next one!" cried Polly eagerly.

"Yes, I shall always remember — you may be sure of that. I shall not forget my lesson!"

They had reached the door, and Polly shook hands with him and said good-bye.

She went straight to Miss Sterling.

"Well, it's done!" she said soberly, taking her favorite seat.

"What is done?"

"My talk with Mr. Parcell."

"Did *you* go?"

"Yes, I had to. Father would n't."

"What did you say? How did he take it? Tell me!"

"Oh, he took it all right! I guess he did n't really like it at first. I was pretty hard on him, I suppose. But he needed it! I did n't go there to give him sugar-plums!"

"Polly!"

"Well, I did n't! It had got to be said, and I thought I might as well say it plain at the start!"

"Oh, Polly! Polly!" Miss Sterling chuckled softly.

"Why, Miss Nita, you 're laughing!" Polly's tone was reproachful. "There is n't anything to laugh at. I almost cried, and so did he!"

"Dear, forgive me! But I could n't help seeing the funny side."

"There is n't any funny side!"

"Go on! I won't offend again."

"There is not much to tell. Oh, I do wish Miss Twining could have heard him praise her poems — after he had read them! Do you know, Miss Nita, he had n't even looked in the book! He thought it was trash — not worth his while! Think of it — those lovely poems! But I found the book for him — He did n't even remember where he'd put it! — and I told him to read it, and he did!"

"Polly! you mean you asked him!"

"I guess I told him all right — I was mad just about then. And he read steady, by the clock, 'most twenty-five minutes! I don't know as he'd have stopped by now if the telephone had n't rung."

"And he liked them?"

"Oh, he thinks they're beautiful! He was awfully sorry he had n't thanked her — I know he was! But he is going to write her a note, and I told him he could say 'thank you' to the next one, and he said he should."

Juanita Sterling disgraced herself the second time. She dropped back in her chair with a stifled laugh.

"Miss Nita!" began Polly plaintively.

"I know, dear! But to think of your saying such things to that dignified man!" She chuckled again.

"Don't, Miss Nita! It hurts. His dignity is all on the outside, I guess. Anyway, it went off before I left."

"Oh, Polly!"

"I don't see a thing to laugh at. It was as solemn as — as a sermon."

"I rather think it was a sermon — to him!"

"Perhaps. Anyway, I'm glad I went."

"I wonder that your father and mother allowed you to go."

Polly smiled, a tiny, flushed smile. "They don't know it."

"Why, Polly Dudley!"

"Well, it had to be done, and there was nobody but me to do it. I did n't dare say anything beforehand, for fear they would n't let me. Now I'm going home, to tell them all about it."

Miss Sterling smiled. "You'll do, Polly! When I have a hard errand on hand, I'll commit it to you."

CHAPTER XXVII

"I LOVE YOU, DAVID!"

POLLY happened to answer the doorbell when David rang.

"Hallo, David!" she said brightly.

His face was troubled.

"Is your father at home?"

"Why, yes,—that is, he is in the hospital somewhere. Who is sick?"

"Aunt Juliet, and she won't have anybody but Dr. Dudley. We've been trying to get him by telephone, and finally they thought I'd better come up. Otto brought me, and he'll take the Doctor back."

"Oh, the hospital telephones are out of commission, so they're using ours about all the time. Sit down, and I'll find him."

From ward to ward went Polly, following the Doctor. She caught him at last on the upper floor, and he drove off with Colonel Gresham's man.

"Stay a while, can't you, David?" invited

256

Polly. "You'll have to walk home anyway, and there's no need of your hurrying."

"They may want me," he hesitated, fingering his cap.

"No, they won't! There are plenty to take care of Mrs. Gresham. I haven't seen you in an age."

David's face reddened. "I've — been pretty busy," he faltered in excuse.

Polly ignored his embarrassment. "I am sorry for Mrs. Gresham. She's not very sick, is she?"

"I'm afraid she is. She was in terrible pain when I left home."

"I guess father'll fix her up all right," said Polly comfortably.

David smiled. Polly's faith in her father was a standing joke among her friends.

"Oh, you may laugh!" she cried. "It doesn't disturb me a mite. He pulled you out of a tight place once."

"Yes, he did," agreed the boy. "I presume I have about as much faith in him as you have."

They talked for a while in commonplaces. David seemed interested in nothing. He grew restless and once or twice said something about

257

going home. Still he stayed. Finally he got up. Then suddenly he sat down and with a visible effort said huskily, "I suppose you think I'm a brute!"

"Oh, no, David!" returned Polly quietly; "but I think you're a little bit foolish."

His cheeks flushed angrily. "Oh, foolish, is it! Pray, what have I done?"

"M—m, not so very much, except to ignore me, when we've always been such good friends."

"It's your own fault!" David's temper was getting the mastery. "Going round with another boy and not paying me any attention at all!"

"Don't let's quarrel, David! I suppose you mean Doodles, and it does seem so silly for you to be jealous of that little boy!"

"You played all his accompaniments, and you did n't play for me," said David in an aggrieved tone.

"He asked me, and you did n't. You know he has n't had a piano very long and can't play as you can. But I would have gladly played for you if I had known you wanted me."

The boy said nothing, and Polly resumed.

"You act as if I belonged to you and must n't look at another boy."

"You do belong to me!" he declared.

"Since when?" laughed Polly.

"Since the first day I saw you," replied David doggedly.

"Oh!" she smiled, "I never knew it! But I don't make a fuss because you call on Patricia or go round with Leonora."

"Of course you don't! You would n't mind if I went with forty girls! You don't care a rap for me." His face was gloomy.

"Oh, David! what do you want me to do?— hang round you all the time and say, 'David, I love you! David, it's true! David, I'll love you all my life through'?"

"Go on!" he said fiercely, "make all the fun you like! It is fun to you, but with me it's life or death!"

"David!"

"You know I never cared for any other girl! You know you are my world! And yet you deliberately make fun of me!"

Polly's dimples vanished. "No, David, I am not making fun of you, but only of your foolishness —"

"Oh, yes, I suppose it's foolish for me to love you as I do when you don't care a straw—"

"Wait! wait!" she interrupted. "I don't mean that at all, and you know it! But for a great, tall fellow like you to be so unreasonably jealous of a little ten-year-old does seem absurd. I love Doodles, of course; everybody does. But, David, you ought to know that's all there is to it."

"He says he's going to marry you!"

Polly laughed outright. "I never heard anything about it before, so I guess I would n't let it worry me, David." She chuckled. "Whatever made him say that! He's a funny little chap!"

"Will you marry me?" David asked abruptly.

Polly's dimples came and went. "Do you mean right off?" she queried soberly. "I rather want to go to school a little longer."

"There you are again!" he grumbled. "You can't take anything in earnest! I may as well go home!"

"But, David, the idea of asking me such a question! And I only thirteen! Can't you see how silly it is?"

"No, I can't! It's the only way to make

260

sure of you! Some other fellow will get ahead of me!"

"No other fellow has yet, David." Polly's voice was sweet and serious.

"Do you mean that," he asked, "honestly?"

"Of course. You know I have always liked you better than any other boy!"

"You like me, but you love Doodles," he mused.

Polly laughed softly. "Oh, dear!" she sighed, "will nothing satisfy you? Well, then," — she was blushing almost to tears, — "I love you, David! I — I think it's mean for you to make me say it!— I — love you better than any other boy I ever saw!" She flung the last words at him with a show of vexation that David could not withstand.

He grinned.

"And now — you laugh at me!" She sprang up and started past him; but he caught her in his arms.

"Polly! Polly! Dear Polly!" he said tenderly. "Forgive me! I am a pig! But to tell me I was mean and that you loved me — all in the same breath! Now say I'm contemptible — or anything! I'll agree to it!"

"Well, you ought to — you are!" she half sobbed, half laughed. Her face was hidden on his shoulder.

Suddenly she threw up her head and started back. "Let me go!" she whispered. "It is ridiculous to stand here like this." She pulled away from him and retreated to her chair.

"I don't see why we can't be engaged," said David. "Promise that you'll marry me, Polly!"

"Oh!" she cried, "I thirteen, and you just fifteen! What a pair of ninnies we should be! David, if you want to keep me, you must let me go free! I shall be sixteen when I'm through high school, and there'll be four years of college. Then — perhaps —! Time enough for that sort of thing after we're twenty!"

David looked at her with smiling eyes, yet he said, "I'm afraid I shan't feel very sure of you."

"You're a funny David!" laughed Polly. "I say, let's forget all this, and just be a boy and girl having a good time!"

"Forget that we love each other, Polly?"

"No, no! but take that for granted, and let it drop!"

"I guess you'll have to teach me how," David laughed.

"All right! Come sing me that song I saw you buying at the music store the other day!"

When David left the house, he stopped on the threshold to finish what he was saying. Then, suddenly, he caught Polly's hands, pressed a kiss squarely on her lips, and sped away.

"David Collins!" she cried.

But David was already down the steps. He looked back with a radiant bow.

CHAPTER XXVIII

A VISIT WITH MRS. TENNEY

THE letter-carrier came early, and Polly ran over to the Home in hopes to be first at the pile of mail on the hall table. She wanted to carry Mr. Parcell's note upstairs herself.

There it was, right on top, "Miss Alice Ely Twining"! Polly caught up the envelope with a glad breath. Then she went hastily through the rest and found a letter for Miss Sterling and one for Miss Crilly.

Mrs. Albright was in the corner room.

"I will deliver these now," she said, "before it is time for Miss Sniffen."

"I'm afraid she'll catch you in there some day," Polly told her with a troubled little nod. "What if she should!"

Mrs. Albright laughed softly. "When I hear anybody coming I slip into the closet — I have done that several times already! I do hope this letter will do Miss Twining good. It looks like a man's handwriting."

Juanita Sterling looked doubtfully at the

address on her own envelope, then she ran a
paper-cutter under the flap.

"An invitation from Mrs. Dick for us all to
spend to-day with her!" she announced disin-
terestedly.

"Oh, let's go!" cried Polly.

"Shall we walk or fly?" The tone was not
encouraging.

"Ride," answered Polly promptly.

"Perhaps you can't get the cars."

"Perhaps I can!" was the retort. "You
don't want to go — that's what!"

"I am not hankering for it," smiled Miss
Sterling dubiously.

"It will do you good," Polly decided. "The
more you get out of this atmosphere, the better. I'll run home and do some telephoning!
Will you ask the others, Miss Nita? Or wait!
We don't know yet how many can go."

Polly was off in a whirl, and for the next half-
hour bells rang, wires snapped and buzzed,
feet flew, and tongues were busy. Then Polly
returned to say that they could have three cars
which would seat fourteen besides the drivers.

Miss Crilly was there and heard the news
with delight.

"I'll run round and ask 'em! Shall I?"

"Yes, please," answered Polly. "Take as many of the ladies as would like to go. We children can stay at home if there is n't room."

"Count me out, for one," said Miss Sterling quickly.

"No, count her in!" ordered Polly.

Miss Crilly laughed. "Sure!" she agreed. "I'll find out who wants to go. You wait, Polly. 'T won't take long."

She was as quick as her promise, but her face was doleful.

"Every blessed one is crazy to go, except Mrs. Crump and Mrs. Post and Miss Leatherland. What can we do!"

Polly counted up. "That makes twelve of you, so Patricia and Leonora can go. David and I will stay home."

"You'll do no such thing!" Miss Sterling's tone was firm. "I'll send Polly in my stead."

"Polly won't go!" she laughed. "You're the one that received the invitation, and the idea of your staying behind! David is coming up, anyway, and we're to play duets if we can't go; so we'll be all right."

Miss Sterling gave Polly a quick glance of

surprise, and Polly threw back a smile, just as Mrs. Albright appeared.

"What time are we going?" she asked. "I have my dress to mend."

"Our car won't be at liberty this forenoon," answered Polly. "Father needs it. But we can start right after luncheon. Will one o'clock do?"

The hour was agreed upon, and Mrs. Albright turned to the door. Then she came back.

"I almost forgot my message for you, Polly! The prospect of a ride makes me good for nothing. That note for Miss Twining was from her minister, Mr. Parcell. It seems, awhile ago, she sent him a book of her own poems, and this was to acknowledge it and beg pardon for his tardiness. It is a beautiful note! She let me read it. He praises her poetry sky-high—he does n't say too much, you know, but just enough. And you ought to see her — she is so pleased! She wanted me to tell you that she had it. When she first read it she cried, and I did n't know but it would upset her; but I guess it has n't. He says he is coming to call on her as soon as she is able to receive visitors. She can't imagine who told him she was sick; but it is n't strange he heard of it — such news flies."

Polly's face was red with guilty blushes; but Mrs. Albright took no heed. She and Miss Crilly hurried away.

"I hope she won't ever find out my part in it," sighed Polly. "But I can't help being glad I went, even if father did scold!"

"I was afraid he would."

"Yes," nodded Polly, with a little regretful scowl.

"But tell me about David!" broke out Miss Sterling eagerly. "Is it made up?"

Polly laughed happily. "No more quarrels forever! Mrs. Gresham was sick, and David came up for father; so I asked him to stay — and we had it out! What do you think that boy wanted? To be engaged — now!"

"Mercy! And you only thirteen!"

"I talked him out of it in a hurry, and I guess he sees it as I do. He's the dearest boy — and the foolishest!"

"Yes, David is a dear boy, the most agreeable of his age I ever knew! He is so thoughtful and winsome."

"That would please David mightily. I shall have to tell him. He has n't much self-esteem— it will do him good. I wonder why he likes me better than other girls," mused Polly. "There's Patricia — ever so much prettier than I am, and Leonora — right in the house — sweet as can be and delighted with his least attention. But no, he likes me best — I — don't — see — why!" She slowly nodded out the words.

Juanita Sterling laughed softly. "Love goes where it is sent, you know. As for me, I don't wonder at all!"

"Oh, well, you are partial!" said Polly with a little blush. "But I can't understand it with him."

"For the same reason that you prefer him to the other boys. I'm glad you have made up."

" I am! I hate fusses! Dear me! I must go back and telephone."

She ran over again shortly before the appointed time.

"David and I are going, after all!" she cried. "At the last minute Mrs. Illingworth had to change her plans for the afternoon, so we can have her other car. Is n't that fine! Will you sit with us? I told David what you said, and he is ready to eat you up!"

The former Mrs. Dick welcomed her friends with cordial hands and tongue.

"I had almost despaired of you," she told Miss Sterling and Polly, as she walked with them into the house. "And I'm glad so many could come. I did n't know how it would be. Awfully sad about Miss Twining, is n't it? I always liked Miss Twining."

"Is n't she lovable?" put in Polly.

"Yes, very. — Take seats, all of you. We were just speaking of Miss Twining — I'm so sorry for her! But if she is losing her mind, perhaps it will be providential for her to go soon."

"'Losing her mind'!" exclaimed Miss Crilly. "Who made up that whopper?"

"Why, is n't she? One of the Board told me — Mrs. Brintnall. I met her in town the other day. I think it came straight from Miss Sniffen. She said she was a great care, now that she has heart disease, and that she is liable to drop away any time. Mrs. Brintnall spoke of her mind's failing as if everybody knew it — that a good many days she would seem as bright as ever, and then again she did n't know much of anything and would be so obstinate and ugly that she'd have to be punished just like a child! Is n't that awful! But you think it is n't true!"

270

"Think! I know it is n't true! not a single word of it!" Polly was too excited to heed Miss Sterling's warning pinch.

"I never saw anything out of the way in her," attested Miss Mullaly. "She has always appeared to me like a very cultured woman."

"She is a perfect lady," asserted Mrs. Winslow Teed.

"Yes, she is!" agreed Miss Castlevaine. "I guess Miss Sniffen's the one that's losing her mind — huh!"

"Is she as bad as ever?" queried Mrs. Tenney anxiously.

"Worse!" declared Miss Major.

"We don't have pie or pudding now — ever!" put in Miss Crilly eagerly. "And we can't talk at table, only just to ask for things!"

"Oh, my!" cried Mrs. Tenney. "What does possess her!"

"Seven devils, I guess!" laughed Miss Crilly.

"Better put it seven hundred and seven!" flashed Polly.

They laughed, and the talk went on. Miss Sterling watched the hostess. She seemed years older than bright, cheery Mrs. Dick of the Home. Sometimes she let the talk pass her by, or she only flung in a bitter little speech. In the course of the afternoon, when the guests had wandered away from the dreary "front room" to the barn, the hennery, the garden, the orchard, Mrs. Tenney contrived to gather together her special cronies, Mrs. Albright, Miss Crilly, Miss Sterling, and Polly.

"Come inside! I want to talk with you," she told them.

"Say," she began, in lowered voice, "do you s'pose there's any chance in Miss Sniffen's taking me back?"

Astonishment was plain on the faces before her.

"Oh, I s'pose you think that's queer!" She laughed nervously. "But I just can't live here any longer! I was the biggest fool to marry that man! I thought I was going to have a good home and plenty to eat and to wear. We do have enough to eat — and good enough, but, my! he has n't bought me anything except one gingham apron since I came, and he growled over that! He's the limit for stinginess! When I was at the Home I used to say I'd rather live in an old kitchen if 't was mine, and now I've got the old kitchen I'd exchange back again in a jiffy! Do you s'pose she'd take me!"

"Do you mean to —" hesitated Mrs. Albright.

"Yes, I mean to run away from the old man! I know you're shocked; but you have n't lived with Sereno Tenney! He'll freeze me out next winter, sure as fate! I'll have to shut up the house, except the kitchen, and stay there, where I can't see even a team pass, with hardly a neighbor in sight. It drives me wild! To think I was such a fool! If he were a poor man, I could stand it; but he's got money enough."

"Why don't you make it fly, then?" broke in Miss Crilly. "Bet you I would!"

"No, you would n't! He had to go with me to pick out the apron, and he fretted like sixty because I would buy one made of decent cloth! I was all in just over that!"

"We s'posed he was a nice, pleasant man — it's too bad!" Miss Crilly was the only one who found words for reply.

"I don't have anything to read," went on the disappointed woman. "He does n't want to know anything. He does take a daily news-

273

paper, but that's all. There was a Bible in the house when I came, and two or three school-books — pretty place to live in!"

"Get a divorce!" advised Miss Crilly.

"I could easy! He'd never fight it — has n't got life enough. But where could I go?"

"I'm afraid you could n't do anything with Miss Sniffen," said Mrs. Albright sadly.

"What do you say, Polly?" smiled Mrs. Tenney. "You look as if you had your advice all ready."

"No," answered Polly sorrowfully. "Only you've promised, and it does n't seem as if you ought to break your promise — just because you don't like it here as well as you thought you would. It is n't that I'm not sorry, Mrs. Dick — I mean, Mrs. Tenney —" Polly hurried to explain. "I'm so sorry I could cry! But it does n't seem right — to me — perhaps it would be, perhaps I don't know." Polly lifted appealing eyes to the woman's flushed face.

"I guess you see things clearer than I do, child! We'll put it to vote. Mrs. Albright, what do you think?"

"I hardly know, and, anyway, I can't decide it for you. I suppose I should incline to Polly's opinion."

"Miss Sterling? You hold the controlling vote, so be careful!" Mrs. Tenney laughed uncertainly.

"It is a hard question, Mrs. Dick. I can hardly imagine a worse hell than having to live with such a man as you picture him, and yet —"

"I know! It's three against two! Good-bye, June Holiday Home, with your steam heat and Miss Sniffen! We must adjourn — there's Mrs. Grace and Mrs. Winslow Teed!"

For the ride home Polly sat between Miss Crilly and David in Dr. Dudley's car.

"Is n't that a great bluff of Miss Sniffen's?" Miss Crilly's tone was too confidential even for Polly's quick ears. The repeated question carried as far as David — Polly knew from his sudden change of expression. But Miss Crilly talked on. "Seemed as if I must tell! I never was so stirred up in my life! It's the last thing I should thought of!"

Polly gave her a cautionary smile.

"O-o-h!" Miss Crilly cast a frightened glance in David's direction.

"A motor-car is n't the best place for talking secrets," he laughed. "But I won't peep!"

"I have n't let any cat out!" retorted Miss Crilly.

She and David tossed merry sallies back and forth; but Polly was uncomfortable. David would think she did not trust him. She wished Miss Crilly had not referred to the matter.

"Come on down to dinner!" invited David, after they had said good-bye to Miss Sterling and Miss Crilly.

"Oh, I'd love to!" beamed Polly. "I'll run in and ask mother."

He hailed his uncle's chauffeur, and bade him wait.

In a moment she was back and they stepped into Colonel Gresham's car.

"I am going to share my secret with you," David smiled, glancing doubtfully at the man ahead.

"Otto," he said tentatively, without raising his voice above the tone he had used for Polly. The man did not stir. "Otto," a little louder. No answer.

He nodded complacently. "I wanted to make sure of him," he smiled. "Now I'll go on."

"The other is n't my secret, David, or I'd tell you!" Polly hastened to explain.

"That's all right!" laughed David. "Perhaps this chimes in with yours, and perhaps it does n't. Last night I went up to Billy Marble's, and when I was along by Ford Street I noticed a man and a woman a little distance ahead. I was walking pretty fast, and as I came up behind them and was wondering which way I'd go by, — you know the sidewalk is narrow there, — a light struck across the woman's face, and I saw it was Mrs. Nobbs. I did n't know the man. Has she relatives here?"

"A brother, I think, a bachelor brother."

"Tall, is he?"

"Yes."

"This man was. Probably it was he. I had on my sneaks — that's why they did n't hear me. I was pretty near, when I caught something that excited my curiosity. I heard the words distinctly, — 'I would n't be in her shoes for all the money she has made out of June Holiday Home!' — 'And that's no small sum, I'll warrant!' the man replied. — 'Small!' she exclaimed; 'she's robbing them every day of her life! But she's in a terrible fix now, and I

guess she knows it! I can't be thankful enough
that for once she did n't make a cat's-paw of
me! I said, "When there's any flogging to be
done, you will do it!" She was mad, and I half
expected her to discharge me on the spot, but
I know too much for her to dare to go too far.
I've done piles of dirty work for Amelia Sniffen!' — 'Better cut it out,' said the man. —
'Can't, as long as I stay,' she replied. 'That's
what I'm there for! But I've got so nervous
since this happened, I don't know what to do!
I start every time I see one of the Board come
into the house. What if they should find out!
You don't suppose they could hold me for —
anything, do you? I'd give a farm to know
how much Mrs. Albright has heard, but I'm
afraid to quiz her. She's the one that rooms
across the hall and tried to get in when they
were having the time — she's got more grit
than the others. I don't think Miss Twining
would dare tell, and I don't see how she could
— she is locked in all the time, ostensibly to
keep her from visitors! I thought if Mrs. Albright did find out she'd go right to the Board;
but there has n't been a word yet. That woman
needs a doctor if ever anybody did. Lucky for

us that she did n't die when —' And that's all I heard. They stopped before they came to the Home entrance, and I was afraid of being caught, so I cut across the avenue into the shadows. I was amazed!" He drew a long breath. "But I fancy it is n't much news to you."

"Some of it is," Polly replied. "I never thought of Miss Sniffen's being dishonest — with money. I don't see how she can —"

"Easy enough in a place like that. But this other is pretty bad business. If Miss Twining should happen to die without any doctor, and the authorities should find out that Miss Sniffen beat —"

"No, she did n't!" interrupted Polly. "I suppose she meant to, but Miss Twining fainted and that put a stop to it. I'd tell you everything, David, only Miss Nita and Mrs. Albright and Miss Crilly and I agreed not to say a word to anybody."

"Never mind! I can guess enough. Something should be done about it, Polly. If Miss Twining needs a doctor, she ought to have one immediately."

"I know it!" Her voice was troubled. "I

wanted to tell Mr. Randolph; but they won't let me, for fear he'll take the Home's part, or something, and get them into trouble. I don't know what to do!"

The car stopped at the Gresham door, and Polly forgot disagreeable things in the pleasure of Mrs. Collins's cordial welcome.

CHAPTER XXIX

DISAPPOINTMENT

Miss Twining was worse. Dr. Gunnip had been called late in the afternoon. It was now nearly six o'clock, and the third-floor corner room was discussing the situation.

"I guess you'd better see Mr. Randolph to-morrow," Mrs. Albright was saying.

"Why not make it this evening?" returned Polly. "She may not live till morning!" Tears were in her voice.

"No, the Doctor didn't think she'd give out right away; he said she might last a good while."

"Little he knows about it!" scorned Polly.

"Well, he said it right up and down!" put in Miss Crilly.

"It is too bad!" Polly drew a long, sighing breath. "I don't believe she'd have had any heart trouble at all, if Miss Sniffen hadn't made this fuss!"

"The excitement has no doubt aggravated it," commented Mrs. Albright.

281

"Is that all Dr. Gunnip said, that she had heart disease?" queried Polly.

"He did n't stay long enough to say anything!" sputtered Miss Crilly. "He walked in and walked out — I wish I 'd timed him!"

"You 'd have had to look in a hurry," remarked Mrs. Albright quietly.

"Guess he 's like a doctor my mother used to tell about," observed Miss Crilly. "You had to catch hold of his coat-tails if you wanted to ask him a question. And he never would have consultation, no matter how sick anybody was. He said, one could play on a fiddle better than two."

A quick little smile ran round the group; but nobody laughed. The present question was too serious.

"Miss Twining did n't tell me much," resumed Mrs. Albright. "The Doctor had just gone, and I was in a fidget for fear Miss Sniffen would come back. But I could see that he had upset her completely. I don't think, from what she did say, that he gave her any particulars. He said she had got to be extremely careful. She feels as if it was about over with her."

"I wish father could see her," fretted Polly.

282

DISAPPOINTMENT

"He would n't frighten her so, even if he did have to tell her that her heart was in bad shape! I hate Dr. Gunnip worse than ever! Did he leave her any medicine?"

"Oh, yes! I saw two little piles of tablets on the table."

"Likely as not they'll make her worse!" Polly got up. "I'm going to see Mr. Randolph to-night!" she announced determinedly.

"No, no!" objected Mrs. Albright. "Wait until morning! It would only excite her more to have another doctor now. She'd think she was in a worse condition than she is."

"I'd wait if I were you," agreed Miss Sterling. "I think it will be better all round."

"Well," yielded Polly reluctantly, and sat down again.

"What you going to tell him, anyway?" questioned Miss Crilly a bit anxiously.

"Why — everything!" Polly's hands flew apart with expressive gesture.

"I'm afraid he won't want to interfere."

"He is n't a fool!" retorted Polly. "And when I've told him all I'm going to tell him, if he does n't interfere — if he is n't aching to interfere — he will be one!"

283

Miss Crilly giggled. "You're the greatest!" she said admiringly.

The next morning Polly awoke with the vague consciousness that something of importance was at hand. Then she remembered. To-day she was to see Mr. Randolph!

During breakfast the matter was discussed.

"You seem suddenly to have become a woman of affairs," playfully remarked Dr. Dudley.

"There is n't anybody else to do things," said Polly plaintively. "Miss Crilly would n't amount to anything if she went. She'd get scared first thing and make a regular fizzle of it. Mrs. Albright has pluck enough in some ways; but she could n't be hired to see Mr. Randolph. Of course, Miss Nita'd do it all right; but she just won't! And somebody must!"

"It is full time," the Doctor agreed; "but it looks a big load for your shoulders."

"Oh, I don't mind this!" Polly said brightly. "It was hard, going to Mr. Parcell's; but this is — different, you know."

"Decidedly different."

Polly glanced up from under her eyelashes.

284

DISAPPOINTMENT

She knew what he thought of her visit to the minister's, and now she sighed a little in remembrance of his fatherly comments.

"Of course, Mr. Randolph will be surprised — shocked, I guess; but he is n't to blame, and he's a lovely man to talk to. I think I'm going to enjoy it."

Mrs. Dudley caught the twinkle in her husband's eyes, and laughed.

"What have I said out of the way now?" Polly laid down her fork.

"Nothing," her father answered gravely.

"I don't see why mother was laughing, then." She glanced from one to the other.

They sipped their coffee in silence, but the girl detected a lingering bit of a smile on her mother's lips.

As soon as she had put her room in trim for the day, Polly ran over to the Home for a final talk with Miss Sterling before making her appointment with Mr. Randolph.

She found both Mrs. Albright and Miss Crilly in the corner room. A little excitement was in the air.

"Have you heard?" asked Miss Crilly.

Polly's eyes went frightened.

"No — what?" she said weakly.

"Don't be scared, child! It is nothing!" Mrs. Albright put an arm around her. "It is only that Mr. Randolph is sick."

"O-o-h!" mourned Polly.

"It's in the morning paper," added Miss Crilly. "It says, 'seriously ill.'"

"Yet he may not be," interposed Miss Sterling. "The papers seldom get it right."

"It is too bad!" Polly sat down. "Our paper was late," she explained, "and father did n't have time to read it, — he was called off from breakfast, — and I was thinking so much about going that I forgot the paper. Is that all it says?"

"Yes. It does n't tell what the matter is."

"Now we shall have to wait!" said Polly dismally. "How is Miss Twining?"

"A little brighter, I think," answered Mrs. Albright.

"Dear me! I hope Mr. Randolph won't die!" Miss Crilly's face was despairing. "There is n't another one we 'd dare tell!"

"No," agreed Polly, "he's the only man we can trust. We can't do a single thing till he gets well."

CHAPTER XXX

DOODLES SINGS

Doodles had heard of Nelson Randolph's illness, yet he was unprepared for the additional tidings that came to him when he was on a downtown errand.

"Oh, he suffers something terrible!" exclaimed the boy who brought the news. "Carl Harris told me about it. He's down there in the paper office, and they say if he don't get better pretty soon he's got to die! The Doctor can't stop the pain."

Doodles walked away thinking hard. "Guess I'll go," he told himself. "He liked my singing the other night up here, and perhaps it would make him forget. Anyhow, I can go!"

An hour later Doodles stood at the door of the Randolph home.

"He's sick. He can't see anybody," said the maid who answered his ring.

"Is he able to talk?" queried the lad.

The girl nodded.

"Then will you please ask him if he would like to have Doodles Stickney sing to him."

" 'T won't do no good," she replied indifferently. "The nurse won't let anybody see him."

A man came slowly up the steps, and the boy turned to recognize a well-known physician.

"Oh, Dr. Temple!" he began eagerly, "do you think Mr. Randolph would like to have me sing for him?"

The physician looked the lad over gravely. He was so long about it, Doodles wondered if his boots were dusty and the Doctor were disapproving them. Then came the answer.

"Probably not."

"But he did like to hear me sing the other night when he was at our house. He said so. And when I heard how he is suffering, I thought perhaps I could make him forget it." His appealing brown eyes looked straight into those keen blue ones that the physician's admirers thought saw everything.

Dr. Temple considered a moment. "Come in!" he said.

Doodles followed where he led, which was into the first room beyond the entrance.

"Sing!" was the order.

288

Doodles, not in the least abashed, stood where he was, in the middle of the reception room, and began.

Soft, soft as the crooning of a mother bird, came the first notes.

"Peace . . . peace . . . peace I leave with you." Gently the music rose, the lad's voice beautifully modulated to suit the time and place. "My peace . . . my peace I give unto you: . . . not as the world giveth . . . not as the world giveth . . . give I unto you. Let not your heart be troubled . . . let not your heart be troubled . . . let not your heart be troubled, neither let it be afraid."

The physician sat still for a moment, as if reluctant to break the spell. Then he got up quickly. "Come!" he bade.

Doodles followed, up the velvet-covered stairs, with never the sound of a footstep, and to the end of a wide corridor.

"Wait here, please!" Dr. Temple motioned him to a chair by the window, and after knocking at a door disappeared behind it.

Presently he returned. "You may sing what you sang downstairs." He went back, leaving the door ajar.

Again Doodles sang. At the end he waited, wondering if he were to keep on.

A white-clad young woman came out of the room, smiling to him under her pretty white cap.

"Mr. Randolph would like to have you sing some more," she said.

"The Lord is my Shepherd," "Come unto Me," "I will lift up mine eyes," "The Lord bless thee and keep thee," — these and others Doodles sang, while not a sound came from the room beyond.

Then the young woman appeared again.

"Mr. Randolph says he wishes you would sing 'Old Folks at Home,'" she told him.

At the close of the song the nurse came to the door and beckoned him in.

The president of the Paper Company put out a feeble hand.

"Thank you, Doodles!" he smiled. "I suppose you came all the way from Foxford just to sing for me!"

"Oh, that is n't anything!" said the boy lightly. "I am glad to do it, Mr. Randolph. I do hope you will get better!"

"I am better now! You have done me good, Doodles!"

"I'm so glad! May I come again?" eagerly.

"I should be mighty glad if you could! I will send my car for you any day."

"Thank you!" The lad's face was radiant. "To-morrow?" He glanced at Dr. Temple.

The Doctor gave him a smiling nod.

"This same time?"

"Better than the afternoon," assented the physician.

Doodles was downstairs when the nurse came out to speak to him.

"Mr. Randolph says to wait and he will have his man take you home."

So Doodles rode to Foxford in Mr. Randolph's sumptuous roadster, to the astonishment of Blue whom he met not far from home.

CHAPTER XXXI

SHUT OUT

Miss Sterling was not in her room. Polly had knocked and knocked. Finally she turned away and went slowly downstairs.

"Is Miss Nita out?" she asked of Miss Sniffen in the lower hall.

"I don't know," was the answer. She did not offer to look at the day-book on the desk.

Miss Lily came by, on her way upstairs, and said good-morning as she passed.

Polly had reached the door, when a little cry arrested her. She turned to see Miss Lily half kneeling on the stairs, clutching the rail.

"Oh! are you hurt?" Polly ran up to her.

"Not much, I guess," was the tremulous answer. "I can't see, and the stairs are so wide! I fall every day or so!"

Polly helped her up. "I'd go close to the balustrade, if I were you."

"Oh, no! I must n't!" Miss Lily whispered, glancing down into the hall.

"She's gone," said Polly softly. "Come

right up here! Afraid of scratching? 'T won't do any harm — with your soft slippers."

"She won't let me!" breathed the frightened woman.

"Oh, I guess she won't mind!" returned Polly easily. "That's what rails are made for — to cling to."

"What's the matter now!" broke in a cutting voice.

"Why, Miss Lily fell, and I'm trying to make her come up close to the rail, so she can get a good, firm hold; but she's afraid of scratching the stairs."

"Of course it will scratch — to go tramping over that polished wood! She's to step on the carpet, as I told her! You're always interfering, Polly Dudley!"

"Miss Sniffen, I did n't mean to interfere; but Miss Lily can't see as well as you can, and—"

"She can see well enough! Her eyesight is good. There is no need of her falling."

"But she can't get hold of the rail away off in the middle!"

"Certainly she can reach it! Don't stand there talking nonsense!"

Miss Lily turned and hastened up the long

flight. Polly watched her for a moment and then walked slowly down the stairs.

The superintendent waited at the foot, her face flushed and stern.

"You have made trouble enough round here," she said bitingly. "Now I think we'll stop it!"

"Why, Miss Sniffen, what have I done?"

"You're putting foolish notions into the heads of these old women — petting and pampering them in the way you do! To organize a walking-club for them, when they've got one foot in the grave — it's absurd!"

"Oh, they're not old — all of them!" broke in Polly. "Miss Nita isn't old! — or Miss Crilly! — or — "

"You need not enumerate! I know how old they are, and I know how old they say they are! To think of your coaxing them into such disgraceful escapades as you have! Those gray-haired women dancing out in a pasture lot! Oh, you need n't look so surprised! I know what you're up to, if I do stay home here! You were saucy on that occasion, and bold, too! Calling to passing automobilists to come and dance with you! It was scandalous!"

"Why, Miss Sniffen," — Polly's tone was gently explanatory, — "you can't have heard it straight! We did n't do a single thing out of the way! And I did n't call anybody! Mr. Randolph and Miss Puddicombe drove along, and Mr. Randolph said it looked too tempting, and wanted to know if they could n't come and dance. That was all!"

The superintendent primmed her lips. "We won't discuss it any further. All I wish to say is that hereafter you may confine your calls to Wednesday afternoon, when we receive visitors."

Polly stood for an instant, dumb with surprise and dismay; then she took a step forward.

"Good-bye, Miss Sniffen!" she said in a low, tense voice, and passed swiftly out into the sunshine.

She walked along, regardless of anything besides her own tumultuous thoughts, until, as she was turning in at her home entrance, she heard the old familiar call, "Pollee, Pollee, Pollee-e-e!"

David was only a few yards ahead, and she waited.

"What is it?" he asked as he came up.

The ghost of a smile flickered on Polly's face.

"I've just been shut out of the Home!" she said with almost a sob.

An angry light leaped in the boy's eyes; but he spoke no word, only clinched his teeth.

They went up the walk together, Polly talking fast. Mrs. Dudley met them in the hall, and the story was begun again.

"That woman!" cried the boy; "I'd like to go over and knock her down!"

"David!" chuckled Polly, with an admiring glance at his broad shoulders and athletic frame.

"It is terrible to think of those dear people being in her power!"

"Something must be done." Mrs. Dudley looked troubled.

"If only Mr. Randolph had n't been sick!" said Polly plaintively. "But Doodles says he is better!" Her face brightened. "Oh, David! did you know Doodles has been singing to him?"

"No. I suppose that cured him." There was a little warning tone in the rich voice.

296

"It has helped," Polly replied gently. "It makes him forget the pain. Mr. Randolph sends after him every day and has his man take him home again — is n't that nice?"

"M—hm," nodded David.

"Doodles was here this noon," Polly went on. "Something was the matter with the car, and so he ran over while Murray was fixing it. The Doctor says Mr. Randolph may go to ride to-morrow if it is pleasant."

"When shall you see him?" asked David.

"Soon as ever I can — to think of Miss Nita's being shut up there, and my not being able to get to her!"

"It would n't do any good to telephone," mused David, "or to write a note."

"I'm afraid!" Polly shook her head. "If she'd grab those cards from Mr. Randolph's boxes of roses, she'd take a letter. What do you suppose she did it for?"

"Did n't want her to know who sent them."

"But why?"

"Oh, probably she's in love with him," replied David carelessly.

"Miss Sniffen?" Polly's voice was flooded with astonishment.

"Anything very surprising about that?" laughed David.

"Why, the idea! He could n't!"

"No, he could n't, but she could."

"I have thought of that," assented Mrs. Dudley. "I cannot account for her actions in any other way."

"It's so funny!" giggled Polly. "And she probably knows he is engaged to Blanche Puddicombe!"

"That is what stumps me!" exclaimed David. "Such a girl!"

"They say she has a fortune in her own name," put in Mrs. Dudley.

"Fortune!" scorned the boy. "I would n't marry her if she would give me a hundred million!"

Mrs. Dudley laughed.

"She'd be better than Miss Sniffen," said Polly.

"But to think of coming home to such a wife as she'll make!" cried David.

"And sitting down to dinner with her!" went on Polly.

David shook his head. "A man might stand it for one day, but for a lifetime — good-bye!"

"It does n't seem as if he would marry just for money," sighed Polly.

"That's what most men think of first. Is n't it, Mrs. Dudley?"

"Some of them," she agreed. "I can't believe they are in the majority."

"She'll make the very crotchetiest wife!" asserted Polly. "He'll have to keep her in a glass case! See how she went on up in the pasture! The sun was too hot and the wind was too cool, her stone seat was too hard, and the ground was too rough to dance on! Everything was too something! She was n't contented till she got her 'Nelson' out of reach of Miss Nita. I guess men have to run more risk than girls do."

"Uncle David would n't agree with you," smiled David. "Aunt Juliet tells a story about him — long before he was married. A girl — I think it was a trained nurse, anyhow somebody he knew pretty well — asked him what he thought of her marrying. He waited a moment, and then said, in his deliberate way, 'Well, I don't know more than three or four decent men anyway, and you would n't be likely to get any of them!' She had to tell of that, and Aunt

Juliet heard it. Uncle David looks solemn at first, when she begins it — then he chuckles."

"That sounds just like Colonel Gresham," laughed Mrs. Dudley.

"He's such a nice man!" praised Polly with emphasis. "And so is Mr. Randolph, just as lovable! — I would n't mind marrying him myself."

"You would n't!" flashed David.

"No," maintained Polly; "but I shan't have a chance," she chuckled.

Her mother heard the Doctor calling and went to him.

"You ought to go in there and hear those children talking about marriage," she whispered; "it is better than a circus!"

The Doctor looked through to where they sat, and smiled.

Meantime the talk in the living-room had taken a personal turn.

"I suppose you'd marry any of the fellows," David was grumbling.

"I should prefer to choose," laughed Polly. "Oh, David! it is funny to hear you go off!" She dimpled over it.

"'Funny'!" he scorned. "That Wilmerding

dude will be walking down to school with you, same as last year! Carrying your books, too!" David frowned. "And you'll let him!"

"He might as well be of use. It's lots easier than to carry them myself."

"Wish your father'd send you down in the car."

"He thinks it better for me to walk," she smiled.

"You'll talk and laugh," David fretted on, "till he'll think you're dead in love with him! You jolly with all the boys more than you do with me!"

Polly's face sobered. "David," she said, "in some things you are wonderfully wise; but you don't seem to know very much about girls. I am not always the happiest when I'm laughing. You talk as if you'd like to keep me in prison, same as Miss Sniffen keeps those poor dears over there. I know better, but it sounds that way."

"Forgive me! I'm getting piggish again!"

"No, but I wish you weren't quite so suspicious. I'll have to make a bargain with you, — how will this do? If anybody steals my heart away, I'll notify you at once."

301

David stood up straight. "I must go," he said. "It is later than I thought. No, Polly, you need n't promise me anything! I can trust you. Only —" He smiled, looking down at her. "Good-bye!"

CHAPTER XXXII

THE TALE IS TOLD

NELSON RANDOLPH gained steadily, — so Polly heard through Doodles, — and she planned to see him soon. Then, one morning, the boy appeared with a sorrowful face. Even before he spoke Polly guessed that something was wrong.

"I can't go to see Mr. Randolph any more," announced the little lad mournfully.

"Why not? What's the matter?"

"That Miss Puddicombe!" The boy's face told more than his words. "She said Mr. Randolph was worse, and for me not to come again till he got well."

"O-o-h!" cried Polly. "What has she got to do about it! She'd better wait till she's married before she begins to dictate!"

Doodles shook his head sorrowfully. "I don't see how my singing could hurt him. She talked as if it was all my fault!"

"Nonsense!" scorned Polly. "More likely it is she herself! Don't worry, Doodles! He will

303

get well pretty soon, and then things will be all right again; but — oh, dear, I wish he would hurry up!"

The next evening David brought the dismaying word that the president of the Paper Company had gone to Atlantic City for several weeks.

Polly was distressed over the situation until her mother suggested the happy thought that no doubt he would recover more rapidly than at home. Then Polly smiled again and was ready to enjoy David's new flute solo.

In her weeks of waiting Polly came to a new appreciation of David. Her closest girl friends were out of town, her mother unusually busy with some church work, her intercourse with Juanita Sterling limited to a few perfunctory calls; and except for David's cheery visits she would have been lonely indeed. Not a day but the boy appeared, often with flute or banjo, and he made himself so delightfully entertaining that Polly would forget the June Holiday Home and its troubles.

Lurking in the background, however, ready to leap forward as soon as she should be alone, was the torturing fact that Miss Sniffen still kept cruel wardship over her prisoners, and she counted over and over, joyfully marking them off one by one on her calendar, the days before Mr. Randolph would be at home again.

Still, it was not a very long waiting time, after all, and one bright morning Polly entered the private office of the president of the Paper Company.

Now that she was actually there, face to face with the "lovable man" in whom she found so much to admire, she hardly knew how to begin. But, suddenly realizing that the president's time was precious, she dashed into the matter at once.

"It is about the Home, Mr. Randolph, that I have been wanting to see you for so long. I was coming right after Miss Twining got sick, and then you were ill yourself. Before you were well enough to see visitors you went away, and there has n't been a single chance until now. Oh, Mr. Randolph, do you know how affairs are going on over there? Have n't you ever guessed?"

"Why — what do you mean, Polly? Nothing wrong, is there?"

"Everything!" Polly's hands dropped with

emphasis into her lap. "None of the ladies have dared say a word, because if they find any fault they are liable to be turned out. So they have borne it all as well as they could. I wanted to come to you a good while ago, but they would n't hear to it. Finally things got to such a pass that we four, Miss Nita, Mrs. Albright, Miss Crilly, and I, said that something must be done. We thought you were the best one to tell, for you have always been such a friend — we could trust you!"

"You can, Polly!" He smiled across to her. "You need not be afraid of my divulging the source of my information."

"Oh, I don't care if folks do know my part in it, but the others would rather you would n't give their names — unless it is necessary. Miss Sniffen turned me out weeks ago!"

"Turned you out? For what?"

"Oh, because I told Miss Lily to cling to the balustrade so she would n't fall! That is, it started there. She said I'd got the ladies into all sorts of scrapes. She scolded me for lots of things — one was that dance in the pasture. She said it was scandalous. I don't care so much what she does to me, only my not seeing

306

Miss Nita. But the ladies are actually afraid of
their lives! When Miss Twining was abused so,
those that knew wondered whose turn would
come next. Why, Mr. Randolph, Miss Sniffen
almost killed Miss Twining! — Oh, of course,
she did n't mean to!" For the man had started
up with an exclamation of horror. "I think she
was thoroughly frightened when Miss Twining
fainted."

"But what did she do?"

"Why, she went up to Miss Twining's room,
late one night, and carried a riding-whip, — she
had threatened that afternoon to 'flog' her —
and it upset Miss Twining and brought on a
fainting turn. Now Miss Sniffen keeps her
locked in all the time! I don't know what she
would do if it were n't for Mrs. Albright! She
rooms right across the hall, and her key fits the
lock; so she goes in every little while. There's
a card on her door, saying she's too ill to see
visitors."

"That is the feeble-minded one, is n't it?"

"No!" flashed Polly. "She's not feeble-
minded any more than you are! That's just a
bluff! Miss Sniffen got scared and made up all
that rubbish! Miss Twining is beautiful. I love

her — oh, I love her dearly! She writes the nicest poetry! Father says it is real poetry, too."

"Why did Miss Sniffen wish to whip her?"

"Just because she would n't tell who gave her some money. She could n't — she had promised not to! And it was her own money! But I must begin at the beginning, or you can't understand."

Polly drew a long breath, and recounted the details of the sad story.

"The next morning I happened to go over to see Miss Nita," she concluded, "and Mrs. Albright told me this. Miss Crilly was there, too. Miss Crilly rooms right next to Miss Twining and heard a good deal; but she did n't dare to stir."

Nelson Randolph gazed at Polly with troubled eyes, and rested his arm upon his desk.

"David Collins overheard something one night," she went on. "He was going up Edgewood Avenue when he came upon Mrs. Nobbs and a man, — probably her brother, — and what Mrs. Nobbs was saying made him keep along behind them, instead of passing as he was intending to do."

As the talk was repeated, the listener's face grew stern, and when Polly came to the end of her story he fingered the little silver elephant upon his desk before he spoke.

"You say that the board is not what it should be?"

"It is poor, dreadfully poor, Mr. Randolph. Lately they've had stale meat and sour bread — and hardly any fruit or green vegetables all summer long!"

"Yet her accounts stand for expensive roasts, lamb chops, early fruits when they are highest in price — the best of everything!"

"They never get on the table," asserted Polly. "Miss Nita and the others have spoken again and again of their wretched living. And the cooking is awful!"

"I am told that she pays her cook fifty dollars a month."

"I don't know what she pays," Polly replied, "but they seldom have good cooking. She is changing help all the time."

"We have trusted her implicitly," the president mused. "Her father was a man of undoubted honor."

"I don't see that it would be much worse to

steal from the Home than to take Miss Twining's money or Miss Nita's cards or —"

"Cards? From Miss Sterling?" broke in Nelson Randolph quickly.

"Did n't you put your cards in those boxes of roses you sent her?" asked Polly.

"Certainly."

"She never saw any! Miss Castlevaine was going upstairs and happened to see that first box of roses on the hall desk. Miss Sniffen was fingering a card. When Miss Nita received the box there was no card there. That was why she was so long in saying 'thank you,' — she did n't know where they came from. We finally found out through the boy who brought them."

Nelson Randolph frowned. "A pretty state of affairs!" he muttered.

"And she never got one of your telephone messages!" Polly went on.

"What!" the man exclaimed.

"She did n't!" Polly reiterated.

"But Miss Sterling gave me no hint of such a thing!"

"No," Polly returned sadly. "I guess she did n't dare."

"Surely she was not afraid of me!"

"I don't know," replied Polly dissatisfiedly and with emphasis. "It really seems sometimes as if she were."

"There must have been some tremendous lying," he mused. "They gave me messages purporting to come from Miss Sterling. Why should she be singled out in this way?" He looked across at Polly, as if he expected her to answer the question.

The red in her cheeks grew redder. She remembered the reason David had given.

"I think it is no uncommon thing for the ladies not to get their telephone messages," she replied evasively. "That was one reason why Mrs. Dick ran away with the milkman. She was so upset at not receiving an invitation to a wedding that had been sent her by telephone."

"It is high time that something was done!" The president lifted his little elephant and brought it down hard. "We have been inexcusably blind!"

"I wish Miss Twining could have some good doctor," ventured Polly.

"She shall!" he promised. "Be patient for a few days, and I will hurry up things as fast as practicable. You say she is a little better?"

"Mrs. Albright thinks so. She is over her scare a little. Dr. Gunnip frightened her half to death! He won't let her try to get up. Don't you hate Dr. Gunnip?"

Mr. Randolph smiled. "I don't know him personally," he replied. "I never thought I should want him for a physician." He shook his head musingly.

"I will lay the matter before the trustees and managers at once," he said, as Polly rose to go. "I need not ask you," he went on, "to be whist about this, since I have proof that you can keep a secret under trying conditions. I thank you more than you will ever know."

CHAPTER XXXIII

THE PRINCESS AND THE DRAGON

JUANITA STERLING moved restlessly about her room, doing this and that which had no need of being done. It was a mild day for late September, and she thought of a walk. No, it was nearly time for the afternoon mail, she would wait. If she could only get a note from Polly — or from David! One of Polly's notes had never reached the third-floor corner room! Since that, notes had been conceded to be dangerous. How she missed Polly's visits! She wondered now if Polly's interview with Mr. Randolph were really over. That report could not be entrusted to paper. She wished that her windows were on the front. She might go into Mrs. Albright's room — no, she had better remain at home, somebody might come. She took a book and sat down in the easiest chair; but her thoughts were not on the printed page. She slammed it back in its place with a mutter of scorn — scorn for herself.

"Shall I ever stop thinking — of him!"

Meantime, downstairs, the front doorbell had rung. Miss Sniffen answered it. She usually answered the bell nowadays.

Nelson Randolph stood waiting.

"Good afternoon!" he smiled. "I want to run up to those corner rooms and see how the light is, now that the windows are shut up. I think we may have to put in other windows on the side."

"Oh, no, Mr. Randolph, the light is very good, indeed! I don't think more windows will be necessary."

"Well, maybe not, then; but I'll just take a look at it, seeing I'm here."

She moved back slowly. "I think Miss Sterling is out; but you can see the first-floor room."

They went in together, but as the man turned to speak he found that he was alone. With a smile he cast a leisurely eye around, and then strode along the hall to the upper staircase.

The superintendent was coming down.

"No use your going up," she said in an unnecessarily low tone. "One of the ladies says she is out, so we shan't be able to get in."

"Oh, that won't matter!" he replied carelessly. "I'm a good deal of a burglar; I always

314

carry a skeleton key in my pocket — it will unlock almost anything. You ought to have one."

"We have never needed it," she responded coldly, quickly preceding him.

She tapped softly on the door.

"Oh, you're in, after all!" she exclaimed in a voice of sweet surprise. "They said you had gone out."

"I have been here since dinner. — How do you do, Mr. Randolph! Are you quite well again?"

"Should n't know I had ever been sick — except for the doctor's bill!" he replied. "Now, how about this light, Miss Sterling? Do you find the addition in the way?"

"Why, of course, it is n't quite so pleasant," she admitted; "but I don't mind it very much."

"I think it would make things a little better to put a window in, say about here."

"Oh, that would be lovely!" she cried.

"I will suggest it, at any rate. I never like to spoil one room for the sake of another." He ran his eyes over the wall. "We might make it one broad window, here and in the room below, to match the one on the first floor — it would n't be a bad plan. We 'll see." He turned to go, then halted and looked at his watch.

"I'm afraid you stay in too much, Miss Sterling," he said carelessly. "Suppose you put on your things and come for a ride. It is very mild out."

"Oh, thank you!" The red rushed to her cheeks. "I'll be ready in a minute."

Left alone, Juanita Sterling hastily brought out hat and coat. Her heart was pounding with excitement and — yes, joy! She chided herself in no uncertain words.

"Little fool!" she muttered. "He wishes to ask questions about the Home, questions that I am better able to answer than Polly — that is all! He is engaged to Blanche Puddicombe — remember that, and don't be a — dear, dear, where are those gray gloves! Oh!" as the needed articles were brought to sight.

She ran downstairs and directly out of the big door, meeting no one.

As the car rolled up the avenue she felt a delicious sense of freedom. She remarked upon the changing foliage and the unusual warmth of the day, the man at her side making only brief assents.

"That Dragon," he finally broke out, "did n't mean to let the Princess be seen to-day!"

Miss Sterling met his whimsical look with puzzled eyes. Then, as the meaning dawned, "Oh!" she cried, a little blushing laugh keeping the word company.

"Do you always lock your door when you go away?"

"Never," she answered, — "then or at any time; we are not allowed to lock our rooms."

"She told me you were out, and that your door would be locked; but I said I had a skeleton key in my pocket, and went on."

"You quite outwitted her," she laughed. "I don't understand why she should lie about it."

"I have been there several times and inquired for you," he resumed; "and was always told that you were not in."

A flush of surprise pinked her face. "I never heard anything of it," she said regretfully.

"So Polly Dudley told me. I saw her this morning."

"Oh, did you!" she cried eagerly.

"She was in my office for an hour or two. We have been blind as moles, the whole gang of us!" he added in a disgusted tone. "We have trusted that woman with everything — to your sorrow and ours! I hope the officers will see it as I do, but — I don't know. Miss Sterling," —he turned to her with a brighter tone in his voice, — "do you remember when I used to come to your house to consult your father— and you would entertain me while I was waiting for him?"

"Oh, yes!" she answered, "I remember perfectly; but I did n't suppose you recollected — it is so long ago."

"I don't forget easily. You were a schoolgirl then, were n't you?"

"I was just through the high school."

"It was the winter before I was married," he said reminiscently. "It seems a lifetime since then. Yet it is only some twenty or more years ago. Your father was a very wise man, and I was pretty green in those days. I remember I wanted to sue somebody that had cheated me in a small way, and your father advised me strongly against it. I chafed a good deal at his decision; but I have thought of it a good many times since, how much better things turned out for me than if I had had my own way. Too bad he had to go so young! We need such men. I wish we had a few like him on the Home Board." He turned toward his companion with a rueful smile. "I am rather glad that happened down at the Home to-day. It has given me a little personal experience with the Dragon that may be convenient to have." He smiled again at her, that kindly, whimsical little smile that so well became him.

She smiled, too, and then, when he had turned back, she frowned. She wished he would n't smile that way — to her. He should keep such smiles for his fiancée.

"By the way," she began, "how is Miss Puddicombe? I have n't seen her lately."

"She is very well, much better than she was during the summer. She is in New York at present, visiting her aunt for a fortnight."

Ah, that was why he was able to take her to ride! She wondered if she ought to offer her congratulations, but finally decided to keep silent. She was not supposed to know of his engagement.

The road wound up through a maze of yellow. Tall trees on either side sifted their gold down upon the travelers. Juanita Sterling caught a leaf in her hand and held it.

"How beautiful it is!" she said, and drew a deep breath.

The man turned to look at her trophy.

"Oh, no! I mean the way," she explained. "It is strange, but it makes me think of heaven."

"The streets of gold?" he smiled.

"M—no," she replied doubtfully. "I can't quite tell myself; but I think it is the peace and the glory of it — the spirit of the place."

His eyes were on her face, and the car bumped over a stone.

"There! That's because I was looking at you!" he laughed. "A motorman should n't gaze at a princess."

She gave a little gurgling laugh; then she grew grave again.

"What do you say," he asked abruptly, "to keeping on over the mountain to Bryston and have dinner?"

Her heart gave a joyful leap, yet she answered quietly, "I am afraid—I'd better not."

"Oh, yes," he urged, "let's keep on! I am selfish, I know; but I'd rather eat dinner with you than to eat it at home alone, and I'm sure that Squirrel Inn will give you a more appetizing meal than the Dragon will furnish."

320

"I dare say," she responded. "What a bewitching name for an inn! Is it as captivating as it sounds?"

"More," he smiled. "It is the inn that has made Belgian hare famous."

She laughed softly, and he speeded the car.

"I took Mrs. Puddicombe up there one day, and she has raved about it ever since. The house itself is very old, with little windows and a gambrel roof, and a well-sweep in the rear. They say, half of the garret is given over to the squirrels."

"What a delightful place! I shall love it, I know!" Inwardly, however, she amended, "Maybe I shan't!" thinking of Mrs. Puddicombe.

But once seated at the quaint little table, in the old high-backed chair, eating what tasted better than the best chicken that ever went into an oven, Juanita Sterling forgot Mrs. Puddicombe and her daughter Blanche, and smiled upon everything.

"I am having more dinners to-day than my share," she observed over the pumpkin pie and cheese. "We have ours at twelve, you know."

"What did you have?"

"Codfish balls and pickles and stale bread and butter."

"No dessert?"

"No," she laughed; "that was cut out months ago."

He shook his head gravely. "I did n't suppose it was as bad as that."

"This makes up," she said gayly.

It was a leisurely meal; and when it had come to an end the memory of it was not the least of its delights.

The air had cooled decidedly, and meeting the stiff breeze Juanita Sterling shivered. She turned up her coat collar about her neck.

"Are you cold?" he questioned.

"Not much. I shall get used to it in a minute. It was pretty warm in there."

He stopped the car and jumped out. "There are some light-weight robes somewhere," he said.

"Don't bother!" she protested. "I rarely take cold."

But he continued his search.

"There!" he said, putting it around her shoulders, "is n't that better?"

"Delightful! Thank you!" It was cozily warm and comfortable.

322

She drew a deep, happy breath. The car skimmed along as if on wings. She could meet the wind with pleasure now. The stars twinkled down their glad greeting. Probably she would never see the like of this again. But to-night it was hers! It should not be spoiled by Blanche Puddicombe! She let her enjoyment have its way and talked and laughed freely.

"How can you keep so cheerful in the Dragon's prison?" Nelson Randolph asked at length. "I should think all of you would have been dead from gloom before this time."

"Polly Dudley has done a great deal toward keeping us up, and we have several very bright ladies there. Mrs. Albright and Miss Crilly would make a dungeon sunshiny."

"Happy companionship is everything," he assented. "That is what I am denied. My home is about the most desolate place on earth!"

"It looks delightful from the outside."

"Oh, the house is well enough! But what is the good of a house with nobody to speak to! I stay at the club evening after evening, because I dread to go back to that lonely place I call home." He spoke drearily. After a moment he went on. "I started out this afternoon with a good deal of hope; but you have thrown most of it to the winds!"

"I? Why, Mr. Randolph!" She gazed at him in surprise.

"Impolite," he nodded, with an apologetic smile. "But, Miss Sterling, you know that I love you! You must have known it all summer! And you try to be friendly — that's all! You didn't want to go to Bryston, and I was self-ish enough to keep on! I suppose it is too much to expect, that you will care for an old fellow like me; but — oh, Miss Sterling! can't you?"

For a moment memory was swept away in the flood of astonishment and joy that over-whelmed her. Then, like a menace, the haughty girl of the sheep pasture loomed before her.

"Oh! no! no!" she gasped. "Why do you say such things to me? — *you* — engaged to Blanche Puddicombe!"

"O-h!" — It held a note of exultation. "Has that absurd story reached you? Miss Sterling, there is not an atom of truth in it!" The words tumbled from his lips. "Mrs. Pud-dicombe's grandmother and my grandfather were sister and brother. The families have always been friendly. Last summer Blanche was in such wretched health that her mother wanted me to take her to ride as often as I could. So whenever I went off on business I would carry Blanche along. That is all there is to it!"

They were moving slowly now. A great car came honking up behind, roared past, and became a red star in the distance. Another flashed out ahead, glared down upon them, and whizzed by. Nelson Randolph spoke again.

"Have you no hope for me?"

"Oh, yes!" It barely rose through the purring of the car.

His right hand left the wheel and closed over the two little gray-gloved ones folded so quietly.

"You shall never regret it!" he promised. "I will try to make you forget this year of misery."

The talk ran on. As they passed through the outskirts of Fair Harbor, he said: —

"I expect to go to New York to-morrow morning on the 6.30 train. If I can get through my business in time I shall come back in the evening; but I am afraid it will be too late for a ride. That will have to wait until Thursday.

I don't know how I am going to communicate with you. I cannot bear to leave you without any means of letting me know if you are in trouble."

"I don't think there will be any trouble," she said contentedly.

"There might be. How would it do for me to tell the Dragon that you belong to me and that you are to be free to go and come as you please or to use the telephone whenever you like?"

"Oh, don't!" A note of fear was in her voice.

"You had better lock your door at night, then. There is a key?"

"Yes, but it is subject to rules."

"Ignore rules and lock the door! Dragons are not to be trusted. And remember, if there should be any trouble whatever, call me at once, — in some way, — and I will drop everything and come."

"Thank you! You are so good!"

He laughed softly. "Good to myself!"

They sped along Edgewood Avenue, and the car stopped in the shadow of a great maple. Miss Sterling threw off her borrowed wrap.

He stepped to the ground and put out his

326

arms. What could she do but walk into them?

"I will go in with you," he said, as he set her gently down.

Her face was still aflame with his kisses when they entered the big door together.

Miss Sniffen met them in the hall.

"You are late," she said with a half smile. "Have you had an accident?"

"Oh, no!" Nelson Randolph answered. "We went up to Bryston to dinner, that is all. Miss Sterling thought she had better return home early, but I coaxed her to keep on and find out how Belgian hare tasted." He laughed lightly and said good-night.

Miss Sterling's foot was on the stair when the superintendent arrested her.

"You are too late for chapel," she said severely.

"I was afraid I would be," was the reply.

"This must not occur again. Do you know that Mr. Randolph is to marry Miss Puddicombe?"

"I heard so," she smiled.

"The wedding-day is set!"

"So I was told."

"Did he tell you?"

"Oh, no! I heard it a good while ago."

Miss Sniffen looked a little disappointed and turned down the hall.

Juanita Sterling closed the door of her room, struck a light, and threw her hat and coat across a chair.

On a small table a twin frame held photographs of a man and a woman.

She took it in both hands.

"Father, mother, — dears! do you know that your 'little girl' is happy? — happier than she has been since you went away?"

The last words broke in a sob; but the eyes that looked up into hers were smiling.

CHAPTER XXXIV

A MIDNIGHT ANNOUNCEMENT

JUANITA STERLING was forced to hear much bantering in regard to her prolonged ride with the Home president; but she received it with the utmost good humor. Not even to Mrs. Albright did she hint of the happiness that had come to her. It would be known soon enough; to-day the joy was hers and hers alone.

"What would Blanche Puddicombe have said to see you go gallivant'n' off to Bryston with her lover!" cried Miss Crilly. "I wish she could have, I just wish she could have! 'T would have been a picnic, sure! Are you goin' again, Miss Sterling?"

Juanita Sterling laughed, her cheeks coloring prettily. "He did n't ask me to go to-day."

"Too bad!" cried the tease. "But she blushes, so I guess she'll go when he does ask her."

"Perhaps she's trying to cut out Miss Puddicombe," suggested Miss Major.

"She has n't told us a thing he said to her,"

329

winked Miss Mullaly. "They had time for lots of love scenes all those long miles!"

"An auto is n't the best place in the world for love-makin'," giggled Miss Crilly.

"Now you stop bothering her!" cried Mrs. Albright. "We'd every one of us give our eye-teeth for such a ride with the president, and you know it!"

"My! I guess we would!" Miss Crilly performed a pirouette. "I'd run my feet off to get into the car!"

"Well, what did you talk about?" queried Miss Mullaly coaxingly.

"Yes, we want to hear," urged Miss Crilly; "so when we go with him we shall know what to say."

"No danger of your not knowing what to say!" laughed Miss Major.

"Some of the time we talked about Belgian hare," answered Miss Sterling demurely.

"Belgian hare!" grinned Miss Crilly. "I bet you did n't talk five or six hours about Belgian hare!"

Juanita Sterling chuckled gayly. "He asked what I had for dinner yesterday, and I told him!"

"Honest?" gasped Miss Mullaly.

"Yes," nodded the other.

"What did he say?"

"I don't remember just what; but he was surprised."

"I guess he was! I hope it will set him to thinking."

"Well, if I stay here fooling away all the forenoon, I shan't get a credit mark for having my bed made early!" And Miss Crilly tripped off.

The rest soon scattered, and Miss Sterling was left alone to dream over her joy and to wonder what her friends would say when the truth came out.

In the afternoon she called at Dr. Dudley's, and was disappointed not to find Polly. The day was cold, with a raw wind, very unlike the day before; so after a short walk she returned home.

Mrs. Albright met her in the upper hall.

"Miss Crilly is sick," she said anxiously. "She is in terrible pain, and nothing relieves her. She wants Dr. Dudley; but Miss Sniffen says it is not necessary. I don't know what to do!"

"Sh!" Miss Sterling held her answer to listen. "I thought I heard a footstep," she whispered. "Is Miss Sniffen downstairs?"

"She went down. I don't care if she does hear me! I'm getting desperate."

"She ought to have a doctor," Miss Sterling said, with wrinkled forehead. "I wonder if I can be of any use — I'll come right up."

The combined resources of the two were of no avail. Miss Crilly grew worse.

"I shall die — I know I shall! — just as poor Miss Twining is going to!" wailed the sufferer.

"No, you won't!" returned Mrs. Albright. "You haven't any heart trouble."

"I've got something!" insisted Miss Crilly, writhing with pain.

Miss Sniffen appeared at the door with a bowl of steaming water and a bundle of cloths. "I'm going to put these on," she announced briskly.

"I tried hot water first thing," said Mrs. Albright. "It didn't do any good."

The superintendent gave no response. She was busy administering the remedy.

"Don't make such a fuss!" she reprimanded. "Pain never killed anybody yet."

"You'd better go back to your room, Miss

Sterling," she turned to say. "No need of your staying here."

There did not seem to be, and the request was obeyed without reply.

Later Mrs. Albright came upstairs to say that Miss Crilly was a little easier. "I think she's going to get on now," she concluded.

"I hope so," was the reply; "but call me if she should grow worse."

"Yes, I will, — though you could n't do any good," she amended.

"I could get a doctor for her."

"I don't see how!" Mrs. Albright gazed questioningly into the steady gray eyes. This was a new Miss Sterling. "You can't do anything with Miss Sniffen."

"There are other people in the world besides Miss Sniffen. If she needs a doctor she shall have one. So let me know if the pain comes on again."

Miss Sterling had been abed an hour or more when she was awakened by a gentle rap.

Mrs. Albright softly opened the door.

"She's worse than ever; but Miss Sniffen won't hear to calling the doctor. She says if she is n't any better in the morning she will send for him; but Miss Crilly insists that she can't live till morning in such agony. Miss Sniffen thinks she is scared to death, and of course fear does n't help matters. But she does need a doctor — I know that!"

Miss Sterling began to dress. "Where is Miss Sniffen now?"

"She went downstairs."

"I will keep watch till she gets still, then I'll go down."

"What can you do?"

"I'm going for Dr. Dudley."

"Suppose she sees you?"

"I know how to run!"

"She might catch you!"

"She shan't!"

"I'm afraid to let you try it." She lingered irresolute.

"You need n't. I'll let myself! Go back to Miss Crilly, and tell her to keep up courage a little longer and I'll have Dr. Dudley here as soon as I can."

She put on her softest slippers and crept carefully down the stairs. All was dark. Not a sound came to her keen ears. She crossed the hall and reached the heavy front door. Cautiously she passed her hand from lock to lock —

something squeaked! She frowned, and hastily slid the last bolt — A light flared behind her!

"What are you doing? — Miss Sterling!" Miss Sniffen came quickly towards her.

"I am going for the doctor!" She was out the door.

Miss Sniffen was almost as quick. "Come back!" she cried. "Come back this minute!"

Juanita Sterling was on the long flight of granite steps, so was Miss Sniffen. The lithe little figure ran swiftly along the walk to the street; the pursuer was close behind. The feet ahead seemed heavy and slow; the steps that followed came nearer, nearer! Miss Sterling could almost feel the big hand upon her shoulder! Her heart beat suffocatingly, her ears thundered defeat, she must drop or die! Then she thought of Nelson Randolph and grew strong! She bounded forward — she was nearly there! No, she was only passing the corner! On, on, on! She reached the gate, bumped against it, sped along the walk, stumbled up the steps, and pushed the bell button — not until then did she venture a backward glance.

A tall figure was walking slowly, very slowly up the street!

"Out — of — breath!" she said softly, with a chuckle that was half a sob.

A light flashed inside, and Mrs. Dudley opened the door.

"Why, Miss Sterling!"

"Is — Doctor — home?" she puffed.

"No, he is n't. He's out of town. Come in! Somebody sick?"

Mrs. Dudley put her into an easy-chair, felt her pulse, smiled in happy assurance, and waited for the story.

Before it was finished, Polly peeped in.

"I thought it was your voice! What *is* the matter, Miss Nita?" She drew up a chair and sat down, folding her crimson robe about her.

Part of the tale was hurriedly retold.

"Doctor may come on the 11.55 train; if not, he can't get here before one o'clock."

"And Dr. Vera is watching with Dorothy!" cried Polly.

"So I told her," said Mrs. Dudley. "Dorothy is a very sick child; he cannot leave her. I would go over if I thought I could do any good."

"I'm afraid Miss Sniffen would n't let us in," returned Miss Sterling. "I think I'd better call up Mr. Randolph. He said to do it if — there

336

was any trouble." Her face rivaled in color Polly's robe.

The young girl's eyes widened.

"When did he —" she began; but her mother interrupted.

"Yes, by all means, telephone!"

Miss Sterling darted into the next room, while Polly sprang to turn on the light.

"Hallo! Is it Mr. Randolph?" came to Polly's ears. "Juanita Sterling is talking. I am at Dr. Dudley's. Miss Crilly is very sick, and I came over for the Doctor; but he is out of town. Can you come up? Yes. Yes. Good-bye! — He says he will be here in less than ten minutes." She returned to the chair she had left, and Polly cuddled down beside her, while Mrs. Dudley went to put her dress in better order.

"I'll stay till he comes," said Polly comfortably. "Then I can run and leave you to let him in — you won't mind, will you? Do tell me more about that race, Miss Nita. Oh, don't I wish I had seen it!"

She laughed over the superintendent's probable discomfiture, and lamented Miss Crilly's illness.

"It is too bad father isn't at home," she said

musingly; "but, oh, Miss Nita! what made you think of calling up Mr. Randolph? When did he tell you any such thing?"

"I went to ride with him yesterday," was the quiet answer.

"You did! Was n't that lovely! Where did you go?"

"Over to Bryston. We took dinner at Squirrel Inn."

"Oh, my!" chuckled Polly. "What will Blanche Puddicombe say?"

"I don't care what she says. Polly, he is not engaged to her."

"He is n't? Oh, I am so glad, I don't know what to do! I did n't want him to be engaged one bit!"

"I did n't say he was n't engaged," returned the other demurely. "I only said he was not engaged to Miss Puddicombe."

Polly's face fell. "Oh, dear!" she cried in a vexed tone, "I never thought of his being engaged to anybody else! Who is it? — I don't know that I care, but I may as well know!" Polly looked cross.

Miss Sterling laughed softly. "What a little fire-box you are!" she said.

"Oh, yes, laugh!" pouted Polly. "Of course, you don't care, because you don't like him as I do; but I think it is mean for him to be engaged — just when I was so glad he was n't! You have n't told me who it is yet — anybody I know?"

"Yes."

"Somebody here in town, then?"

"Yes, right here."

"I don't see who it can be. I never saw him riding with anybody but Blanche Puddicombe. Why don't you tell me?" cried Polly impatiently.

"I said she was right here." The little woman in gray sat very still. Her eyes were following the pattern of the rug. Her cheeks grew red and redder.

"Why, I don't see —" began Polly. Then she started forward. "Oh, Miss Nita! you don't mean —"

Juanita Sterling met the bright eyes, and nodded smilingly.

"Oh, Miss Nita! Miss Nita!" — Polly squeezed her friend's arm in ecstasy — "I can't believe it! It's too lovely for anything! I want to hop right over the moon! How did he say it,

339

Miss Nita? Do tell me how he said it! I've always wanted to know how they said it, and mother won't tell me, and father won't, and unless you do I never shall know!"

"You — with a lover like David!" laughed the other.

"Oh, well, David's only a boy! Please — there's his car! It's turning round!" She started and her eyes fell upon the clock. "Just after midnight! I did n't notice its striking. Good-morning, Miss Nita! How funny it will seem to say Mrs. Randolph!"

"Polly!" the other expostulated.

Polly laughed and flung her arms round Miss Sterling's neck. "Remember! I'm not going to let you off! You must tell me how he said it!"

"Charmingly, Polly, charmingly!"

"No, that won't do! — There's the bell!" And the crimson-robed little figure fled.

Juanita Sterling had wondered what she would say when they met the next time. How different this was from her dream!

Nelson Randolph took her hand in a warm clasp. "I am glad you let me come," he said.

Briefly she explained the situation.

"Better call Dr. Temple."

"I thought of him, but I did n't like to take any more responsibility."

"Where is the telephone?"

She led the way and made a light.

"Yes, it's Randolph," she heard him say. "I am at Dr. Dudley's. He is out of town. A woman at the Home is very sick. Can you come up? Yes, I will wait here and go over with you."

He settled himself in a big rocker, and regarded her smilingly.

"So the Princess had a race with the Dragon! That is more than I anticipated. Was she frightened?"

Miss Sterling blushed. "Not much — a little," she admitted. "Once — for a long minute — I was afraid the 'Dragon' was going to catch me!"

"But she did n't! I am proud of you!" He grasped the hand that rested on the arm of her chair.

She pulled away and ran across the room. "I'm going to sit here!" she announced, smiling to him. To hold her hand that way — when at any moment Mrs. Dudley might appear!

He surveyed her with amusement. "Was that an unforgivable sin?" he twinkled.

"M — no," demurely. "The Doctor may come."

"He won't come in at the window," he laughed. "Don't you think you are a little unkind, when I have been so far away all day and have n't had a glimpse of you since last night?"

"You can see me just as well over here. There have been other days when you have not seen me." A mischievous light gleamed in her eyes.

"It was n't my fault," he smiled. "I tried pretty hard to see you!"

She went back, blushing like a school-girl.

"Thank you! I 'll be good! I can't realize that you are coming to make my lonely home such a place of delight!"

She could not look up to meet the eyes that she knew were dwelling upon her.

"I want to take you over there to-morrow," he went on. "There are a few changes I propose making, and you may like to suggest some on your own account. You can have it any way you please."

342

She glanced up now, her cheeks still aflame, her face flooded with joy.

"I shall like to go," she said; "but I think I'll leave the changes to you. The outside looks beautiful to me just as it is. The wide lawn on the south side, with the background of evergreens, is magnificent!"

"I am glad you like that. I never tire of it. So you don't want me to trim the trees up — as some folks advise?"

"O-h!" she gasped. "The effect would be ruined!"

He smiled. "I might have done it to please you, but I think I'd have argued a little first."

"I should have argued more than a little if you had suggested it," she laughed.

"I am going to build out a big veranda from the dining-room, put in windows for the winter, and then give them over to screens through the summer."

He paused to listen. "Dr. Temple, I presume," as a car whizzed up and stopped. He went to the door, while Miss Sterling threw on her coat.

Mrs. Dudley joined them, and the four proceeded to the Home.

The superintendent opened the door to them, smiling a little when she saw Nelson Randolph.

"There is probably no real need of routing people from their beds at this hour," she said; "but, of course, we wish to do all we can when any one is suffering. The patient will be glad to see you," she added, addressing the Doctor.

The physician was swift in his diagnosis. "It is a case that calls for quick work," he told Mrs. Dudley. "There must be an operation at once. You think your husband will be here on the 1.03 express?"

"I feel sure of it."

"Then we will wait for him."

"She can be taken over to the hospital now; — we need not wait for that."

Mrs. Dudley returned home to make the needful preparations, and Juanita Sterling went to encourage Miss Crilly for the coming ordeal.

The patient was tearful, but brave.

"Probably I never shall come back," she said; "but you are awful good to try to save me, Miss Sterling! I'd like to live long enough to show you how much I appreciate it."

"Nonsense, that wasn't anything! And of

course you're coming back! Dr. Temple says
you have every chance in your favor if it's done
right away. He thinks you are in splendid condition. Now don't you worry a single minute!"

"I'll try not to! I wish I were as brave as
you. I'd never have dared to go — with her
chasin' me! My! I wish I could have seen you
two leggin' it!"

Miss Sterling laughed. "That is what Polly
wished. But as for my being brave, Miss
Crilly, I'm afraid I'm not. I am going to tell
you my big secret — I have told only Polly yet;
but maybe it will give you something to think
of, — I expect to marry Mr. Randolph!"

"O-h, Miss Sterling! Oh, my! Isn't that
perfectly beautiful! Well, you *have* given me
something to think of! Why, I 'most forgot
already what's comin'! And I'm going to keep
thinking of it hard, so's I won't worry! The
idea of your marryin' the president! I do'
know's I wonder you were n't scared o' Miss
Sniffen! And to think how I jollied you only
this morning — about him! Why, I never
thought of such a thing!"

"Of course not! But it didn't trouble me."

"It didn't — really?"

345

"No, I quite enjoyed it!"

"You're awful good to say so! But what about Miss Puddicombe? I thought he was —"

"No, he wasn't. It was a mistake. They're cousins, distant cousins, that's all."

"Well, well, isn't that funny! And I'm so glad for you that I don't know what to do! — O-h! my! that was a pretty big pain! But I can bear it better now — will you kiss me once, just once, Miss Sterling?"

She bent and kissed her, and smiled cheerily.

"What's that! I guess they're after me! Oh, if I don't come back —"

"But you are coming back!"

"Maybe — but if I shouldn't, remember I'll always love you for what you've done for me!"

The patient was wrapped up quickly by one of the hospital nurses, and two orderlies bore her away. She was still smiling.

Juanita Sterling stood watching her out of sight, when a light step close behind made her start.

"Did I frighten you?" smiled Mrs. Albright. "It's about Miss Twining — Has Dr. Temple gone?"

A MIDNIGHT ANNOUNCEMENT

"He was in the hall talking with Mr. Randolph. I'll see."

She ran down a few steps, and then back again.

"They're there still. Is she worse?"

"I don't know. She heard the commotion and after they'd gone called me in. She got nervous, lying there and imagining everything. I wish the Doctor could see her. Should you dare ask?"

"Yes —" She was on the stairs.

Nelson Randolph saw her coming and put out his hand. But he dropped hers suddenly, as his fingers touched it.

The sparkles of amusement were still in her eyes when she told her errand.

Dr. Temple looked at his watch.

"Time enough?" inquired the president.

"Plenty."

Mr. Randolph approached the superintendent who was busying herself at her desk.

In a moment he returned. "Mrs. Nobbs will go up with you," he said.

Juanita Sterling did not wait; she hastened upstairs to insure Mrs. Albright's safe exit from the corner room.

347

The door was left partly open as Mrs. Nobbs and the physician entered, and the two in the opposite apartment moved out of range.

The low voices of doctor and patient did not carry beyond the corridor; but at a step Miss Sterling bent forward.

Dr. Temple was taking an instrument from his bag.

"Stethoscope," she whispered.

For several minutes no sound came from the sick-room. The listeners breathed anxiously.

"Good as anybody's!" The tone was emphatic.

Miss Sterling caught Mrs. Albright's hand in a rapturous squeeze.

"Do you mean — no heart disease?" Miss Twining's soft voice was shrilled with incredulous joy.

They could not catch the reply; but they smiled to each other in delight.

Shortly Mrs. Nobbs and the Doctor went downstairs, leaving the door free.

The others hurried across.

Miss Twining was tearfully excited. "Oh! did you hear? He says my heart is all right, and in the morning I can go down to breakfast!

He'll insure my living to be a hundred years old—as if I ever would!" She laughed quiveringly. "Those pink tablets I'm to take after meals, and the brown ones if I should feel bad—I never shall again! I believe it is two hours apart—you see! He says it is just a little nervous breakdown—There isn't any anodyne in them! Oh, I'm so glad you called him!"

CHAPTER XXXV

A NEW WIRE

Early the next morning Juanita Sterling was awakened by a heavy thud. Where was it? It came again. She sprang out of bed, threw a robe around her, and ran over to the window.

Some distance below appeared a grinning face. A man was coming up a ladder.

"Don't be scared, ma'am! I'm only going to put on the loop. Is n't this the room where the 'phone's to be?"

"Why — I don't know," she hesitated.

"It's to go in Miss Sterling's room."

"Who ordered it?"

"Nelson Randolph of the Paper Company."

"Oh, yes!" she cried, "that's all right."

"Where will you have it? On this side?"

"I — guess so —" She looked around. "Yes, here 'll be a good place."

"All right, ma'am! Another man 'll be up to do the wiring. I'm only putt'n' on the loop. Orders were to rush it through — that's why

350

I'm so early." He grinned. "Hope I have n't disturbed you, ma'am."

She assured him that she was not in the least disturbed. She drew down the shades and turned back to the room. It was not yet six o'clock.

A telephone of her very own! Delightful possibilities loomed before her through all her dressing. No more dreading of stormy days when she would be shut in the house; no more fears to torture her in the wakeful hours of the night. Help and protection would be hers at call!—And she could talk with Polly! She wanted to dance for very joy. And only two days ago her heart was aching! She felt as if it would never ache again.

At breakfast she heard many surmises regarding the strange noises about the building, before the workmen on the L were there. She decided to keep silent unless she were asked. It would be known early enough.

The electrician had come and gone, leaving on a table by the window the little instrument which seemed to its happy possessor to be almost alive. She stood looking at it and wondering how soon it would be in working order, when Mrs. Albright came in.

At once she saw the telephone, and stared in astonishment.

Miss Sterling laughed. "No more midnight troubles!"

"I am so surprised I don't know what to say." The visitor sat down.

"It isn't usable yet," Miss Sterling told her. "The man said he had to do some wiring in the cellar, make connections, and so on."

"Won't it be lovely for you!" cried Mrs. Albright.

"For all of us," amended the other. "I want the ladies to feel that it belongs to them as well as to me, and to come and use it whenever they wish."

"That is good of you! I'm sure it is needed badly enough. Isn't it nice that Miss Crilly is doing so well?"

"Yes, I'm glad as can be! I felt she would come out all right, but it is better to know it."

"She owes her life to you. I never should have dared to brave Miss Sniffen's anger, as you did."

"I guess I shouldn't have dared, if I hadn't known there was somebody ready to stand by me in case of need."

"That must have helped. Miss Sterling, I could n't keep from hearing what you told Miss Crilly last night."

"I supposed you would; in fact, I meant you should hear."

"Well, I am so glad! You don't know how glad! Only I can't bear the thought of losing you."

"Don't begin to worry yet! I shall not go at present."

"Well, I wish you all possible joy, and I feel sure you'll have it — with such a good man. My married life was short, — only one year, — but it was packed full of happiness. I have had the memory of that all these years."

"Was it sudden?"

"Like that!" She snapped her fingers. "We were in New York — on a pleasure trip!" She smiled sadly. "A runaway horse struck him down — he was gone in an instant!"

Tears sprang to the eyes of the listener.

"Now I ought not to have told you!" Mrs. Albright said regretfully.

"Yes, you ought! I am glad you did! I knew you had had sorrow; but I did n't know just what it was."

"Death is n't the worst thing that can happen," she smiled. "I try to think only of the happiness I've had, instead of the rest. And, my dear, I cannot wish you any greater joy than I had as long as Jack was with me."

"It must be good to have that to remember. Sometimes —"

"Ting! ting! Ting! ting!"

"Why! — I wonder —" Miss Sterling ran over to the telephone.

"Hallo!" she called.

"Good-morning, Juanita!"

"Oh, Mr. Randolph! Good-morning!"

"My name is Nelson."

She laughed softly. "Good-morning — Nelson!"

"Thank you! It is pleasant to hear you say it."

"I did n't know the wire was usable yet."

"I told them to call me up as soon as it was in working order."

"It was such a surprise! I can't tell you what a joy it is to me!"

"I could n't think of a better way out of the difficulty."

"It is the best of anything."

354

"I shall feel safer about you. Are you alone?"

"Yes, I am now. Mrs. Albright was here when you called; but I see she has slipped away."

"It is delightful to be able to talk with you at any time. You cannot realize what you are to me!"

She smiled into the mouth-piece. "You think, then, that a woman is incapable of the same feeling?"

"Oh, no, not incapable, but — I thought — that, perhaps —"

"You think I don't feel quite as you do — is that it?"

"Yes. I don't see how it is possible!"

"I am glad you think it is my heart that's at fault, instead of my brain."

"No, no, not at fault! I can't explain here. I'll wait till I see you."

"Oh, let's finish it up right now! This is a private wire, is n't it?"

"Certainly."

"We'll go ahead, then. What makes you think I don't feel as I ought?"

"I did n't say just that! You're all right, anyway!"

355

"Thank you! But why do you think I don't feel as you feel?"

"Well, in the first place, there is no reason why you should."

"Is n't there? And in the second place?"

"Why, you — you — were n't anxious to go to ride with me!"

"How do you know? Miss Sniffen got the invitations, not I!"

"I gave you one, face to face!"

"O-h, up in the pasture!"

"Yes. You offered no reason for your refusal."

"I could n't! I supposed that you were engaged to Miss Puddicombe."

"And you were afraid she would n't like it?"

"You are not a good guesser. I think I did n't consider her very much," with a little laugh.

"Then you thought I ought not to ask you?"

"Don't ever enter a guessing contest — you would n't win!"

"I suppose not," meekly. "Can't you help me out?"

The red in her cheeks crept up to her hair, she frowned a little. "I — I could not give you the real reason, Mr. Randolph, and I did n't want to lie!" She ran ahead hurriedly. "I was try-ing to forget, and —"

"Wait a minute! A train is going through the cut, and I did n't hear that last. . . . Now go on, please."

"I don't want to! It was bad enough to say it once!"

"You need not repeat, then. Though I should like to hear."

"I said — I — had been trying —"

"Just a minute! Somebody is knocking."

She sighed. She had a mind to run away — she hated the telephone!

"Hallo!"

No answer.

"Princess, are you there?"

"Yes," faintly.

"Sorry I had to keep you waiting. Now I am all ears!"

"I wish you were n't!"

"Never mind, then! Let it go till I see you this afternoon."

"Mercy! no! — I said — I — oh, I'm not going to tell you! You can guess it out for your-self."

"Perhaps I can't."

"Never mind! You won't miss much. Good-bye!"

"Wait a minute! Juanita!"

"Yes."

"I'll be there about three, but I'd better call you up before I start. I'm sorry you won't tell me."

"It does n't need to be told. Anybody could guess!"

"I can't see any clue."

She laughed. "I'm the clue! Good-bye."

CHAPTER XXXVI

POLLY DUDLEY TO CHRISTOPHER MORROW

Saturday Morning.

DEAR CHRIS, —

I have such an avalanche of news, I don't know where to begin. First, I must thank you for your dear letter and the wild flowers. They are lovely. We were immensely interested in hearing about your school, it is all so different from ours. What do you think father said, Chris Morrow! He put the sheets carefully back in the envelope, and as he laid it on the table he exclaimed, "That boy is a born letter-writer!" It ought to make you very proud, but I know it won't. He never said that over a letter of mine! But I am not jealous. I do wish you were here. I wish it every day. But I'm glad you are so happy with your father, and that he has such a splendid position. Now for my news!

I ought to be dusting my room this very minute! My desk is so dusty — it blew in last evening, I guess, when the window was open, the

dust, I mean — and it stares me in the face
and makes me feel guilty. I can't do as Mrs.
Albright does when her room is dusty and she
does n't feel like dusting. I went to see her one
day, and she was sitting by the window, smiling as usual. She said, "Don't look around,
dear, for I presume the dust is thick on everything. I was too tired to dust after my walk,
so I took off my glasses and have been having
a really beautiful time in spite of the dust."

Later.

There! I feel better. Everything is bright as
new! Now I shan't be in terror if the doorbell
rings.

I wonder what I'd better take first. I wrote
you all about Miss Crilly and what a time Miss
Nita had getting a doctor. Miss Crilly is back
at the Home now, perfectly well, and you can't
see her ten minutes before she will get in something about Miss Nita's saving her life. She
did, too! Father says that if she had waited till
morning it would have been too late. Poor Miss
Sniffen! I'm glad she did n't have any more to
answer for! Mr. Randolph put a private wire
up to Miss Sterling's room, and she felt fixed

all right. It was funny! If he'd waited till the next week he would n't have needed to do it, though it was very nice for her as long as she was there. Well, a week after the telephone was in, Mabel ran up to Miss Major's room before she was up, frightened half to death. She said, "Oh, Miss Major!" — woke her out of a sound sleep — "Miss Sniffen has gone! And Mrs. Nobbs has gone! And Bridget has gone!" Bridget was the cook. "How do you know?" Miss Major asked. "'Cause they ain't anywhere!" Mabel cried. "We've looked all over, Nellie and me! In Miss Sniffen's room and Mrs. Nobbs's room and Bridget's room! They ain't anywhere at all!" Of course, that roused the house, and everybody was running round half-dressed, and they hunted everywhere, and they could n't find a trace of the three. Their trunks had disappeared ånd every vestige of their belongings! The servants did n't know what to do, and they stood around helpless, till Miss Major and Mrs. Albright went into the kitchen and began to get breakfast. Miss Nita telephoned to Mr. Randolph, and he came up and appointed Miss Major to have charge of things till they could get new officers. In the middle

361

of the forenoon who should appear but Mrs.
Dick! — Mrs. Tenney, I should say. Her husband had died a month or so before, and she
had tried to get back into the Home, but Miss
Sniffen would n't have her, and she had n't
dared to apply to anybody else. As soon as she
came in and found out they'd gone, she took off
her things and went right into the kitchen to
help. She started to make some bread; but the
flour was sour and wormy, and she would n't
use it. So Mr. Randolph sent up some new, and
told her to order anything she needed. You can
imagine they had a good dinner! It was a first-
class meal, they all said, the best they had had
in years. Miss Nita called me up early, and I
ran over before school. They were having a
regular jubilation, — as happy as a flock of
kids!

Now they've got a superintendent that is
worth while! She is just lovely! The matron is
nice, too, so motherly. And what do you think!
They have a trained nurse — all the time —
and they are going to fix up an infirmary on the
top floor, so those that are sick can be quiet
without the well ones having to be whist. Dr.
Temple has been appointed House Physician —

oh, I tell you, things are mightily changed at the Home!

I think I wrote you about Miss Twining and her "resurrection." That night when Dr. Temple contradicted so emphatically what Dr. Gunnip had told her she says she felt as if she had been dead and buried all those dreadful weeks and had come back to life. Miss Crilly insists that if it had n't been for Miss Twining's "martyrdom" we never should have had "spunk" enough to go to Mr. Randolph with our awful story. I guess she is right. That stirred us up to do something. Miss Twining is pretty well now. She writes nearly every day, and as she can sell as much as she likes she earns a good deal. She told me once how she had always longed to hear one of her poems read in church. Well, last Sunday Mr. Parcell finished up his sermon with her "Peter the Great." It is beautiful — I'll copy it for you some day. He repeated it splendidly. I could n't resist glancing over at Miss Twining—you ought to have seen her! She looked just like a saint — or an angel!

Have I told you how father all but scolded me for talking to the minister in that way? He did n't like it a little bit! I shan't dare to tell ministers what I think after this! But I do believe it did Mr. Parcell good. He has been lovely to me ever since. He is n't half so cold and top-lofty as he used to be.

I'm getting down pretty near the weddings, I guess. We've had two! They're celebrating birthdays now at the Home, and Mrs. Adlerfeld's happened to be the first one. Miss Churchill had a lovely birthday cake for her, and chrysanthemums. The table looked beautiful. But little Mrs. Adlerfeld gave them a surprise. Of course, Miss Churchill and the matron knew all about it, and Mrs. Albright and Miss Nita and I; but the majority did not dream of such a thing. At eight o'clock Mrs. Adlerfeld, who had slipped away to put on her traveling dress, walked in on the arm of Mr. Von Dalin, and there was a minister, and they were married! Colonel Gresham gave her away, and we had such a nice time! She is living in New York. Oh, she was so sweet! I wish you could have seen her. In speaking of Mr. Von Dalin she said, "He is always a glad man. I could not marry a man who was not glad." Is n't that dear? It was hard to lose her. I am thankful

Miss Nita did n't have to go away — I don't know what I should have done!

Now comes *her* wedding! It was so pretty, everybody said. I was in it, so I could n't tell so well. The chapel and all the rooms were beautifully decorated with flowers, and the bride wore a simple tailored suit of dark blue, hat and boots to match. They looked splendid together, he is so tall and handsome and she is so slender and pretty. You don't know how much prettier she is since she has curled her hair! I always thought she would be. Almost all the ladies went right to curling their hair as soon as Miss Sniffen had skipped out, and it is a great improvement. Father gave away the bride, and David was Mr. Randolph's best man. I was the maid of honor. I felt as if I had been married myself. David said he did n't, but he wished he had been. Does n't that sound just like him? He is the queerest boy! Do you know, he comes away up here almost every morning, so as to walk down to school with me and cut out Todd Wilmerding! He knows I don't care a rap for Todd, but he hates to see him carrying my books!

Miss Nita says I must call her simply "Nita"

now, but it is hard to change. Mr. Randolph sometimes calls her "Princess," and she always smiles and blushes — I wonder why! "Princess" just fits her, does n't it? He declares he shall feel slighted if I don't call him "Nelson"! As if I would — that dignified man! Nita insists that he is n't dignified one bit, but I don't agree with her. Anyway, I shan't leave off the "Mr." to-day! They were only gone a week. I go over there nearly every day. The house has been altered a good deal. A beautiful, big veranda, or addition, has been built off the dining-room, sides all glass, and heated so that it can be used in the coldest weather. I ate dinner there last week. Nita has two servants, so she does n't have to work hard. There is a new music room, too, out of the hall, with a magnificent new piano in it! Miss Nita enjoys that. Oh, I forgot to tell you that they are going to have a piano at the Home! Mrs. Winslow Teed is delighted. And they have new china for the table. Miss Churchill could n't stand that old heavy stuff, and the good had all been broken. You would n't know the place. The ladies can go and come as they please, making a note of where they are going, or not, just as they choose. There are hardly any rules, and visitors are allowed every afternoon between two o'clock and six. I guess Mr. Randolph means to make up to them for all they have suffered through Miss Sniffen. One thing I am glad of! The ladies have some new dresses! And Mrs. Crump and Miss Castlevaine have new winter coats. They were the worst dressed of anybody, as they had been there longest. And I am almost gladdest of this,—each lady has five dollars a month for spending money! They are expected to buy their own shoes and stockings and gloves and neckwear and hats; but they'll have plenty left for themselves.

Mrs. Albright's birthday comes next week, and we are planning a big time. But the cream of the birthdays comes next summer, when we expect to celebrate June Holiday's birthday. It will be a grand outdoor affair. Some of the ladies have chosen their parts already. Everybody is to represent something in a June day, and the children — trustees' and managers' children, you know — are going to be butterflies and bumblebees. They want me to be Morning — in light pink. Miss Crilly is going to be South Wind — won't she be breezy? She has n't quite decided about her costume, but it is to be of some gauzy stuff. I think Miss Lily will be Blue Sky and White Clouds. She will be sweet in blue and white. Then there are going to be lots of flowers and birds and all sorts of characters. I wish you could be here! Can't you come across? What do you think Blue says he is going to be? A hop-toad! Is n't that like him! If he does he 'll carry it out so he 'll keep everybody laughing. There is Patricia coming! I must say good-bye in a hurry. Loads of love from us all.

POLLY MAY DUDLEY.

P.S. Patricia has just gone. She brought some news. Doodles is going to be soprano soloist in the boy choir at Trinity Church! Is n't that worth while! Of course, it is Mr. Randolph's doing. He is one of the head men there, and what he says, goes. He thinks Doodles's singing is about right. So Nita will hear him every Sunday. Mother says you 'll have to stay home from school the day you read this, for there won't be time for anything else. More love from

POLLY.

CHAPTER XXXVII

HOLLY AND MISTLETOE

June Holiday Home awoke early on the 24th of December, for everybody — which means fifteen of the residents — was going to spend the day with Mrs. Randolph. "From directly after breakfast until midnight," the invitation ran, and the president's car was to be at the Home by eight o'clock.

Such a profusion of curls and crimps, of new dresses and waists and fichus, added to new shoes and hats and coats, would have shocked the former superintendent of the Home; but Miss Churchill and Miss Ely even offered their services in the putting on of frills and furbelows, to the astonishment of those not yet grown familiar with kindness.

Mrs. Post, being unable to walk, had at first considered herself as entirely out of the fun; but Mrs. Randolph won the enduring love of that eldest member of the Home circle by saying that she should send an extra man with the chauffeur, so that Mrs. Post might have no fears regarding her trip from Edgewood Avenue to Courtney Street.

The Randolph home looked a bower of Christmas greenery and blossoms when the guests entered it that chill morning.

"My! is n't it beautiful!" cried Miss Crilly, sniffing the pungent, woodsy odors. "Smells like you were right there!" She grasped her hostess by the shoulders. "Now, solemn true! Are n't you the happiest mortal on earth?"

Mrs. Randolph smiled, blushing a little, too.

"I don't know how happy other people may be," she answered; "I only hope that they are as happy as I am."

"There! I knew it!" Miss Crilly exulted, as if she had just disclosed a secret.

The others laughed, the thin ice of conventionality was swept away, and at once all were merry.

"I think the new ladies wished they were coming when they heard us talking about it," said Miss Mullaly.

"They said they were invited to spend the day with relatives," returned the hostess.

"Yes, but they won't have half so good a time as we shall." Miss Crilly wagged her head expectantly. "They'll just sit around stiff and poky — most of them look as if they would. Is n't Polly coming, Mis' Randolph?"

"This evening."

"Won't that be lovely! She always makes things fly!"

During the forenoon the house was inspected from the quaint little rooms under the eaves to the cold-storage apartment below ground, Miss Crilly insisting that she wanted to see the head and the foot of it; and no new mistress of her own home would have been human not to be pleased with the praise that came from all lips, even including Miss Castlevaine's and Mrs. Crump's. In fact, these two fault-finders appeared to have been won over from their most unpleasant habits by the changes at the Home, which went to prove that Colonel Gresham was not wholly wrong.

"The clouds are chiming in with the rest of the world," called Miss Mullaly from the sunshine-room, just as the sun was setting. "Come here, every one of you, and see this sky!"

Informality was the watchword of the day, the guests having early been given the freedom of the house, and Miss Mullaly had strayed away from the others into the windowed room.

"My sakes!" exclaimed Miss Crilly. "Isn't that a real Christmas celebration!"

After the first outburst, the little party watched the gorgeous display almost in silence.

"It is too grand for words," breathed Miss Major.

Mrs. Randolph caught sight of Miss Twining's face, and it turned her from the distant glory. She told Mrs. Albright afterwards that she looked as if it were given her to see what was not visible to the others — a glimpse of heaven itself.

Mrs. Bonnyman broke the spell.

"Let's go back before it fades," she suggested. And the majority followed her into the firelit living-room.

"You missed the lovely purple tints," Miss Mullaly told them, as the remaining quartette filed back to join the rest.

"We'd rather have the picture of that magnificent sky of mottled crimson," declared Mrs. Grace.

"Nothing could be finer than that," observed Mrs. Tenney.

372

"Look out!" broke in a rich voice. "I shan't let you say there's anything finer than this!"

"Not even a sunset?" laughed Miss Crilly, as Nelson Randolph appeared in the doorway.

"A sunset is all right in its proper place," he smiled; "but when I want to ornament a chandelier I prefer this." He held up a large spray of mistletoe. "What do you think?" he challenged Miss Crilly.

"I guess you've got me this time!" she laughed.

"And I may get you again, my girl, before the evening is out!" He shook a warning finger in her direction.

"Dear me!" she cried, "I'm glad I came! To be called a 'girl'! I, an old maid of — I won't tell how many 'summers'! Thank you, Mr. Randolph!"

"If all old maids were as young as you there would n't be any," he responded gallantly.

She laughed her blushing protest, while he went for a stepladder.

The mistletoe, in its place of honor among the evergreens, brought forth many expressions of admiration.

The host surveyed it with satisfaction.

"I think that's a pretty nice piece of mistletoe," he said slowly. "It ought to be, I paid a good price for it. But I expect to get my reward before midnight," he twinkled to the smiling company.

"Don't be too sure, Mr. Randolph!" cautioned Miss Crilly.

"I am an expert at this business," he announced gravely, "and all I have to say is, Look out!"

The ladies were still laughing when they sat down to dinner. Luncheon had been in the sunshine-room, but dinner was served in the dining-room, a big, beautiful apartment all in oak, with a fire crackling at one end. The favors were knots of mistletoe and holly, and a roasted goose held the place of honor upon the table. All were in gayest holiday humor, from the mirthful host to quiet Miss Leatherland, who came far enough out of her shy self to show her friends that she possessed a goodly amount of fun and only needed the opportune moment to display it.

As the guests sauntered back to the living-room, they made a wide détour, rather than risk crossing the space beneath the brilliant chandelier with its innocent adornment. The host, after carefully depositing the cripple in the easiest chair, smiled over to Miss Crilly.

"Too bad to cause you so many unnecessary steps!" he said.

"My feet are not tired," she smiled back at him.

"Then let's have a waltz!" he cried, coming up with outstretched hands.

"Too soon after dinner," she laughed.

"No, it's a good time!" he twinkled gravely.

She hesitated, considering him with doubt on her face.

"Don't you trust him!" called Mrs. Randolph. "He is longing to waltz you under the mistletoe!"

He strode across to his wife.

"How dare you blacken my reputation in the face of all these ladies!" he cried sternly.

She laughed up at him with fearless, roguish eyes.

"Have I suggested anything that was not in your mind to do?"

A burst of laughter assailed him, while he walked off muttering, — quite audibly, — "These women! these women!"

The jingling of sleighbells set the keener-eared of the guests to listening.

"Polly would n't come in a sleigh, would she?" queried one.

"They're stopping here!" announced Miss Castlevaine from a front window. "But it is n't Polly," she added, "it's — goodness! — it's Santa Claus!"

"Santa Claus!" echoed the roomful.

And regardless of mistletoe, there was a rush across to the windows, while Nelson Randolph went to welcome his guests.

In they came, the strange little party of six, and were presented to the company as Santa Claus and Madam Santa Claus and four of the little Santa Clauses.

"Who can they be?" whispered Miss Mullaly to her neighbor.

"More'n I know," returned Mrs. Crump. "I guess Polly 's one of 'em, but which!"

Santa Claus was the same rotund, pudgy old fellow — with the long white beard and the laughing face — that children love, and on his broad back was the proverbial pack of presents. His wife, in fur from head to foot, wore a frilled fur cap, and, safely hidden behind her spectacled, rosy-cheeked mask, looked the veritable mother of all the little Santa Clauses attributed to her. The children stood silently by in their picturesque costumes, looking round the room, as children will, while their father and mother conversed with the host and hostess.

Finally they were all seated, and Madam Santa Claus began in quite a motherly way to talk about her children.

"It's Polly Dudley," whispered Mrs. Tenney to Mrs. Prindle. "I know her voice. And I'm pretty sure that little one is Doodles. Don't they look funny?"

They were all clad in red and white. The girls wore scarlet frocks reaching almost to the floor, with short white fur coats, and caps to match. The boys had long red trousers, and coats like those of their sisters. As they looked around on the company they bore a strong resemblance to their parents, with their rosy cheeks and laughing lips.

"I had to leave most of the children at home," the mother was saying. "Lambkin is too young to come out such a cold night, so Eagle stayed to take care of her; and at the very last minute Monkey broke his arm, and of course Brother could n't come without his twin. It only served Monkey right, he's so careless — though I'm not quite sure that it is Monkey! I never can tell those boys apart." Mother Santa Claus wagged her head cheerfully. "Then, Mousey and Deer have sore throats, and I thought the rest had better stay and keep the sick ones company. They'll have a good Christmas Eve all together, even if they are sick."

"Please, can I take off my coat?" asked one of the girls, coming to her mother's side.

"Not yet, Starling. Sit down and be quiet!"

"Your children have unusual names," twinkled the host gravely.

"That's what people say," the mother returned. "But we simply name them according to their characteristics. This one," nodding to the girl who had just gone back to her seat, "we call Starling, because she talks so much, and her sister there is Dove, because she is so gentle. Squirrel is the nimblest of them all and he is never still a minute. See him wiggling round now! This little one," reaching out a hand to the smallest of the four, "is Lark, because he

378

sings so sweetly. — Can't you sing your new carol, dear?"

So the youngest of the Santa Clauses stood up obediently and sung a beautiful Christmas song about the Baby Christ. The applause was long and insistent.

"He'll sing again for you pretty soon," promised Mother Santa Claus. "I think father is ready to distribute the presents now. Come, children, run along and help him, and mind you all step lively!"

The rosy-cheeked Saint took up a big parcel, and read off, in a clear voice, "Miss Katharine Crilly."

Starling was nearest, and took the package; but Miss Crilly, a little upset at being the owner of the first name called, jumped up and hurried across the room for her present, unheedful of mistletoe and the eyes that were watching her. Just inside the enchanted circle, the sudden hush of the room gave her its warning. She caught the eager glances directed beyond her, and turning her head uttered a startled cry. Almost at the same instant an arm shot toward her, missing its aim by scarce an inch. With one bound she cleared the invisible

379

line of danger, and, scudding straight past Starling and her inviting parcel, stopped only at the detaining hand of her laughing hostess.

"Mercy sakes!" she cried, and her face rivaled in color the Santa Claus reds, as she met the laughing eyes of her host.

She came back with her parcel, much flurried and still scarlet of face, while squeals of laughter and gay sallies rang about her.

After that there was more heed, and the distribution of presents went on without further hindrance.

The big bag was empty at last, and Santa Claus exclaimed with a sigh: "Oh, but it's hot! I say, let's get off some of this toggery!" He slipped himself out of his fur coat, pulled off his cap and his mask — and there was David Collins, smiling blithely to the company!

The others were quick in following his example, and Madam Santa Claus stood revealed as laughing Polly, with Patricia, Leonora, Blue, and Doodles clustered round her.

Then there was plenty to say, many thanks to be given, and much chatter and laughter. In the midst of it all, Nelson Randolph made himself heard: —

"Ye men-folk, listen! I am glad to share my rewards with you, so go ahead, David and Blue and Doodles, and obtain as much tribute as possible under the mistletoe!"

"How can you share what you have n't got and never had and don't know as you ever will have?" laughed Miss Crilly.

He turned toward the saucy speaker and shook his finger sternly.

"Jilting me, and then taunting me of my failure! Katharine Crilly, perhaps before midnight the slipper will be on the other foot!"

This brought a hubbub of applause and merriment, and the ladies backed away from the charmed circle and giggled and talked gayly among themselves.

But Christmas presents are bewitching things, and it was not long before mistletoe was all forgotten in the beauties of fine needlework, the mysteries of new stitches, and the attractions of dainty knickknacks. David and Blue and Doodles succeeded in making momentary captives of Mrs. Tenney, Mrs. Winslow Teed, and Miss Lily, while Polly and Patricia were several times arrested on their heedless ways across the room.

Nelson Randolph seemed to have eyes only for Miss Crilly, although once Polly almost walked into his hands. A short but exciting race she led him before dodging behind Miss Mullaly's chair and asking breathlessly if the mistletoe was all over the room.

He halted and looked round on the laughing company.

"My word of honor! I forgot!—Lady Polly, I humbly beg your gracious pardon!" He bowed low.

"Granted, Sir Rogue!" she replied, dropping a curtsy.

Full of the spirit of mischief, Patricia slipped away to the piano. And so the waltzing began.

Of course, everybody knew what to expect from their "men-folk" partners unless they were exceedingly wary, and only an occasional couple whirled into the enchanted circle.

Ice cream and cakes were succeeded by music and the singing of carols, until somebody suggested that it was time to go home.

The host took out his watch.

"I shall not open the door for anybody yet," he declared. "Only ten o'clock! Master Lark will give us another song!"

But before the command had been obeyed, the telephone rang lustily.

"Oh, is it!" Mrs. Randolph heard her husband say. "Thank you all, and a Merry Christmas to every one of you!"

When he returned he nodded smilingly to her, and then Doodles gave a funny little sleepy song that none of the others had heard, — "The Land of I-dunno-where."

Afterwards came more carols, until Blue and Doodles had to hurry away lest they miss the last car to Foxford.

The all-day guests began to put on their wraps, word was sent to bring up the car, and all was bustle and happy words and Merry Christmases in abundance. Each guest carried a pretty basket filled with gifts from the host and hostess, and it was nearly eleven before the last load was off, with the sleighful of young folks to keep it company.

Nelson Randolph and his wife went silently back to the deserted living-room.

"Seems kind of lonely, does n't it?" she said.

"Not a bit!" he replied, leading her under the mistletoe and claiming his reward.

"They did have a good time," she said happily.

"The best, I'll warrant, that they've had for a decade." He looked down at his wife searchingly.

"What is it?" she smiled.

"You did n't care, did you?"

"For what?"

He tossed his head toward the branch above them.

"No, indeed!" she replied. "Why should I?"

"I did n't think you would," he said slowly; "but some women would have had a fit!"

"I was n't built that way," she laughed. "I think I enjoyed it more than any of the rest of you!"

"My dearest wife!" he said gravely, while his lips found their favorite spot where a curl strayed over her forehead, — "My dearest wife!"

She heard with almost a start. Did he realize his words, or was it simply an impulsive phrase? A story had been told her once — but, no, that did not belong to Christmas Eve!

"It was all a happening," he went on. "I spied the mistletoe when I was coming home,

384

and it set me to wondering if it would n't help
out; so I brought it along. I wanted those dear
women to have a real Christmas merry-making,
not a sham affair. Take such folks, they 'll generally sit around and talk, and laugh a little,
and think they are celebrating something. I
wanted them to have a young Christmas. And
I did n't catch anybody after all," he ended, a
plaintive note in his voice.

"You did n't try to catch anybody, did you?"
she smiled.

"Whatever put such a thing into your head?"
he demanded fiercely.

She laughed. "I have seen you a few times
before to-night."

He frowned — then broke into a chuckle.

"Bless you!" he said fervently.

"Nelson Randolph!" she suddenly cried out,
trying to break away from him, "The windows!
I forgot!"

"What's the matter with them?" he twinkled. "They 're all shut."

"But the shades! They 're up! — Nelson!"

"What if they are?" he returned comfortably.

"Somebody may look in!"

He smilingly held her tight. "If any wanderer is abroad in this cold, he ought to be rewarded with a picture of domestic bliss."

"But if Mrs. Betts should be coming home late! —"

"She'd probably be disappointed that it was only I, instead of some other woman's husband."

"Nelson, do let me go! . . . I think we might find easier seats," she laughed, as she came back to him.

He turned her toward the little mantel clock. It was two minutes of twelve.

"Almost Christmas morning!" she said softly. "I wonder if they'll call us up to-night."

"Hardly. We should have heard before. Everything was complete at ten o'clock."

"How surprised they were!" she mused smilingly. "I'm so glad you did it for them."

"I am glad *you* did it!" he amended.

She started to reply, but he lifted a detaining finger. The city hall clock was striking the hour.

"My princess," — his lips touched her own, — "I wish you the joyfulest Christmas —"

"Ting! ting! Ting! ti-i-ng!" broke in imperiously.

"Go," he urged, loosing his clasp.

386

"Oh, Mis' Randolph! is that you?" came in Miss Crilly's clear voice. "We all wish you a merry, merry Christmas, and we thank you more than we can ever tell if we live to be a hundred years old! They piled into my room to wait till Christmas morning, for they would have me do the talking, though I can't do it half so well as some of the rest of 'em! Oh, you don't know how surprised we were! We stood talking in my door, Mis' Albright and Miss Mullaly and Miss Major and I, and I said, 'Come in and sit down!' So I struck a light, and happened to glance this way! Well, I gave one scream, and looked round to make sure where I was; and Miss Mullaly she squealed out, 'How came that here?' Then I spun across the room lively! And when I picked up your card with its dear little piece of mistletoe — well, you could have knocked me down easy! We heard little shouts and laughs all up and down, and Miss Major said, 'I wonder —' and ran right off to her room quick. Then the others caught on, and they went! I had to follow, of course, to see! And when we found there was a 'phone in every room — we just did n't know what to do! Why, if I wake up in the night I shall want to run over here to feel of it, just to make sure it is true! To think of your doing it for us!"

"I did n't! It is Mr. Randolph you ought to be thanking, not me! He —"

There was a dash across the room and the receiver was caught from her hand.

"No, no! I had nothing to do with it! I only filled my wife's order — that's all!"

"Nelson Randolph!" she expostulated. "Let me have the telephone!"

But he shook his head. "Thank you, Miss Crilly, on her behalf! I'm mighty glad you like them. What's that? Oh, well, if she did, I should be there beside her, thanking Him for giving me so good a wife!"

"What are you talking about? I want to know!"

With a smile he relinquished the instrument.

"I heard you say that! I told him that Miss Mullaly said you ought to get down on your knees every day of your life and thank the Lord for giving you such a good husband."

"You can tell Miss Mullaly that is just what I do!"

"My! I will. Is n't this fun, to be talking

388

with you this way!—and at midnight, too!
Oh, why did n't I think of it when he was there!
Well, you thank him for us all! You ought to
have heard us gabble when we found those five-
dollar gold pieces in our baskets! It was lovely
of him to do it! And those shoes you gave me
—did you crochet them yourself?"

"Certainly."

"All those stitches for me! They're beautiful! I've always wished I had some of that
kind. And—just think!—I should n't be
here to-night if it had n't been for you! Oh, I
could n't thank you enough if I should live to
be a thousand years old! You'll be sure and
come to our tree, won't you?"

"We will look in on you some time during
the evening. We can run away from the Dud-
leys' for a little while."

"Well, I am so full of happiness I believe one
drop more would make my eyes spill over! I
never thought I should chime in with Mis'
Puddicombe, but to-night I do! June Holiday
Home *is* the gate of heaven—and all because
of you and Polly!"

THE END

KATHLEEN NORRIS' STORIES

MOTHER.   Illustrated by F. C. Yohn.

This book has a fairy-story touch, [counterbalanced by the sturdy reality of struggle, sacrifice, and resulting peace and power of a mother's experiences.

SATURDAY'S CHILD.

Frontispiece by F. Graham Cootes.

Out on the Pacific coast a normal girl, obscure and lovely, makes a quest for happiness. She passes through three stages—poverty, wealth and service—and works out a creditable salvation.

THE RICH MRS. BURGOYNE.

Illustrated by Lucius H. Hitchcock.

The story [of a sensible woman who keeps within her means, refuses to be swamped by social engagements, lives a normal human life of varied interests, and has her own romance.

THE STORY OF JULIA PAGE.

Frontispiece by Allan Gilbert.

How Julia Page, reared in rather unpromising surroundings, lifted herself through sheer determination to a higher plane of life.

THE HEART OF RACHAEL.

Frontispiece by Charles E. Chambers.

Rachael is called upon to solve many problems, and in working out these, there is shown the beauty and strength of soul of one of fiction's most appealing characters.